P9-DUB-515

McLEAN SEES IT THROUGH

When Raymond Bosanquet, a wealthy, unpleasant man, is found shot dead in his study after lunch one day, Chief Inspector McLean of Scotland Yard travels to Pevensey to investigate. Could the murderer be one of Raymond's two teenage sons? Or is it Robert Grant, who is in love with Raymond's lovely, young second wife, Dorinda? Is Dorinda herself an accomplice? And why didn't the gardener see anyone running from the crime scene? McLean seems to be getting nowhere with his enquiries at first, but he gradually unravels the complex mystery.

Books by George Goodchild
Published by The House of Ulverscroft:

THE DANGER LINE
McLEAN DISPOSES
THE LAST REDOUBT
THE EFFORD TANGLE
NEXT OF KIN
McLEAN INVESTIGATES
COMPANION TO SIRIUS
SAVAGE ENCOUNTER
FALSE INTRUDER
DEAR CONSPIRATOR
TIGER, TIGER
LADY TAKE CARE
McLEAN AT THE GOLDEN OWL
THE TRIUMPH OF McLEAN
MAD MIKE
McLEAN TO THE DARK TOWER CAME

GEORGE GOODCHILD

McLEAN SEES IT THROUGH

Complete and Unabridged

ULVERSCROFT
Leicester

First published in Great Britain

First Large Print Edition
published 2000

The characters in this book are entirely imaginary,
and have no relation to any living person.

British Library CIP Data

Goodchild, George, *1988* –
    McLean sees it through.—Large print ed.—
    Ulverscroft large print series: mystery
    1. McLean, Inspector (Fictitious character)—Fiction
    2. Detective and mystery stories
    3. Large type books
    I. Title
    823.9′12 [F]

    ISBN 0–7089–4296–2

Published by
F. A. Thorpe (Publishing)
Anstey, Leicestershire
Set by Words & Graphics Ltd.
Anstey, Leicestershire
Printed and bound in Great Britain by
T. J. International Ltd., Padstow, Cornwall

This book is printed on acid-free paper

1

When Raymond Bosanquet took unto himself a second wife, it was natural that the press — that section of the press which thrives on tittle-tattle and emotions — should take notice of it. Actually there was nothing very remarkable in a man of fifty-five marrying a girl of twenty-five, but the girl happened to be particularly attractive, and Bosanquet was well-known as a zoologist, and a writer of books chiefly on Natural History. He was happily indifferent to the sales of these works, since his father had amassed a fortune at the beginning of the century, and had ultimately left it all to his only son.

Bosanquet's second marriage was an extremely hasty affair. He went abroad for a three months' holiday, and came back with his new wife, whom he had met in Paris, and married before the British Consul in Rome. His friends crowded to his Sussex house on his homecoming, in response to invitations to meet his wife. Some of them had visualised her as a middle-aged spectacled blue-stocking, of frigid demeanour and austere disposition. To their great surprise they were introduced to a woman who was little more than a girl — a sensitive, rather sad-eyed blonde, who betrayed her nervousness at every handshake, and who swiftly won the hearts of all the men, and the envy of most of the women.

Her two stepsons had been present, and they seemed as nervous with their step-mother, as she was with them. John was eighteen and just about to go to Oxford. Jasper was three years younger and at a public school, from which he had managed to get a special *exeat*. Between the boys and their father there was an unbridgeable abyss. Both sides were aware of it, and no real attempt was ever made to cross it.

Very diffidently the boys had called their father's wife 'mother' for some time. But subtly this changed and she became Dorinda, to them as well as to her husband. Three years passed and during that time much water flowed under the psychological bridges. The sensitive timid bride changed, as everything changes. The big house on the East Sussex coast became the scene of intense friction and disharmony. Bosanquet, with his fish-ponds and aquaria, and his very circumscribed interests, began to live a solitary life. His young wife found little to interest her in the neighbourhood, because

Bosanquet was unsociable except with his own academical friends, who were all old and frightfully learned.

He spent much of his life in his large study, where in addition to innumerable works on subjects dear to him, there were aquaria containing both British and tropical fishes. He ran the house on the smallest possible staff — a butler, three maids and a gardener, who was also chauffeur when occasion demanded. Rich as he was, he exercised the most rigid economy in every direction, except in the sphere of his most intense interest.

Thousands of pounds were spent in the excavation of fish-ponds, and the installation of electrically heated aquaria. He would pay vast sums for specimens of rare fishes, which he endeavoured to breed in artificial surroundings, and then start a quarrel with his wife over some quite necessary small bills covering clothing for herself and the two boys. Prout, the butler, was continually on the carpet in respect of housekeeping items, and the family car was five years old, with no hope of being replaced.

It was August and both John and Jasper were home from college and school. John was taking his final examination in June and was still waiting for the result. Jasper was in the same position regarding the Higher Certificate, which his father had insisted on his taking.

'It really doesn't matter a damn,' he said to his stepmother. 'Father's not sending me to the University, and if you want to get a job the only thing they ask is whether you've got the school 'cert.' '

'Your father's probably right,' said Dorinda.

'But what's he going to do with me?'

'He's thinking about that.'

'Time he made up his mind. I'll tell you one thing. I won't sit again for the higher 'cert.' '

'Let's hope it won't be necessary,' said Dorinda with a smile.

'It's not going to be. If father won't set me up in some kind of business, I'm clearing out.'

'Clearing out where, Jasper?'

'Anywhere. Perhaps I could work my way to America and get a job there. One thing I won't do — and that is sit in some lousy office and write figures in books. I know father's been writing to that Insurance company in which he holds shares. If he's trying to work me into a job there he's making a big mistake. I won't go — and I mean to tell him so.'

'Don't worry, Jasper,' she begged. 'Perhaps

4

everything will turn out all right.'

Jasper seemed to have doubts about that. He turned towards the door with his hands thrust deep into his pockets, then hesitated and came back again.

'You may as well know,' he said. 'I mucked the examination. There's no earthly chance of my getting through. I haven't been working, and I may as well admit it.'

Dorinda tried to look stern.

'Why didn't you work, Jasper?' she asked. 'After all, public schools are expensive, and your father — '

'I never wanted to go there. I could have got into the Army easily if father had entered me for Sandhurst at the right time. But he hated the Army, and went mad with rage when I suggested it. Dorinda, what's wrong with him?'

'Wrong with whom?'

'Father.'

'There's nothing wrong with him. He's preoccupied with his new book, and — '

'You always try to excuse him,' cut in Jasper. 'I suppose it's a sense of loyalty. But isn't it better to be candid — truthful?'

'I don't understand what you mean.'

'You do. John and I often talk about it. You're as unhappy as we are, and the fault is father's.'

5

'Now listen, Jasper, I won't discuss your father — '

She stopped as the elder boy entered the lounge. He was tall and of athletic build, and much less seriously disposed than his younger brother. At that moment his attire was far from conventional, for he wore a pair of shorts that ended almost as soon as they began, and above this there was nothing but a rowing vest. There was a strong resemblance to his father in his eyes and nose, but it was doubtful whether Bosanquet had ever been so well-built, or so good-looking.

'Hooray!' he said. 'He's just gone into Eastbourne, so we can tinkle the bell. Gosh, it's hot!'

He thereupon pushed a bell-button, and flung himself into a settee, from which he looked up and regarded his brother and stepmother.

'Is Jasper on the mat for something?' he asked.

'Oh no,' replied Dorinda with a smile. 'He was telling me about the school.'

She stopped short as Prout entered. He was a man of about thirty-five, with small regular features, and extremely neat attire.

'Did you ring, madam?' he inquired of Dorinda.

'Mr. John did.'

'Oh, Prout,' said John. 'This weather is getting us down. Bring some drinks, will you? Whisky, gin — '

'Beer for me,' said Jasper.

'And a bottle of beer, and plenty of ice.'

'Pardon, sir,' said Prout. 'But we have only soft drinks.'

'Soft drinks!' ejaculated John. 'But hang it, I saw the wine merchant delivering all kinds of stuff yesterday.'

The butler looked a trifle uneasy. He gave a soft cough and then tried to explain.

'There are alcoholic drinks in the house,' he said. 'But I have no key to the wine cupboard. Mr. Bosanquet was under the impression that the staff were helping themselves, and — er — he took over the key.'

Dorinda winced at this, and John looked positively fierce, but he deemed it advisable to save the situation from deteriorating.

'Very well, Prout. Bring some soft drinks and glasses.'

'Immediately, sir.'

As the door closed John exploded. What the hell did his father take them for? What if the servants did have a drink or two on the quiet? Clearly none of them were trusted, or Prout would have been allowed to have the key. He had just about had enough of the old man's miserliness. And having got so far he went further.

'Mother,' he said, lapsing into the old form of address. 'For three years I haven't had as much pocket money as the milk-boy. At college you're supposed to do something in the nature of entertainment. People drop in at all times, and expect a drink. It's been rotten for me, having to make lying excuses. I've had to refrain from going to parties because I've never had the money to throw one myself, and to make matters worse at the beginning of every new term I'm hauled up before the Proctor because my college bill hasn't been paid. Father only pays it when I write to him and tell him what has happened.'

'Perhaps he's lost some of his money,' suggested Dorinda.

'No, he hasn't. It was only yesterday I saw an Income Tax demand for the second instalment. Do you know how much he is due to pay?'

'Your father and I never discuss money,' said Dorinda.

'Well, the demand was for £1,600 — and that was only for half a year. I'm not a complete fool at mathematics — even though I do read Classics. It means his last year's income was assessed at something like

£12,000 — and that doesn't mean it mightn't be more.'

'John!'

John walked up and down, and as he walked his left big toe would insist on pushing up through a hole in his tennis shoe.

'We've got to do something about it,' said John, coming to a halt, and sitting down again. 'We've got to tell father that we won't stand it any longer. This business of locking up the drinks is about the last straw. He's treating all of us as if we were dirt. Every week he gets stingier and harder. I vote we have it out with him — and the sooner the better.'

'Hear! Hear!' said Jasper.

Prout came in with the drinks, and a large bowl of ice from the refrigerator. John watched him as he uncorked a fresh bottle of lime juice with dexterous fingers, and then met their various demands.

'Will that be all, madam?' he asked.

'Thank you, Prout,' said Dorinda.

John ignored the two straws and drank deeply from the tall glass.

'Prout's a marvel,' he said.

'Why?' asked Dorinda.

'Nothing seems to disturb him. I've heard father ticking him off about things, and Prout never turns a hair. When he came here I had a bet with myself that he wouldn't stay three months, and yet he's suffered in silence for two years. He ought to be awarded the Victoria Cross.'

Dorinda was stirring her drink reflectively with the two straws. The sort of conversation that was taking place was obviously painful to her. But the boys were growing up, and taking notice. It was useless to pretend that Castle House was the abode of peace and contentment — useless to attempt to conceal from either of them the fact that she and their father were temperamentally and psychologically poles apart. John was staring at her.

'What's on your mind, Dorinda?' he asked quietly.

'You two boys. I think you don't try to understand your father.'

'It's the other way round,' argued Jasper. 'He doesn't try to understand us. He has a contempt for us — '

'Oh no. He's proud of you both.'

'Proud my hat!' scoffed John. 'The fact is we don't reach up to his standard — or he thinks we don't. Jasper only just managed to scrape through the school 'cert,' and father was disappointed. He expected credits in all subjects. I think I'll get my degree, but it will only be a 'pass.' In father's mind all that counts are diplomas. I know he got a double-first when he was up at the varsity, but he got it by neglecting everything else. Maybe we've only got third class brains, but whose fault is that? Why should he take it out of us because we haven't inherited his cleverness — call it genius if you like?'

'But he's not taking it out of you,' protested Dorinda.

'Then why does he keep us short of money? Why are we staying here in August, when we ought to be on holiday? Why does he refuse to let me take that American trip until he hears the result of the examination?'

'He's very busy just now.'

'Yes, busy tying another knot in the purse strings,' put in Jasper. 'It's time something was done about it, and I think we should have it out with him this evening.'

Dorinda shook her head doubtfully, and then the telephone bell rang. John, who was nearest the instrument, took up the receiver.

'Yes,' he said. 'What name? Grant? Oh yes, I'll tell her.'

He handed the receiver to Dorinda, who took it rather nervously. The conversation which followed was noticeably monosyllabic on her part, and finally she said she would let him know. As she hung up the receiver she saw John's questioning glance.

'Was that the Mr. Grant who called here?' asked John.

'Yes.'

'I liked him,' said John. 'He's an engineer, isn't he?'

'Yes — from Egypt. I knew him many years ago. I hadn't seen him for four years before he called.'

'He's amazingly good at tennis,' said John. 'You remember he played a set with me. I just managed to win, but then he played with an old racket which I dug out, and he hadn't played on a grass court for years. I wouldn't back myself to win the next time. Can't you invite him down for a week end?'

'I'm sure he can't spare the time,' said Dorinda. 'You see, his leave is nearly at an end. Now I must go into the village, or lunch will be late.'

She left the two boys sitting in the lounge. John stretched himself and wandered to the piano. For a few minutes he played with some uncertainty a Chopin Study, and then broke into jazz, at which he was much more proficient. Finally he swung round on the stool.

'Tell you what,' he said. 'Dorinda's about as miserable as hell. I believe her marriage to father is about the biggest flop that any marriage ever suffered.'

'But she sticks up for him.'

'That's natural enough. Having made a hell of a mistake she's not keen on advertising the fact — even to us. But we know what father is. Mother had no better time than Dorinda has. It was always father's home, father's money, father's children, father's wife — father's everything. Father has never risen above the joy of possessing.'

'Probably we'd be the same if we had anything to possess — but we haven't,' replied Jasper, with a scowl. 'I say, John, who was your fat letter from?'

'Don't be so damned inquisitive,' remonstrated John, and played a few more bars on the piano.

'You needn't be so secretive. I know it was from a girl. They all write the same sort of ghastly fist. What's her name? What does she do? And what does she look like?'

John's reply was to play the piano louder and louder.

2

Bosanquet's visit to Eastbourne had as its object business of the greatest importance. Mr. Pole, of Pole & Wonham, solicitors, had given up the most comfortable chair to his wealthy client, and was waiting to hear what was clearly agitating him. Bosanquet produced from his pocket a long envelope containing a folded blue document.

'I wished to see you about my will,' he said. 'The existing will was executed three years ago — shortly after my marriage.'

'I remember the occasion quite well.'

'Changed circumstances necessitate certain changes in the provisions of the will. They are such that I think a new will is called for.'

'As you wish, Mr. Bosanquet. One is naturally bound by circumstances. What are your wishes in this matter?'

'Under the present will there is a trust fund created whereby my two sons will enjoy an income of a thousand pounds a year each.'

'I remember that. Do you wish to decrease, or increase those benefits?'

'No. They can stand.'

Mr. Pole made a note on his pad.

'Good!' he said.

'My wife under the present will is to enjoy the residue of the estate, but I want that altered.'

'Certainly.'

'She will on my death inherit the sum of two hundred pounds per annum — '

'Did you say two hundred?' inquired Pole, with surprised eyes.

'Yes — two hundred pounds per annum, which sum she will forfeit in the event of her marrying again.'

Mr. Pole commenced to write, but he didn't get very far. He had known Bosanquet for a very long time, and had advised him on many matters. It seemed to him that the terms of the new will as they affected Mrs. Bosanquet were incredibly harsh.

'You surely can't mean that' he said. 'How could she possibly subsist on that amount? You would only succeed in bringing about the contingency you apparently wish to prevent — her re-marriage.'

'My mind is made up. I have my own reasons. Now as to the residue of my estate — I wish to endow a number of scholarships for students in zoology. These scholarships will be known as the Bosanquet scholarships. I propose to appoint the requisite trustees, the names of whom I will give you later. They can be added to the draft.'

Mr. Pole made his notes with tight lips.

'Any change in the servants' legacies?' he asked.

'No. They may stand. I think that is all. I should like to see the new draft as soon as possible.'

Mr. Pole nodded and made some remark about the weather. Clearly he disapproved of his client's vindictiveness towards his young wife, but it was obvious that if he wanted to keep his client's business tact was essential. He showed Bosanquet to the door, and then wished him good morning.

Bosanquet's next call was at the police station, where he asked to see Superintendent John Ball. He was kept waiting a few minutes and then shown into the Superintendent's office. Ball was an elderly intelligent officer with a high regard for his visitor's great learning and social position.

'I hope you're keeping well, sir,' he said pleasantly.

'Not very well. I hate this hot weather. I should have telephoned you first.'

'Not at all. I've been investigating that little matter — as quietly as possible, of course, but so far, I'm sorry to say, without result. If there are any further developments — '

'There are,' interrupted Bosanquet. 'I

16

received this letter by the morning post.'

He produced an envelope from his pocket, and handed it to the Superintendent. Ball extracted a single sheet of notepaper and read what was written on it:

Why don't you behave more like a human being? You only succeed in causing unhappiness, and making bitter enemies. You treat your wife like a chattel, and your sons like cattle. Your friends are becoming wise to your insufferable selfishness and unforgiving nature. Be warned in time or calamity may overtake you.

The Superintendent looked up from the letter to see Bosanquet's grim face. He then begged to be excused and went to a file from which he extracted two other letters. He compared them with the last one.

'Same handwriting,' he said. 'And all of them posted in London. I've had an expert busy on the first two. He's of the opinion that they are not the normal handwriting of the person who wrote them — that they were probably done with the left hand. The paper on which all are written is of a very common type, torn from a cheap writing pad. This letter is in stronger terms than the others.'

'Yes. I take the last sentence to be a direct threat.'

'It may not be meant in that way,' argued the Superintendent.

'What other way can it be meant?'

'People are notoriously loose in their language. But I agree the matter is not such as can be ignored. Have you no idea at all as to the identity of the writer?'

Bosanquet did not reply at once. He walked to the window and looked out into the street. Then he came back again and sat down by the Superintendent's table

'I think I should be frank with you,' he said. 'Two months ago an old friend of my wife came home from abroad. His name is Robert Grant, and he is an engineer of some sort in Egypt. I think that my wife and Grant were very close friends before she was married. I got the impression that Grant was bitterly disappointed to find her married to me. He made but one stay at the house, but my wife has been to London several times since, and I'm quite certain they have met again, although she has never admitted it.'

'Is he a young man?'

'Yes — about thirty I should imagine.'

'Do you know where he is staying?'

'The Duchess Hotel, in Sackville Street, London.'

'You say it was two months ago when he came to England?'

'Just about two months. I can't give you the exact date.'

The Superintendent scrutinised the postmark on the earliest of the letters.

'The first one was posted six weeks ago,' he said. 'Mr. Bosanquet — forgive the question, but would your wife be likely to speak ill of you to Grant? I mean, has she perhaps some imaginary grudge — something which she might discuss with an old friend?'

'No,' replied Bosanquet sharply. 'On the contrary she has cause to be grateful to me. I met her at a time when she was in desperate straits, and undoubtedly saved her from destitution. I have given her a good home, the society of eminent personages, a background of culture and refinement. But she hasn't settled down as well as I might wish. If she has taken this man into her confidence it can only be because of an unwarrantable desire to injure me.'

'Thank you,' said the Superintendent. 'I'll investigate this gentleman — secretly, of course. I should like to keep this letter with the other two.'

'Certainly.'

'I presume you haven't mentioned this

matter to any member of your family?'

'Not yet.'

'I think that is wise.'

Bosanquet drove back along the coast road to Pevensey. Across the low-lying green meadows he could see the ruins of the old castle which dated back to Roman times, and where William the Conqueror landed in 1066. It was a pleasant background to what otherwise would have been a monotonous waste, where two thousand years ago the sea had covered everything. Between the road and the present coastline were ruined Martello Towers — those relics of the Napoleonic threat to Britain, which marched across the marshes as a standing memorial of the grim days when Britain faced the possibility of invasion. Now everything was peaceful enough — except in Bosanquet's soul. Everywhere there were flowers and plundering butterflies. From the point of view of the botanist the district was unique. From the bare shingle seaward there grew many plants that thrived despite the arid conditions. Great areas were given over to seakale, and viper's bugloss, and here and there more delicate flowers defied the harsh conditions, and braved the strong sea wind. It was essentially placid, friendly country, and one could easily forget the distant past when fierce wars had raged in the far-flung marshes.

At the Bay the car turned left and ran for a while alongside the ancient canal to the delectable village, beyond which, on high ground, reposed Castle House. On the tennis court John and Jasper were fighting out a battle. They were almost naked, for the heat was tremendous, and the younger boy was kept running up and down the back line in a worthy attempt to return John's terrific drives. Neither of them saw the returning car, and it was doubtful whether Bosanquet saw them, for his mind was occupied with other matters.

On entering the house he went straight to his study, which was a large room on the ground floor, with French windows leading out to the wide terrace, from which there was an uninterrupted view to the sea, and to the high land above Hastings to the East, and Beachy Head to the West. Above the wide fireplace an electrically heated aquarium had been built in. It was kaleidoscopic with moving fishes of incredible colouring, ranging in size from Angel Fish of large dimensions to almost microscopic specimens from the China Seas, some of which had cost him twenty guineas each. He looked at the thermometer on the outside of the aquarium, and satisfied himself that the water temperature was correct. Then he opened a bureau, and took from it a pile of manuscript which he carried to the large table between the two French windows. Piled up at the back of the table were many books, some with their wrappers still on, and others bearing the red label of 'The London Library.' The part manuscript bore the title of *The Coloration of Fishes*. He glanced at the last written page, and then took some sheets of manuscript paper and a pen.

For a few minutes he wrote slowly in a tidy but not easily decipherable hand. The long sentence was involved and he did not appear to be pleased with it as he read it. Away to his right was a very large bowl of beautiful goldfish. They were acclimatised and no heating was required. Bosanquet had taken them out of his various garden ponds, and they were his particular pride so far as coloration was concerned.

He had bred them himself, and he regarded them as the best specimens of their type. His glance went to them now, and their lazy movements and changing contours seemed to hypnotise him, for his gaze remained on the bowl for a quite inordinate time. It was Dorinda who caused him to raise his eye, and extend his focus to the garden.

He saw her below the terrace, talking to the two boys who had just finished their tennis match, and were leaving the court.

The affectionate relationship between his wife and her stepsons should have pleased him, but it had just the opposite result. He bit the ends of his moustache savagely as he watched the trio mounting the series of steps that would bring them to the terrace, and noted that Jasper was demonstrating a back-hand half-volley which he had had the good fortune to bring off against his more expert brother. They were all laughing, as indeed befitted the excellence of the day. But Bosanquet did not laugh.

3

Superintendent Ball never missed an excuse to go to London, and Bosanquet's visit to him afforded him such an excuse. Sussex might be a desirable spot for jaded Londoners, but as Ball would say with enthusiasm, 'Give me good old London every time.' His associations there were many, for on several occasions he had worked in conjunction with the Metropolitan Police, and being a good mixer he had as many friends there as in his own particular force.

Ball knew just where he was most likely to meet those friends, and he chose a train which would land him in London round about lunch time. He took a taxi to a comparatively small restaurant not far from the Thames Embankment, and as he expected he saw a number of men whom he knew, and who welcomed him warmly. He was about to accept an invitation to lunch with two of them when he suddenly saw a man sitting alone at a table in a corner — a youngish man with very regular features, and a mass of wavy dark hair.

'Isn't that McLean?' he asked.

'Yes, but he won't stand you a lunch. He's Scotch.'

Ball laughed, and said he hoped they would excuse him as he really wanted to see McLean. He thereupon approached the table in the corner and soon came under the scrutiny of McLean's deep-set keen eyes.

'Hullo, Ball,' said McLean. 'After Hunt's cruel libel you'll simply have to be my guest.'

'Thanks, but he didn't think you heard.'

'The whole world can hear him when he whispers. What brings you to this sink of iniquity?'

'Business.'

'The last time you came you lost your watch. That was definitely bad business. Wicked city this.'

'You seem to thrive on it,' replied Ball, as he surveyed the menu. 'I intended calling on you, so I'm lucky to have fallen up against you. Ever heard of Raymond Bosanquet?'

McLean was reflective for a few moments. He possessed the useful faculty of being able to rescue almost anything from his subconscious mind — given time.

'A literary man,' he said. 'Naturalist, isn't he?'

'Partly I suppose, but he calls himself a zoologist.'

'Oh, yes. I remember now. He's an

25

authority on fishes, especially the tropical varieties. Spent some years exploring the Great Barrier Reef, and the China Seas. Why do you ask?'

'He lives near me — at Pevensey to be precise. Tons of money and a very nice house — and wife.'

'Why drag her in?'

'She may be involved. You see, Bosanquet has been in receipt of letters of a scurrilous character, and has requested our help. There may be a link here in London. I'm not sure yet. In fact I'm not sure that the matter is really serious. It depends upon what kind of interpretation one puts on the substance of the letters. I've got one with me. Take a look at it.'

He handed McLean the letter which Bosanquet had recently handed to him, and McLean read it.

'In London we shouldn't pay much attention to it,' he said. 'But I suppose you take a different view, where the recipient is wealthy and presumably influential.'

Ball wasn't pleased by this remark. He persuaded himself that it wasn't true that the County police showed any partiality. If a washerwoman had brought the matter to his notice he would have felt it incumbent upon him to take some action. He was about to make that defence, but refrained at the last moment, because he was certain McLean wouldn't believe him.

'Wouldn't you read the last sentence as a direct threat?' he asked.

'Not necessarily. The calamity which the writer mentions might be psychological. It's rather like saying 'virtue is its own reward.' Conversely selfishness brings its own dangers.'

'I appreciate the point, but there have been other letters, and they are causing the recipient some anxiety. He suspects a man who is a friend of his wife — a young man home from the East.'

'Why not the wife herself, if she's unhappy? Tell me more about them.'

Ball quickly put McLean in receipt of all the relevant facts, so far as he knew them. He had discovered that there was a lot of family friction, that Bosanquet was not popular with the servants, and that in fact he was a very difficult man for anyone to get on with.

'With so much ill-feeling about him the letters may have originated in the house,' said McLean.

'I have not overlooked that possibility, but they were all posted in London.'

'That doesn't mean a thing. Have you taken any steps to eliminate everyone actually living in the house?'

'No. That's not easy.'

McLean scanned the letter again very closely.

'It shouldn't be difficult — in a certain event.'

'What event?'

'The arrival of another letter.'

'How will that help matters? We have three of them already.'

'You know that this letter was written with an ordinary pen — and not a fountain pen?'

'Yes. The handwriting expert pointed that out.'

'Then I think your next step is clear. If someone in the house is responsible he probably writes the letters there, with a pen and ink found on the premises. If you'll look in at my office later I'll give you a bottle of ink containing some very unusual ingredients. You must ask Bosanquet to make sure that all the existing ink in the house is replaced by the stuff I'll give you. Then, if he receives another letter it will be quite easy to find out whether it was written in the house or not.'

'That's great!' said Ball, enthusiastically. 'You're a clever devil, Mac. I'll have that ink changed by tomorrow morning.'

'How's the steak?' asked McLean.

'First-rate. Of course I shall still continue

my investigation in London.'

'Naturally. How's Eastbourne looking?'

'Pretty good, but it's a nice change to get up to London. If I had my time all over again I'd join the Metropolitan Police force. But now I'm on the verge of retirement. I say, what about doing a show when I've finished with the young gentleman from the East?'

'I've got a show on of my own,' said McLean. 'A nice raid at midnight on a most offensive nightclub. Look here, don't hurry your own meal, but I must go. Call some time this afternoon for that bottle of ink. If I'm not available I'll leave it with Sergeant Brook. And let me know if the scheme works.'

Ball shook hands warmly, and thanked McLean again for his good advice. Later he went to the Duchess Hotel and started some underground inquiries. To a certain extent these were satisfactory, for he was given a description of a young lady who had twice been seen at the hotel, lunching with Grant. The description was so good that he had no difficulty in identifying Mrs. Bosanquet. The members of the staff to whom he spoke were unanimous in their opinion of Mr. Grant, who had stayed on at the hotel ever since he arrived in London. According to them he was a very cheerful, good-natured man, with a kind word for everyone, and deep gratitude for any little service rendered. The lift-boy said he was a 'toff', and added that he couldn't say as much about everyone in the hotel. 'Some of 'em got zip fasteners on their trousis pockets,' he added.

It was not Ball's intention to question Grant personally, but as he was about to leave Grant was pointed out to him, and he scrutinised the object of his inquiries. Grant was tall and fair, with blue eyes, and very regular features. His skin was tanned to the colour of copper, and he seemed to radiate health. Yet he seemed to be immoderately self-centred at that moment. There was none of the cheerfulness which had been referred to by Ball's informants. Indeed, it looked as if Grant were wrestling with a serious personal problem. Ball thought he had done enough for one day, and left the hotel. Later he picked up his bottle of ink, and went to a show, which was supposed to be naughty but was in fact most boring.

On the following morning he saw Bosanquet, and made known the result of his visit to London. He listened attentively, and winced when Ball repeated the description of the woman who had twice lunched with Grant, but he made no comment and Ball was tactful enough not to linger on the point. Ball explained the idea of the ink, the bottle containing which he had brought with him, but quite forgot to mention how it had originated.

'I think it is sound,' said Bosanquet. 'If you will leave me the fluid I will undertake the task of substituting it for the normal ink. Thank you, Superintendent, for your prompt action.'

Ball had left only a few minutes when Dorinda entered her husband's study. He was busy introducing some food into the large aquarium, and paid no attention to her for some time. She waited patiently, and at last he turned to her.

'Did you want me?' he asked in a toneless voice.

'I need some money, Raymond. I've quite a lot of odd shopping to do.'

'I've no cash,' he answered. 'Can't it wait?'

'No. The Chatleighs are coming down for the weekend. If you will give me a cheque I can get it cashed as I pass the bank.'

He nodded and went to his writing table, where he wrote a cheque for a small amount. She folded it and put it into her handbag.

'Wasn't that Superintendent Ball who called just now?' she asked.

'Yes.'

'Is anything wrong?'

'What do you mean? Why should anything be wrong?'

'I wondered if either of the boys had got into trouble with the car — or perhaps the chauffeur.'

'It had nothing to do with the car.'

He was gazing at her fixedly — with an expression in his eyes that was very difficult to interpret. Then he gave a short little laugh and shrugged his shoulders.

'You're a simple woman, aren't you, Dorinda?' he asked.

'I wish you'd be frank,' she said. 'Why are you behaving so strangely?'

'Can't I admire my charming wife?'

'Raymond!'

'Well, you are beautiful you know. My friends have been telling me that ever since you came here. I remember, too, how deeply I was impressed with your beauty the day I first saw you — '

'Raymond — please!'

'Since when have compliments wounded you?'

'Since they were first accompanied by a sneer. What has come over you of late?'

'You've stolen my question. But you needn't answer it. Dorinda, why not increase the weekend party? Why not invite Mr. Grant?'

She gave him a quick glance, and took objection to the leer that had gathered round his mouth.

'Doesn't that suggestion call for an explanation?' she asked with rising anger.

'Isn't it customary to return hospitality? You've been his guest on a number of occasions, I believe?'

'Who told you that?'

'When a man has a young and attractive wife he must be forgiven if he becomes interested in her movements — outside his house.'

'The Superintendent,' she muttered. 'So you've had me watched? This is intolerable — horrible. When Grant stayed here you made it obvious that you disliked him, but to carry that dislike, and your beastly suspicions to the extent of — '

'You needn't shout,' he interrupted. 'I had rather the boys didn't know.'

'Know what?' she said angrily. 'Know that I still manage to retain a few friends of my own? Listen, Raymond — our marriage has been the most dismal failure, and the fault isn't mine. Until I came here I didn't realise what was in your mind — in what light you regarded marriage. I believed it was to be a give and take affair on both sides, as it was during the few months when we were abroad.

But on coming here everything changed. It was soon clear to me that I was to be merely a housekeeper — a substitute mother to your sons, with no rights of my own. I became an item among your possessions, of far less importance than your goldfish, because they engaged your attentions every day. You even write books about them. I will say this — you differentiated very little between me and your sons. We were all your possessions — subject to your caprices, and fits of bad temper. If you have ever had any real affection for either of them I've failed to notice it. You've been disappointed in them because they have only been normal specimens — not like their gifted father. But they're good boys, and deserve something better than you've given them.'

'Don't you dare mention my sons.'

'I must. You've questioned every penny I've spent on their clothing. You've kept them terribly short of pocket money. You've placed them in an entirely false position — especially John, who can never produce enough money to buy a friend a drink. You'll tell me they are your heirs and will inherit nice sums of money when you die. But they are alive now — very much alive, and need your help, companionship and love.'

'My sons are my affair. If they have turned

against me they must have been incited — by someone.'

'How cruel you can be — how unjust! What is there in you which obstructs ordinary decent emotions? In innocent friendship you see nothing but scandal.'

'Why didn't you tell me you had met that man again — lunched with him at his hotel?'

'Because I knew you disliked him.'

'Not because you are in love with him?'

She was excused the need of replying to this hateful question by the arrival of Prout.

'Yes — what is it?' snapped Bosanquet.

'Pardon, sir, but didn't you ring?'

'I did not.'

'Then it must have been the hall door. The indicator has not been working well of late.'

'Get it seen to. I dislike these intrusions.'

Dorinda took the opportunity to leave. Just as she was getting into the waiting car John sidled up to her.

'What was he shouting about?' he asked.

'Oh, nothing much. I think you had better come with me. You simply can't go on wearing those terrible shoes. Get a coat on, and for heaven's sake brush your hair. Don't be long.'

John was out again in a few minutes, looking much tidier. He took the seat beside his red-cheeked stepmother, behind the glass partition.

'It's rotten of him to treat you like this,' he said suddenly.

'You're imagining things, John,' she said with a smile. 'I had to get a cheque out of him, and that's not always easy.'

'I should say not!' He wrinkled his brow. 'Dorinda, as a matter of interest, do you get a regular allowance?'

'Why bother your head about finance, John?'

'But I'd like to know. Do you?'

'No.'

'Why not?'

'There was no arrangement of any kind. I'm afraid I'm not a very good business woman.'

'But father should have seen to that. I call it a miserable way to go on. A wife ought to have a regular allowance from her husband, and be spared the embarrassment of having to cadge a few pounds when she needs them.' He was silent for a few moments, and then he resumed. 'I'll tell you something. It was just the same with mother when she was alive — father spending colossal sums on the garden and his beloved fish, and mother with never a decent frock to wear. Poor mother! She knuckled down to it, until she had no mind of her own. We — Jasper and I — were too young to understand then, but we do now. We didn't take kindly to the idea of a stepmother, but you soon settled all that for us.'

'Did I?'

'Yes. You've been grand — always thinking of us when you've had enough troubles of your own. Why did you do it?'

Dorinda seemed startled by this question, but there was no avoiding it, for John's keen eyes were staring into her own.

'It's rather a silly question isn't it, John?' she asked.

'No — I don't think it is. They say love is blind, but I shouldn't have thought it was as blind as all that.'

'Well, it is,' she said, laughing to cover her real emotions. 'Oh, here's the bank. Will you run in with the cheque?'

John nodded and took the endorsed cheque from her. He was back again in a few minutes.

'Here's the dough. Five miserable pounds. I had a good mind to add a 'y' and a nought,' he grumbled.

'You always were bad at spelling,' she retorted.

'Anyway, I've got to get some money out of him on Monday.'

'Why Monday?'

'I want to run up to London. Haven't been there since I came down. I've got a feeling there's going to be a hell of a row between now and Monday.'

Dorinda was of the same mind, but she said nothing, and very soon the car was running along the promenade at Eastbourne, the chauffeur looking for a place to park it. With the season in full swing it was hopeless to think of shopping by car. Experience had taught Dorinda that it was a saving of time to carry purchases to the car in a shopping basket. At last Penny — the chauffeur — found a narrow space in the long line of parked cars.

'I can get in there, ma'am,' he said.

This he did, and was then left to his own devices. Dorinda and John were crossing the promenade when John suddenly grabbed his stepmother by the arm.

'Look!' he gasped. 'Isn't that Mr. Grant on the pavement outside the restaurant?'

As she looked in the direction indicated the man saw them both, and waved a hand.

'It is,' she said. 'What a coincidence!'

Grant greeted them both cheerily, and explained that this trip was the result of an impulse.

'London was filthy last night,' he said.

'Absolutely no air, and reeked of petrol. This morning it promised to be worse so I got the car out and took the road.'

'Well, it's certainly nice to see you,' said Dorinda. 'We're on shopping bent, as you may have noticed.'

'Yes, but come inside and have a coffee first.'

'If I do, I'll never get through with my shopping. Look at this dreadful list.'

She waved a long slip of paper on which were innumerable pencilled notes. John came to the rescue like a hero.

'Look here,' he said. 'You have your coffee, and I can get most of that stuff. In any case I've got to get those shoes, and I may be able to make a bob or two. I'll dump all I can get into the car and then join you here.'

Dorinda hesitated.

'All right,' she said finally. 'That's very nice of you, John. Better take three pounds. I'll wait for you here, and we can clear up any oddments afterwards.'

John went off with the basket and the money, and Dorinda walked with Grant into the restaurant.

4

'It wasn't quite true,' said Grant, as they sat down by a window which looked out on to the busy promenade. 'I had to see you, but didn't anticipate seeing you like this. There are strange things going on.'

'What do you mean?'

'I'm being investigated. My little pal, the lift-boy at the hotel, confided in me. Someone is interested in my movements, and your movements. It's a new experience to me, and I don't like it.'

'Nor do I. It's my husband, Bob.'

'Has he admitted it?'

'Yes. He knows I had lunch with you, and in his peculiar warped mind he sees sin.'

'And is giving you hell?'

'I can stand it.'

'For how long?'

'I don't know.'

'I intended to telephone you on my arrival, but now that isn't necessary. Dorinda, why go on with it?'

'With what?'

'This misery which you call marriage. If you had waited — '

'I couldn't wait. My mother died — penniless. I had to find a job. I went as a children's nurse in Paris, and was all right for a time. But then the family struck bad times and I was discharged. I found a new job, but it was a bad one. I had to leave it, for I was on the verge of a nervous breakdown. The little money I had saved was used up. I had no one to turn to — '

'Hadn't you a brother?'

'Yes, but he was unable to help me. Then Raymond came along. It was in Paris and we met quite by accident. He seemed charming, and he prolonged his stay there. Later he asked me to marry him. As he wanted to make a long tour on the continent we were married in Rome, and spent our honeymoon travelling about. North Africa, Greece, the Dalmatian Coast, all the most wonderful spots in the world. I thought I was going to be happy despite the great difference in our ages, but it wasn't to be so. He's a strange man — utterly wrapped up in his hobby.'

'His fishes?'

'Yes. He came out of his hard shell for a few months, and then went back again. I tried to understand him — to appreciate his learning and genius, but what I haven't been able to get over is his terrible acquisitiveness, and his shocking meanness. He's very rich and yet he counts and hoards every penny — where his own immediate interests are not concerned. Every bill is scrutinised, and quarrels are frequent. In addition to this there is his insane jealousy. That is absolutely incurable. I oughtn't to tell you this, but it's been eating at my heart so long.'

Grant sat in silence for a few moments. On a previous occasion she had hinted at friction between herself and her husband, but had never got as far as this. In the past they had been good friends — no more, and he had left England to take up the post in Egypt at a time when this friendship was reaching a pass where it might have developed into something much closer. When, after a long delay, he had written to her his letter was returned by the Postal authorities marked 'Gone away. Address unknown.' It was only after a year had passed that a mutual friend had put him in touch with her again, when he learned that she was married to a Mr. Bosanquet. Looking at her now he had to admit that the years had been kind to her. If anything, she was more beautiful than the girl he had left in the Surrey village, and he was conscious of fierce anger against the man who had brought the wistful expression to her eyes.

'What are you going to do about it?' he asked.

'There's nothing one can do.'

'You can leave him.'

'I've grown fond of the boys. They're very good boys.'

'But they're his sons.'

'I feel as if they were mine.'

'John doesn't look much like your son, does he?'

'There's a lot of the boy still in him. I took on a job, Bob. I think I ought to go through with it, at least until the boys are independent.'

'That means years and years. What's he going to do with them?'

'It's all very vague. If he has any definite plans he hasn't told me of them.'

'Dorinda, do you still love him?'

She hesitated and then shook her head slowly.

'Does he realise that?'

'I think he must. We occupy separate rooms — and have done so for the past year.'

'And yet you are prepared to go on living an artificial life?'

'For the boys' sake — yes.'

'While he spies on your movements?'

'One can get used to anything. It's quite surprising how one faces up to new situations. I've scarcely any pride left, but I think I should have less if I ran out on the boys.'

'That's sheer damned silly sentiment. The boys will inherit his money. Their future is safe, but what about yours?'

'Let's drop the subject,' she begged. 'It's so good to see you again. Tell me about your life in Egypt — what you do all day long and all the scandal and gossip that represents so large a slice of existence.'

Grant was willing to fall in with her mood, and for half an hour he amused her with quite superficial conversation. Then back came John.

'I've done the whole lot,' he said. 'Everything is in the car. Can I have an ice?'

He ordered a large ice-cream from the waitress, and was very soon wrapping himself round it.

'What about some tennis, Mr. Grant?' he said. 'The court's getting a bit burnt up, but it ought to be in your favour, if you're used to sand courts.'

Grant took Dorinda's cue and shook his head.

'Sorry,' he said. 'This is just an excursion. I've no racket, or shoes.'

'But we can fix you up.'

'Our guests are arriving this afternoon, John,' said Dorinda.

'What guests?'

'Professor and Mrs. Chatleigh.'

'Oh Lord — I had forgotten. It looks as if it's going to be a particularly dull weekend.'

'John!' remonstrated Dorinda.

'The Professor will talk fish, and Mrs. Chatleigh will burble Art, while the tennis court goes to rot.'

'There's Jasper.'

'He's not half as good as Mr. Grant. You see, I need someone to stretch me right out. I'll never improve my game playing with Jasper. Anyway, it's no use moaning. I'm sorry.'

'Another time perhaps,' said Grant.

He saw them to their car, and a few moments later they were homeward bound by the sea road. Lunch was a tense affair, for Bosanquet had not yet got over the conversation with his young wife. He ate in dead silence, left the table early and went straight to the study, as was his usual practice. The midday meal seemed to have a soporific effect upon him, and he always slept soundly after it, in his particular high-backed chair by the fireplace. It was understood that no one interrupted him during that period of repose.

'The depression over Castle House is now moving south,' said Jasper, with a sigh. 'When do the Chatleighs arrive?'

'On the four-eighteen,' replied Dorinda. 'One of you will have to go to the station with the car. I can't very well ask Penny, as it's Saturday.'

'I went last time,' said Jasper.

'What a lie!' exclaimed John. 'Anyway, I don't mind.'

'Tell you what — we'll both go,' said Jasper.

This arrangement was duly carried out. The train was forty minutes late owing to enormous holiday traffic, and Jasper, who drove back, very nearly had an accident at the acute bend in the road by the Castle. It was entirely his own fault, but he blamed the car brakes which needed re-lining. Finally Professor and Mrs. Chatleigh were safely landed with their hosts, much shaken-up by the nerve-wracking journey.

The Professor was past middle age, and as bald as an egg. He wore gold-rimmed pince-nez over a thin nose, and always looked over them when the object of his scrutiny was outside a range of two yards. His dress was archaic — his coat much too short, and his trousers tapering towards the bottom. But always he was scrupulously neat. John could imitate him with exactitude. His wife was some years younger, and had once been pretty. She was an ex-schoolmistress, and crazy about Art, with a leaning towards the modern school. During tea the conversation was retrospective in character. The Chatleighs had been to Devonshire for a month, and Mrs. Chatleigh went over the whole itinerary, forgetting nothing.

'But it's all so different,' she moaned. 'The dear little places we used to love are ruined by cheap bungalows and tea-houses. One would have thought the west country would have been immune from the spoilers, but, alas, it isn't so. Henry and I used to walk to delightful coves where we were sure of finding complete seclusion. There isn't one left, and they tell me that the servant problem there is now just as acute as in the home counties. It is all very disturbing. Henry, dear!'

The Professor, who was abstractedly eating a well-filled jam tart with his fingers, hastily put it down and seized a knife. Jasper who had been doing the same thing nearly choked.

'How's the new book going, Raymond?' asked the Professor.

'Rather badly at the moment,' replied Bosanquet.

'I think it's the heat. It's been like this for over a fortnight.'

'It's far worse in London,' said Mrs. Chatleigh. 'Personally, I should like to live in the country — preferably by the sea. But Henry is lost if he isn't within walking distance of the British Museum. I'm most anxious to look round your garden.'

'You'll find it very burnt-up, I'm afraid,' said Dorinda. 'Whenever we see a dark cloud we all cheer, but it never comes to anything.'

She rang the bell, and brought in the good-looking butler.

'More hot water, please, Prout,' she said. 'Oh, you've brought it. That was thoughtful of you.'

'So you've still got Prout,' said Mrs. Chatleigh. 'Somehow I didn't think he'd stay.'

'Why not?'

'He's so very desirable — I mean from the point of view of anyone running a house. My experience has been that the good servants are quickly enticed away by one's friends — or so-called friends. We lost the best maid we ever had that way.'

'Do you refer to Mildred?' asked the Professor.

'Yes. She was quite marvellous, but we only kept her two months. She was offered twice the wages we were paying her.'

'Mildred wasn't interested in wages,' grumbled the Professor. 'Later she married her employer, and now she teaches her own servants how to be good employees.'

It was a dull enough weekend for the two boys, but the Chatleighs seemed to be enjoying themselves. The Professor had long discussions on zoology with Bosanquet, and Mrs. Chatleigh was able to expound her views on Picasso to patient Dorinda, who didn't know Picasso from a bull's foot. It was on Sunday evening that John created a mild diversion. After much angling he succeeded in getting his father alone, and thereupon he voiced his need for two pounds.

'Two pounds!' ejaculated Bosanquet. 'Why do you want all this money?'

'I want to go to London tomorrow afternoon.'

'Oh, you do? And you think I'm going to provide you with hard-earned money to fritter away in London?'

'I've had only ten shillings since I came down.'

'When I was your age — '

'But, father, that was donkeys' years ago. Things aren't the same now. I want to see some fellows in town — a kind of farewell party. Some of them I shan't see again perhaps for years.'

'No. I won't encourage you in going to drinking parties. When I hear the result of the examination perhaps — '

'Examinations? I'm sick of examinations.

49

All my life seems to have been filled with examinations. What do they amount to? All the people I've ever met who have passed umpteen examinations have been dead from the neck downwards. I've done my best. I'm ready to go to work — next week if you like. You know I never wanted to go to the University at all. If I hadn't gone by this time I'd be earning enough to keep myself.'

It was the prelude to a first-class row, in which voices raised in anger could be heard from the lounge. Finally John emerged, looking more rebellious than Dorinda had ever seen him before. She took him into the morning room.

'What's wrong, John?' she asked softly.

'He's a mean swine — !'

'John!'

'I wanted a couple of pounds — most importantly. For weeks I haven't asked him for any money, hoping that when I did he'd give me some. But he turned me down, and not in a nice way. Mother, I'm sick of all this. I simply won't stand being treated as if I were a small boy. He's driving me — '

'John, dear!'

He stopped as she placed her arm round his shoulder, and looked up into her sympathetic eyes.

'You want the money to go to London?' she asked.

'Yes — tomorrow. I'll be frank with you, because you've always been so decent to me. It's a girl. I met her up at Oxford, and made this appointment. Just a dinner together somewhere. She's at one of the girl's colleges, and there was never much chance in term to do anything. She's rather nice.'

'I'm sure she is. I can let you have the money, John. But for heaven's sake give her a good dinner. Two pounds won't go far, with the railway fare to be paid. You should have at least three pounds. Wait a moment.'

She left him, and returned a minute or two later with three one-pound notes.

'There you are.'

'But — are you sure — '

'Oh yes. Have a good time while you may.'

He stood quite still for a few moments, quite overwhelmed by this magnificent gesture. Then, for the first time since she had come into his life, he kissed her.

'You really are grand,' he said. 'When I get a chance I'll show you that they aren't just words.'

Bosanquet remained adamant, and never mentioned the matter again. To add to his chagrin he received a letter from Jasper's headmaster on the Monday morning. It was advance news of the Higher Certificate results, and Jasper had failed. The headmaster believed that with some coaching Jasper could get through next year, and he trusted that Jasper would stay on at the school and take the examination again. The contents of the letter were revealed to young Jasper.

'It's bitterly disappointing,' said his father. 'If you had worked there was nothing to prevent your passing. Well, it means another year.'

'No,' said Jasper firmly. 'I won't go back there again. If you send me back I'll not stay.'

'Nonsense!'

'I mean it, father. I've been there six solid years. The routine and monotony are enough to drive a fellow mad. Every place worth going to is out of bounds. It's — intolerable.'

'Six hundred other boys don't find it intolerable.'

'Don't they? I'd like you to hear their conversation. Most of 'em hate it like hell. A year or two isn't so bad, but when you've had five or six years of it you get desperate. John's been through it. Ask him, and he'll bear out what I say. It isn't a natural life — just a monastery where your brain gets atrophied. A chap doesn't learn a blessed thing the last two years. He becomes an unpaid master, looking after kids who are as miserable as he is, and some of them take it out of the kids to kill the horrible sameness.'

'I won't listen to such nonsense. I went to the same school myself. It has turned out some splendid men.'

'Yes — and some rotters, but you seldom hear about them.'

'That's quite enough, Jasper. I am writing to the headmaster to agree to the extra coaching — '

'I tell you — '

'That's all I have to say.'

The two boys practised 'putting' on the burnt-up lawn for an hour, and then sought a drink, after learning that Bosanquet had taken his two guests out to see Battle Abbey.

'Have you got charge of that key yet, Prout?' asked John of the butler.

'I'm afraid not,' replied Prout. 'But I managed to smuggle out a couple of bottles of ale last evening when I got the wine.'

'Good man!' said John. 'Jasper, we're in luck.'

'No luck will make up for what's coming to me,' moaned Jasper. 'Another year at school will finish me off.'

'You can get expelled,' said John calmly.

'By jove — that's an idea. But how?'

'The 'Blue Pigeon' is out of bounds. Go there and cause a disturbance. A fellow did that when I was there. He broke up the place, and two days later his father was requested to remove him. As a matter of fact he hated drink, and was one of the quietest fellows alive.'

'Well, it's certainly worth thinking about. Oh, here comes the nectar of the Gods.'

Prout balanced the two bottles and glasses with the ease and dexterity of a conjuror. The corks came out with a bang, and the ale rose in gleaming bubbles above the rim of the bottles. Prout nodded his appreciation.

'I've had them on the ice,' he said. 'You mustn't linger over it, or there may be trouble.'

'Mother wouldn't mind,' said John.

'I was thinking of the master,' said Prout. 'I'll collect the glasses in ten minutes.'

'Thanks, Prout!'

Dorinda entered the room before they had finished, and raised her eyebrows at the half-filled glasses.

'Prout wangled it,' said John. 'It's all right. Father has gone out in the car with the Chatleighs.'

'I know. John dear, I think it would be wise not to tell your father you are going to London.'

'Not likely,' said John. 'I've looked up a train, that will enable me to leave while he's having his nap. We can sneak the car and Jasper can drive it back from the station.'

'Can't be done,' said Jasper. 'I've promised to play golf with a man at the club, and I've got to be on the first tee at half past two. Penny can take you.'

But Dorinda thought this would be inadvisable, as Penny was busy in the garden on a special job, and was wanted at half-past three to take the Chatleighs to the station.

'You can easily catch the bus, John,' she said. 'I'm sure there's one about a quarter past two.'

John checked this up on the time-table, and so the general exodus was arranged.

5

At lunch the Chatleighs expressed their thanks for a very nice time. Mrs. Chatleigh had made copious notes about Battle Abbey, and Pevensey Castle, and the Professor had some notes on butterflies which he had observed.

'Now you must come and stay with us,' said Mrs. Chatleigh to Dorinda. 'I wouldn't advise it at this time of the year, but about the end of September London can be delightful. There's a Russian Ballet coming to Covent Garden, and they're doing an entirely new ballet by Tschaikovsky. There's no one quite like Tschaikovsky. I know Raymond doesn't like ballet, and nor does Henry, but you can trust them to find something mutually interesting.'

The Professor endorsed the invitation, and Dorinda said that she and Raymond would be delighted, and that she would let them know later. Bosanquet seemed to be fast going to sleep, and it was doubtful whether he had heard anything.

'If you'll excuse me, Henry,' he said. 'I'll see you before you leave.'

'Of course. You get your nap,' said the Professor. 'Wish I could sleep after lunch.'

'He can,' put in his wife. 'But he wakes up in such a foul temper, and sleepier than ever.'

So Bosanquet retired, while the others attacked nuts and fruit, which Bosanquet never touched. John looked at his watch and then at Dorinda.

'Yes, John,' she said. 'You ought to leave now if you are going to catch that train.'

'Me too,' said Jasper. 'I've got a golf match on.'

The two boys made their apologies, wished the guests a pleasant journey back to London, and took their leave.

'What is Raymond going to do with them?' asked Mrs. Chatleigh.

'I don't know. Unfortunately Jasper failed to pass the examination for the higher School Certificate, and may have to take it again. John sat for his degree last term, but the results aren't out yet.'

'Starting boys out in the world must be awfully difficult. We only had a girl, you know, and she took instinctively to teaching. Henry, you oughtn't to eat any more nuts.'

'Better than we get at home,' said the Professor. 'Well, my dear, I suppose we ought to start packing.'

'Oh, not yet,' begged Dorinda. 'I've told Prout to serve some China tea in the lounge.'

Mrs. Chatleigh beamed.

'How clever of you, Dorinda, to remember my weakness,' she said. 'I'm afraid it's an incurable habit.'

They passed into that lounge, where Dorinda rang the bell. A few moments passed and then Prout entered carrying a tea-tray and the various necessaries. Mrs. Chatleigh watched him enviously as he poured out the pale fluid.

'Sugar, madam?'

'Oh no, thank you — nor milk.'

The Professor had both sugar and milk in large quantities.

'Isn't it shocking to treat excellent China tea in that manner?' said Mrs. Chatleigh. 'Henry, do be careful, or you'll spill it.'

Prout filled Dorinda's small cup, and was handing it to her when from somewhere outside came a reverberating report. The Professor who had his overfilled cup in his hand, spilled half the contents over his trousers. Mrs. Chatleigh uttered a sharp cry of alarm and Dorinda's face went deathly pale.

'It — it was from the study,' said Prout. 'Excuse me, madam.'

He hurried out, and before the rest of them

could get their breath he was back again, standing by the half-open door, looking as pallid as Dorinda.

'What is it, Prout?' she enquired.

'Something dreadful has happened, madam — in the study.'

Dorinda rose unsteadily.

'Was it a shot?' she asked.

'Yes, madam. The master has been shot.'

'Good God!' ejaculated the Professor and hurried to Dorinda's side.

'I'm — all — right,' she gasped. 'I must go to him.'

She hurried across the hall to the study, with the others close behind her. Bosanquet was sitting in his high-backed chair by the fireplace, with his hands on the two arms. His head was sagging to one side, and as his wife approached him she saw blood on the dark waistcoat. The Professor came forward and supported her swaying form. He then reached out and lifted one of Bosanquet's eyelids. The eye was turned upwards.

'A doctor,' he said to Prout. 'And telephone the police at the same time. Dorinda, you had better — '

An increase in the weight he was supporting made it clear that Dorinda was oblivious to everything. He lifted her to a settee, and turned to his wife.

'Try to bring her round, and then take her to her room.'

From outside he could hear Prout begging the doctor to come at once. Then there was a slight pause while Prout got the police number, and the excited voices of the two maids could be heard. One of them tried to peer round the door, but the Professor forestalled her and told them both to go back to the kitchen, as there had been an accident.

Then Prout came back and announced that both doctor and police were coming at once. Mrs. Chatleigh asked him for some smelling salts and a bottle was brought. Dorinda regained consciousness, and was taken to her bedroom by Mrs. Chatleigh.

'It couldn't have been suicide,' said the Professor. 'For there's no weapon about. It looks as if he were shot from that window.'

He indicated the right hand window, behind the fish-bowl, which was open. The curtain had been drawn to shut out the blazing sun, and it was moving slightly in the sea-breeze.

'That was my impression, sir,' said Prout. 'When I came in and saw what had happened I ran to the window, but I saw no one in the grounds.'

'Unquestionably it was murder. But why — why?'

Prout shook his head sadly.

'Have the two boys left?' asked the Professor.

'I think so, sir, but I'll look.'

He was absent for some minutes and then came back to say that neither of the boys was to be found.

'Ought I to try to get then back at once?' he asked. 'I know that Mister John is on his way to the station, and Master Jasper has gone to play golf.'

The Professor was in a dilemma. Nothing like this had ever happened to him before and correct action was difficult to determine. Before he could make up his mind the doctor arrived, and was shown into the house.

'I'm Professor Chatleigh,' said the Professor. 'And my wife and I are guests here. Mrs. Bosanquet is in her room.'

The doctor nodded and went at once to the high-backed chair. Swiftly he carried out the usual tests, and then shook his head, and consulted his watch.

'Is he — dead?' asked the Professor.

'Yes. Do you make the time two-twenty?'

The Professor looked at his own watch and nodded his head.

'Have the police been informed?' asked the doctor.

'Yes. They are on their way.'

'In that case I had better wait. Unfortunately I have a confinement case, so I hope the police won't be long.'

The Professor hoped so too. He was now experiencing a reaction and wanted nothing so much as to lie down. So he left the doctor and went to his room. His wife came in a few minutes later, wiping her eyes.

'Was that the doctor?' she asked.

'Yes. Poor Raymond is dead.'

'Oh, how terrible! What a finish to a nice weekend! And poor Dorinda — only married a year or two. Henry, we shall be questioned by the police.'

'Of course.'

'I'm worried about something. Do you remember last evening? John had a fearful quarrel with his father. Dorinda didn't comment on it but I overheard them.'

'Well?'

'Ought the police to know about that?'

'My dear, they will ask thousands of questions, and we must reply truthfully.'

'But John — '

'What?'

'Oh, it's all so difficult. If we had caught the morning train as I suggested this wouldn't have happened — to us.'

'It might still have happened to poor

Raymond,' replied the Professor in tones of remonstrance.

'But what am I going to say if the police ask me about the family?'

The Professor sat up and blinked at her — quite oblivious to what was in her mind.

'Why should a few simple questions embarrass you, Harriet?' he asked.

'Oh you men are such fools. The moment I stepped in to this house I knew that something was wrong. There was even a suspicion of it last year when we were here, but it wasn't so edged — so noticeable.'

'What's wrong with the house?'

'Not the house, Henry — the occupants. There's disharmony everywhere. The boys are opposed to their father — or were. Dorinda is miserable. She and Raymond were miles apart.'

The Professor joined issue on this point. He happened to know that poor Raymond thought the world of his pretty young wife. It was horrible to talk like that — most ungenerous. His wife stuck out her chin stubbornly. She knew better. Her whole attitude was so cocksure she disturbed her husband's rest, which he needed so badly. He got off the bed and stared through the window.

'I don't think you're justified in drawing

63

such conclusions,' he grumbled. 'Of course married life isn't one endless rhapsody. Even we have had tiffs, haven't we? And heaven knows I'm the most peaceful-minded man.'

'Not so peaceful,' retorted Mrs. Chatleigh. 'You've been egging on people to compel the Government to intervene in Spain and China. You told — '

'Enough!' pleaded the Professor. 'Let us stick to relevant facts. I say you are woefully mistaken about Raymond and Dorinda, and that you exaggerate the importance of Raymond reprimanding his son. Boys need pulling up occasionally. You should know that.'

Mrs. Chatleigh shot him a superior glance. It was like him to keep his head buried deep in sand. He wasn't interested in other people to the extent that she was. She picked up her handbag, and took a handkerchief from it, also a long strip of pink blotting paper. For a moment she hesitated, and then she thrust the piece of blotting paper at him.

'Perhaps this will make you understand,' she said. 'It was inside the writing desk. I used it when I wrote that card to Alice telling her not to forget to air the beds.'

The Professor blinked over his glasses as he

took the blotting paper from her.

'What is all this, Harriet?' he pleaded.

'Hold it up to the mirror. That's my writing in the corner. The other lines were on it when I used it.'

The Professor's sense of decency was outraged.

'I will do nothing of the kind,' he said. 'It is the reversed impression of someone else's writing, and is private. Harriet, I'm shocked at you.'

Mrs. Chatleigh shrugged her shoulders, took the blotting paper from him, and held it up to the mirror.

'Look!' she said. 'I insist that you look.'

The Professor did look, in a shamefaced way.

'I can't read it,' he mumbled. 'It's too faint.'

'Then I'll read it for you. It says, ' — so please don't telephone me again. He mistrusts all my telephone calls. I'll find some means to see you again. Love, Dorinda.' '

The Professor sat down on the bed, looking very discomfited. His wife regarded him with an air of self-vindication. The Professor jumped up suddenly.

'I call it disgraceful,' he said. 'I would never have believed it of you.'

'Don't be so sensitive,' she replied. 'I didn't

mean to read it. Actually it was reflected in the mirror of my handbag, which was lying in the desk.'

'You must dispose of it.'

Mrs. Chatleigh nodded.

'I'll tear it in small pieces,' she said.

'No, wait!' cried the Professor. 'I don't think we should do that. It would make us accessories after the fact, and liable to prosecution. We are not justified in destroying anything in the nature of evidence. For all we know, that man may be — '

He found it difficult to complete the sentence, but his wife finished it for him.

'The murderer,' she said dramatically. 'But Henry, that might bring Dorinda under suspicion. Ought we to do that?'

'Oh, why did you ever poke your nose into other people's affairs?' groaned the Professor. 'Look what you've done.'

'What have I done?'

'You've involved us — in a manner of speaking. If this had been found by the police — as it doubtless would have been — we should at least have had clear consciences. But now — '

'I can put it back where I found it,' suggested Mrs. Chatleigh.

'Making us contributors to poor Dorinda's embarrassment. Those are the two horns of

66

the dilemma, and you are to blame.'

'Blame or not — what am I to do?'

'Tear it up,' replied the Professor miserably, after a short pause. 'Tear it into small pieces, and set light to it in the fireplace.'

6

Superintendent Ball's reaction to the news of the murder was one of momentary incredulity, followed by utter bewilderment. He had never really taken the threat contained in the letter with any seriousness, and had hoped that McLean's plan which had unfortunately been adopted too late, would result in the arrest of someone in the house, whose object would prove to be plain slander and nothing else. But now, if he could believe his own ears, Raymond Bosanquet had been murdered — shot dead in his own study.

Ball hurried along to Castle House, saw the corpse, heard the details, and quickly realised that here was a first-class case which called for the most expert investigator. Ball had the good sense to know that time was of the utmost importance, and that there would be a better chance of solving the case if Scotland Yard were requested to deal with it at once. He had a long talk with his Chief, and as a result he heard later that Chief Inspector McLean and Sergeant Brook were travelling down by road, and hoped to arrive at Castle House by seven o'clock that evening.

'I'm not jealous of McLean,' he admitted magnanimously. 'That man's got everything.'

The district was new to McLean. He had been to Eastbourne and to Hastings, but the country in between was familiar to him only through books. Brook however had taken his nephew and nieces to Pevensey Bay the preceding summer, on one of his frantic Sundays.

'Not a bad place,' he said. 'But no pier or promenade.'

'Heaven be praised!' said McLean.

'Scared me out of my life — those kids,' he ruminated. 'I had a nap after lunch and missed 'em. Finally I found 'em all — on top of one of those towers — what do they call 'em?'

'Martello?'

'That's it. They climbed up to a kind of door about six feet from the ground, and managed to get to the top. Little devils might have fallen down and broken their necks. But this place we're going to is in the old village, isn't it?'

'Yes. I believe the sea doesn't come within a mile of it now.'

'Wasn't the dead man the one who was receiving anonymous letters, that Superintendent Ball spoke about?'

'He was.'

'Didn't the ink dodge work?'

'There wasn't time.'

The vast bastions of the old Roman walls suddenly came to view, and McLean gasped at the immensity of them. This impressive ruin extended for hundreds of yards, after which they entered the village proper.

'Took the kids to the castle after they missed breaking their necks on the Martello Tower. Office of Works have taken it over now, and have made a fine job of it. By the way, who was Martello?'

'He wasn't a person at all. Don't talk so much now, or you'll ram a charabanc.'

The car was slowed down to negotiate the busy narrow village street, and a few minutes later it reached the drive of Castle House, which lay back from the Hastings Road, on a slight elevation. It was easily the most impressive house in the district, and it commanded splendid views. McLean had time to admire the rockeries and fish-ponds as Brook drove the car by the winding 'drive' to the front entrance. A ring at the bell brought Prout to the door.

'Superintendent Ball is expecting me,' said McLean.

'Yes, sir — this way.'

The two men were conducted to the large study, where the Superintendent was sitting with a subordinate officer, going through some notes.

'Ah, McLean,' he said, rising to his feet. 'Glad to see you — and you, too, Brook. The chief was here a little while ago, but was compelled to leave to attend a conference. He asked me to convey to you his apologies, and hopes to see you later. Well, this is a nice sort of sequel, isn't it?'

'Is this the room where it took place?'

'Yes. Not a single thing has been touched — except the body. That had to be taken away for pathological purposes. I hope to have the bullet this evening. It was deeply embedded. I have taken some evidence, but doubtless, as you're in the case so early, you'd prefer to start all over again.'

McLean nodded, and quickly took in the outstanding details of the room. The large heated aquarium over the fireplace attracted his attention, as it was bound to attract anyone's. He gazed for a minute or two at the beautiful multi-coloured fishes, while Brook disposed of various impedimenta.

'Nice, aren't they?' said Ball. 'He was crazy about fishes. Will you use this room?'

'I think so. It will allow the family to use all the rest of the house. Now tell me — have you made any progress at all?'

'None. Bosanquet was shot dead in that

high-backed chair. I've marked the position of the legs on the floor, and on the back of the chair there is another mark which corresponds with the position of the bullet in the body. Everyone in the house heard the report, also the gardener, who was finishing his lunch in the potting shed. No person was seen leaving the grounds. I think I'd better leave you my notes, and take a bite of food while you run over them. Then you'll know all there is to know about the case up to date. You can get in touch with me at the Bay Hotel — if you want me. Otherwise I'll be back in about an hour.'

McLean was rather glad when Ball and his assistant left, for much as he liked Ball, there were huge differences in their ideas of investigation. Brook shared McLean's point of view. He amused himself watching the antics of the fish while McLean ran through the depositions and notes.

'I'll have to get myself one of those,' he said, indicating the heated aquarium.

McLean paid no heed to him, but made notes as he perused the documents. Finally he turned over the last sheet, and clipped the whole lot together.

'Nothing very exciting there,' he said. 'Two of the chief witnesses have not made any statements. One — the elder son — is in

72

London, at an unknown address, and the other — Mrs. Bosanquet — has been allowed to rest. The one outstanding and incontrovertible fact is that Bosanquet was shot dead while resting — or sleeping — in that chair at approximately 2.15 p.m. to-day. I propose to start taking evidence at once. Find Mr. Prout — the butler, and ask him to come here.'

Brook left the study and returned with Prout a few minutes later.

'Sit down, Mr. Prout,' said McLean. 'I appreciate that you have already made a statement to Superintendent Ball, but it will help me to get a grip of the case if you will answer my questions.'

'Certainly,' replied Prout. 'I am as anxious as everyone else to see the matter cleared up.'

'In your former statement you said you had been in the employ of Mr. Bosanquet for two years, and that during that time you had not observed any ill-will on the part of any member of the staff towards Mr. Bosanquet?'

'That is true. I would point out in support of that statement that no member of the staff has been changed during that period.'

'But a statement has been made to the effect that Mr. Bosanquet was rather harsh in his manner to the servants, and that on occasion he complained bitterly about their incompetence. What truth is there in that?'

73

'I think it is true,' replied Prout quietly. 'But we all knew that Mr. Bosanquet was a very brilliant scientist, and that he didn't mean what he said. Then there was the fact that Mrs. Bosanquet always made up for Mr. Bosanquet's fits of temper.'

'How?'

'She would be particularly nice to us afterwards, and make it clear that she was really apologising for him.'

'But did that remove the ill-feeling?'

'I don't think anyone got so far as ill-feeling. You see, the master didn't play much part in the running of the house. We didn't come into contact with him very often. A great deal of his time was spent in this room — and in the garden. He was very detached from ordinary affairs.'

'Tell me what happened this morning — before and after lunch.'

'The family and the guests had breakfast together at nine o'clock. At about ten o'clock Mr. Bosanquet and Professor and Mrs. Chatleigh went out in the car. I think they went to see Battle Abbey, which is not far from here.'

'Did the chauffeur go?'

'No. He had work to do in the garden. You see, he's really a chauffeur-gardener.'

'Proceed.'

'A little later I saw Mister John and his brother practising putting on the lawn, and at about eleven o'clock they came indoors and asked me for a drink. Mrs. Bosanquet was busy about the house all morning. At about a quarter to one Mr. Bosanquet and the guests returned. We had lunch punctually at one o'clock. At about a quarter to two Mr. Bosanquet left the dining-room, and went to his study.'

'You mean he left his guests having their lunch?'

'Yes. I should explain that it was a habit of his. He wouldn't have done it with a guest less well known to him than the Professor. But the Professor understood Mr. Bosanquet. A nap after lunch seemed to be absolutely essential to his health. If he ever missed it he collapsed during the evening.'

'And for how long did he sleep on these occasions?'

'About an hour. During that time I had strict instructions not to disturb him on any account.'

'Did he always occupy the same chair in the study?'

'Always. Master Jasper used to refer to it as 'Pop's nap chair.' '

'Continue.'

'At about two o'clock Mister John and

Mister Jasper both left the dining-room. Mister John was going to London, and I saw Master Jasper for a moment, about five minutes past two, with his bag of golf clubs.'

'Was he leaving then?'

'I can't say. He was in the hall looking for something.'

'And Mister John — did you see him leave?'

'No.'

'What happened then?'

'I went into the kitchen to make some tea. Mrs. Bosanquet had told me to make China tea for three persons, and to take it to the lounge when she rang. The bell went at ten minutes past two, and I carried the tea into the lounge. The Professor, Mrs. Chatleigh and Madame were there. I was serving the tea when I heard the report of the firearm. It seemed to me to come from the direction of the study, and as Mrs. Bosanquet seemed too terrified to move I hurried through the hall and entered the study.'

He stopped to get his breath, for the narration of the grim story affected him deeply.

'I saw Mr. Bosanquet sitting back in the chair as if he were sleeping,' he said. 'But his head was at a curious angle, and then I saw blood on his waistcoat. I ran to the right-hand French window, which was open, and looked out on the terrace and over the garden. In the distance I saw Penny — the chauffeur — looking out of the potting shed. I shouted to him — asked him if he had seen anyone, as a shot had been fired. He said he hadn't seen anyone — as he had been having his lunch. I told him to search the garden, and then went back to the lounge. The mistress and the Chatleighs came back here with me. The Professor went to Mr. Bosanquet and then said he was dead. He told me to ring the doctor and the police, and I did so. The doctor came quickly and the police later. That's all I know.'

'Mr. Prout — can you think of any reason why Mr. Bosanquet should have been shot?'

'No — none at all.'

'Had he to your knowledge any enemies in or out of this house?'

'Not to my knowledge, sir.'

'Are you aware that prior to this murder Mr. Bosanquet had been in receipt of anonymous letters, one at least of which contained a threat?'

Prout expressed great surprise.

'Why, no,' he said. 'I knew nothing about that.'

'When you came to this house Mrs. Bosanquet had been married to Mr. Bosanquet for about a year, had she not?'

'That was my understanding.'

'Would you, from your experience of the family, say that it was a happy marriage?'

Prout shook his head doubtfully.

'I don't think I should be asked that question, sir,' he said. 'I mean that I've no right to form an opinion on such a matter — especially in a case like this.'

'Why is this case any different?'

'What I mean is that Mr. Bosanquet was many years older than Mrs. Bosanquet, and had been married before. It wouldn't be reasonable to expect them to behave quite like a very young couple, would it?'

'I'll put the question a different way. Have you personally known them to quarrel?'

'I wouldn't say quarrel. They had differences of opinion about Mr. Bosanquet's sons.'

'What kind of differences?'

'Mr. Bosanquet was a strict disciplinarian, but Mrs. Bosanquet was easy with them. I think Mr. Bosanquet was not pleased with their progress at college and school — that he expected rather a lot of them, but Mrs. Bosanquet always stood up for them, and that naturally made for disharmony.'

'Did not that disharmony tend to increase as time went on?'

'Just a little perhaps.'

'Do you remember a Mr. Robert Grant calling here?'

'Yes. He called and stayed one night. That was about two months ago.'

'Has he been here since?'

'Not to my knowledge.'

'Have there been any telephone messages from him?'

'I have taken no message from Mr. Grant.'

'Have you at any time seen a firearm in this house?'

'Never.'

'Has there been a quarrel of any kind in the family?'

'No. Only the disharmony I mentioned.'

'But where was this disharmony — between the sons and their father, or between their father and his wife?'

Prout shook his head, as if he found this question very difficult to answer.

'You make it difficult,' he complained. 'When I said 'disharmony' I merely meant that one missed the kind of pleasant relationship that one would expect to find in a family. I'm inclined to think it was due to a clash of temperaments. Mr. Bosanquet was a very brilliant gentleman, but Mrs. Bosanquet didn't seem to be so much impressed by cleverness as by character.'

'And what do you think of the characters of the two sons?'

'I've always found them very nice young gentlemen. It has been a privilege to perform services for them, and they were always very grateful. I'm sure the other servants will bear out what I say.'

'Where were you employed before you came here?'

'I was butler to an English family at Cannes. They finally went to Rhodesia, and I lost my job. I wanted to get a job in England and gave my name to an agency in London. After a wait of two months I had an interview with Mr. Bosanquet, and he gave me the post.'

'All the present servants were here at that time, were they not?'

'Yes. There have been no changes since I came, but there would have been but for Mrs. Bosanquet. She's wonderful at smoothing people down.'

McLean finally dismissed Prout, and reflected for some time on his evidence, which Brook had taken down in shorthand.

'He's evidently very keen to blow Mrs. Bosanquet's trumpet,' said McLean. 'But that's natural enough if he disliked Bosan-quet, as I'm sure he did. I've a feeling that we shall find that dislike shared by quite a number of persons, and such persons will be prejudiced accordingly. I think I shall have to interrupt Mrs. Bosanquet's rest. Ring that bell.'

The summons brought a very pretty maidservant into the room. She was well aware of what was going on, and looked thoroughly scared.

'What's your name?' asked McLean.

'Violet Broom, sir.'

'Well, Violet, will you go to Mrs. Bosan-quet's room and ask her if she is feeling well enough to come down here?'

Violet went out, and after a wait of several minutes Dorinda entered the study. McLean was very surprised. He had expected someone quite young, but nothing quite so attractive as this. Dorinda looked from one to the other, as Brook produced a chair for her.

'Superintendent Ball has imposed on me the task of introducing myself,' said McLean. 'I am Chief Inspector McLean from Scotland Yard, and this is Sergeant Brook. The case of your husband's death has been handed over to us, and I should like to ask you a few questions.'

'I understand,' she replied. 'The Superintendent told me you were coming'

Brook returned to his seat and opened his shorthand note-book, while McLean referred to his own briefer notes.

'It is on record that you married Mr. Bosanquet in Rome three years ago,' he said. 'Is that correct?'

'Quite correct.'

'Prior to that you were a spinster?'

'Yes.'

'Your husband was thirty years older than you?'

'Just over thirty years.'

'Did you know him before he took that trip to the continent?'

'No.'

'So you met him for the first time in Paris?'

'Yes.'

'Would you care to tell me how you came to be in Paris, and to accompany Mr. Bosanquet to Rome, although at that time you were not married to him?'

'Yes. About a year before that my widowed mother died, and I was compelled to seek a post of some kind. Through a friend I got a post of English governess to some French children. I was happy, but it didn't last long, because the family became impoverished through a bad investment. I had to find another post. But this time the circumstances were not so pleasant. My health gave way and I spent some months in a clinic in the Ardennes. When all my savings were used up I went back to Paris. I met my husband in an unconventional way. Almost every day I used to walk from my cheap lodgings to the Jardin des Plantes.' She smiled wanly. 'The fact was I fell in love with an elephant. At that time he was my one friend in Paris. I used to take him a paper bag full of scraps of bread, and he got to know me very well. On two occasions I saw Raymond — my husband — there, and one morning afterwards we got into conversation. After that we met regularly, and finally he told me that he had postponed going south because of me. He knew I had been ill, and was far from complete recovery. He suggested that I should go south with him, and when I displayed reluctance he told me he loved me and wanted to marry me. It was necessary for him to leave Paris at once, as he had some work to do at the Musée Océanographique at Monaco, but he said it might be possible to get married in Paris at once if I doubted him, otherwise we could be married down south, which would have the advantage of allowing me to get to know him a little better. After some reflection I fell in with the idea, and we were married a month later in Rome.'

'Has that marriage been happy?'

She hesitated for a few moments.

'No,' she said.

'Was there any particular reason for the failure?'

'Yes. Once I came home I realised that he regarded me in the light of a possession. His love for me was no more than the love he had for all the other things he possessed — including his two sons. It was soon plain enough that I had married him without knowing him as he really was.'

'Did his sons display any antipathy towards you?'

'At first just a little. But later that changed, and their love and loyalty have since been my mainstay here.'

There was a rap on the door, and then Prout entered with the information that a special messenger had arrived with a small parcel, which he declined to hand to anyone but either Superintendent Ball or Chief Inspector McLean. McLean asked to be excused and went out to the hall where he took possession of the small package. It was addressed to himself and Ball jointly, and when he opened it he found inside a nickel-plated bullet of medium calibre, and a note to the effect that it had been removed from the corpse. He took the bullet into the study and placed it on the table in the bottom of the open box. Mrs. Bosanquet's gaze went to it, and he saw her wince and close her eyes momentarily.

'I understand that the younger son is in the house, but that the elder one went to London soon after lunch,' said McLean.

'Yes.'

'Did you know that the elder son — John — was going to London?'

'Yes.'

'For what purpose?'

'He wished to meet a girl he had met at Oxford.'

'Do you know this girl?'

'No.'

'Did he mention her name?'

'No.'

'Nor where he was going to meet her?'

'They were going to have dinner together. Where he proposed meeting her he didn't say.'

'When the two boys left the dining-room how long was it before you heard the report of the firearm?'

'I think it was about a quarter of an hour.'

'And during that time where were you and the two guests?'

'We were together — in the dining-room for about half that time and then in the lounge where we went to have some tea.'

'During that interval did you see either of the boys?'

'No.'

'What was Prout doing at the time of the explosion?'

'He was serving tea when we all heard it.'

'And the other servants — where were they?'

'I presume they were in the kitchen. Prout assured me they were. He went into the hall so quickly he says it would have been impossible for them to have got back to the kitchen — without being seen. That is to say if either of them — but, of course, the idea is preposterous.'

McLean picked up the bullet and weighed it in his hand.

'Have you ever seen a firearm in the house, Mrs. Bosanquet?' he asked.

'Oh no — except a very old shotgun.'

'Mrs. Bosanquet, what was the attitude of the sons towards their father?'

Her lovely eyes sought those of McLean, and in them was an unmistakable challenge.

'That's a vague question,' she said.

'I meant it to be. But I'll put it more brutally. Has there been any friction between either of the sons and their father which might conceivably end in violence?'

'No. I'll admit he treated them badly — in view of their age and responsibilities. Naturally they felt it, but I'm certain that neither of them was capable of violence against him.'

'Is there a will in existence?'

'I don't know.'

'Have you never discussed such a matter with your late husband?'

'Never.'

The emphatic negative caused McLean to gaze at her fixedly.

'I put it to you, Mrs. Bosanquet,' he said quietly. 'Your position here was that of wife and stepmother — not wife and mother. It would appear to be to your advantage to have your future assured by some legal document, in view of the fact that your husband was many years older than yourself, yet you tell me you have never even discussed such an important question.'

Dorinda seemed quite hurt by McLean's insistence. Her hitherto quiet eyes flung back her resentment.

'It was not important to me,' she said. 'I wanted nothing from him, but what he himself believed I was entitled to.'

McLean shrugged his shoulders. There was indeed nothing to be said in the face of such a statement. He began to see her personality unfolding itself, and it was the personality of a proud woman — and a very brave woman.

'Who acted for him in legal matters?' he asked.

'A solicitor at Eastbourne named Pole.'

McLean noted the name and then turned to the more delicate side of the investigation.

'Do you know a gentleman named Robert Grant?' he asked.

Dorinda's form became very rigid.

'Yes,' she said.

'I believe he paid you a visit here once?'

'That is true.'

'Have you seen him since then?'

'Yes.'

'Where?'

'At his hotel in London, on two occasions, and more recently in Eastbourne.'

'How recently at Eastbourne?'

'Saturday morning. I met him quite by accident. He told me he had come down for the day because he needed some fresh air.'

'Have you seen him since then?'

'No.'

McLean paced up and down the room for a few moments, for this piece of news had taken him by surprise. Ball had not mentioned the fact, so presumably Ball was ignorant of it. Yet it was in Dorinda's favour that she had admitted seeing Grant in

London — and also in Eastbourne.

'Were you alone when you last saw Mr. Grant?' he asked.

'No. My stepson was with me.'

McLean pursed his lips. It made Dorinda's information less gratuitous.

'Mrs. Bosanquet,' he said. 'Did you know that your husband was receiving anonymous letters of a defamatory character?'

'No.'

'Can you think of any person who might write such letters to him?'

'Certainly not. Why do you ask me such a question?'

McLean took the three letters from a folder, and asked her to read them. As she did so her expression became more and more tense. At last she looked up.

'He never said a word to me,' she asserted.

'Is the handwriting quite unknown to you?'

'Quite.'

'You will appreciate that the writer knew that your relations with your husband were not happy relations, and that the last sentence in the most recent letter can be read as a threat?'

'Yes — I appreciate that,' she replied slowly. 'I appreciate, too, that the questions about Mr. Grant are connected with these letters. My husband went to the police, did he not?'

'He thought that advisable.'

'Yes — the Superintendent called here, and Mr. Grant told me that some — '

She stopped suddenly, but McLean took her up.

'What did Mr. Grant tell you?'

'That inquiries had been made at his London hotel.'

Again McLean was filled with doubt about her. Another of her apparent voluntary answers had lost value so far as it affected her veracity. On the Friday evening Grant had been investigated, and on the Saturday morning he had come to Eastbourne! Mrs. Bosanquet had met him — by accident, she said — but the natural interpretation of Grant's action was a desire to know exactly what was happening at Pevensey — knowledge which she could give him. Certainly Mr. Grant was coming more and more into the picture.

'Was your stepson present during the whole time you were with Grant on Saturday?' he asked.

'No. He went to do some shopping on my account.'

'I see.'

'I doubt if you do,' she said. 'Clearly my

husband suspected Grant of sending those letters, or the Superintendent would never have known of his existence. But that isn't true.'

'How can you be sure?'

'It isn't his handwriting.'

'Have you a specimen of Mr. Grant's handwriting?'

'Yes,' she said, and then added. 'But only an envelope. I wrote some shopping notes on the back of it.'

'And destroyed the letter it contained?'

'Yes.'

'Then will you please find that envelope?'

She said she would do her best and left the room. McLean immediately turned over the pages of the London Telephone Directory which was close at hand.

'Get that number, Brook,' he said. 'The Duchess Hotel — and ask if Mr. Robert Grant is still there.'

'If he is in the hotel, shall I put him through here?'

'No. Just find out if he is there, and leave it at that.'

Brook went to the main instrument which was in the hall, and while he was still absent Dorinda came back, with an envelope addressed to herself from London, and dated a fortnight back. McLean gazed at the neat handwriting. There was no resemblance whatsoever between it and that of the anonymous letters, but that point alone carried little weight.

'I should like to retain this,' he said.

'By all means.'

She sat down again, just as Brook came back with a slip of paper in his hand. He passed this to McLean without a word, and McLean glanced at it. It said:-

G. left hotel Saturday 9 a.m. Not been back since. Telephoned hotel to say he was staying away a few days.

'You must be tired,' he said to Dorinda. 'I don't think I'll worry you with any more questions to-night. I'll see the younger boy in a few minutes, and the elder one when he arrives home. Thank you, very much.'

As soon as she had gone Brook looked up at McLean, with suspicion in his face.

'Looks as if the pressing task is to find Mr. Grant,' he said. 'That meeting by accident sounded just a bit too rich. If we can prove he was round about here to-day — '

A ring at the front door could be plainly heard, followed by men's voices, and the entry of someone into the hall.

'Must be the boy back from London,' said

McLean. 'No, it's too early for him if he was dining there.'

There was a knock and Prout entered the room and closed the door behind him.

'I beg your pardon, Inspector,' he said. 'But Mr. Grant has called to see Mrs. Bosanquet. The Superintendent told me that no one was to be allowed — '

'That's all right,' said McLean. 'Ask Mr. Grant in here.'

'Very good, sir.'

'Well, if that doesn't beat the band!' exclaimed Brook. 'Me talking of him and — '

McLean waved him into silence as Grant entered the room. He looked desperately anxious and very hot, and only remembered his hat at the last moment.

'I thought — ' he commenced.

'That Mrs. Bosanquet was here,' added McLean. 'She was until a few minutes ago. For reasons which may be obvious I wished to have the opportunity of seeing you first. I am Chief Inspector McLean of Scotland Yard, now in charge of this case — by which I mean the murder of Mr. Bosanquet.'

'Glad to meet you,' said Grant. 'I read about it only a few minutes ago and came here straight away.'

'To see Mrs. Bosanquet?'

'Naturally.'

'Why naturally?'

'I am an old friend of hers.'

'And her husband?'

'No. He could never be a friend of mine. You may as well know that right away. I met him but once, and never wanted to repeat the ordeal.'

'Were you ever in love with Mrs. Bosanquet?' asked McLean with a suddenness which made even Brook blink.

'I'm not sure. I think I was without really knowing it.'

'Are you in love with her now?'

Grant stared hard at McLean.

'I know nothing about laws of evidence,' he said. 'Your question seems a bit blunt, but I'll answer it. Yes — I am in love with her. That statement ought to remove a lot of misunderstanding.'

'Have you told her so?'

'No.'

'But doubtless she knows?'

'You're wrong. I don't think she does know. I know nothing of the details of this murder, but I thought I might be of help to her, and that's why I called. Have you any objection to my seeing her?'

'Not at all, but I should prefer getting answers to a few questions first.'

'Any questions you like. Go ahead.'

'Have you ever written letters to Mr. Bosanquet, accusing him of selfishness and mental cruelty?'

'I have not.'

'Did Mrs. Bosanquet tell you, or cause you to believe, she was unhappy?'

'Yes. I drew that conclusion the first time I saw her husband, and later she admitted it.'

'You remember meeting her on Saturday morning?'

'Yes. It was in Eastbourne.'

'Have you seen her since then?'

'No.'

'Nor communicated with her?'

'I telephoned her on Saturday evening, telling her that I was staying at Eastbourne over the weekend. I asked if there was any chance of seeing her without coming here, and she said there wasn't as her guests wouldn't be leaving until Monday afternoon at the earliest.'

'Why did you wish to see her?'

'I had had time to think things over. I wanted to tell her that I loved her, and to persuade her to seek a divorce.'

'How was the matter left?'

'She said she would get in touch with me when her guests had gone.'

There was silence for a few moments while

McLean consulted his notes, and then he suddenly put the critical question.

'Mr. Grant, will you tell me exactly what you were doing at a quarter-past two this afternoon?'

'A quarter past two,' mused Grant. 'Yes, that's easy. I was sitting on the beach at Eastbourne, throwing stones into the sea.'

'Alone?'

'With about ten thousand other persons.'

'I mean, had you a companion with you, who can verify that statement?'

'No. We lunched at one o'clock, and I left the dining-room of the hotel at a quarter to two, and walked across the promenade to the beach. I sat there for about an hour.'

'Have you a car?'

'Yes. I drove it down here.'

'Where was the car during lunch?'

'Parked along the promenade opposite the hotel.'

'So there was nothing to prevent your getting into the car and driving here?'

'Nothing — except the desire to do so. Dorinda had begged me not to call, in view of her husband's insane jealousy.'

'But it wasn't groundless, was it?'

'It was at the time. His cruel and unjust suspicion of her is the cause of my change of mind. Had he taken our friendship for what it really was he had nothing to fear, but the moment he set eyes on me, and knew that I was an old friend of his wife, he marked me down as a secret lover. But if you think I had anything to do with his death — '

'I am only concerned with relevant evidence,' interrupted McLean. 'It is of the utmost importance for you to establish where you were at a quarter-past two to-day, because at approximately that time Bosanquet was shot dead.'

'I've told you where I was.'

'Your statement has been recorded,' said McLean. 'If you can provide corroboration of it, I shall be happy.'

Grant thought for a moment, and then shook his head.

'There must be thousands of people who couldn't absolutely prove where they were at that time,' he said.

'That point is appreciated,' replied McLean. 'My immediate object is to eliminate as many possible suspects as I can. You must blame circumstances if you come into that category, not me.'

'I'm not blaming anybody. Can I now see Mrs. Bosanquet?'

'Yes.'

McLean pushed the bell button, and the immaculate Prout stole into the room.

'Mr. Grant wishes to see Mrs. Bosanquet,' said McLean.

'Very good, Inspector. This way, sir.'

Brook was getting intensely interested in the case. Usually such cases were not so close-knit, and Brook found difficulty in holding together the loose ends, but now he had actually noted an important point in Grant's statements, which he imagined McLean had overlooked.

'Mrs. B. dropped a brick,' he said.

McLean nodded and took all the wind out of Brook's sails.

'She should have told us about Grant's telephone call,' added McLean, 'instead of giving us to understand that she believed Grant had come down to Eastbourne for the day only.'

'Wasn't that an attempt to cover him up?'

'I think it was. But at that juncture it was quite clear what we were driving at.'

'Doesn't it mean that she has considered the possibility of Grant being the murderer?'

'Not necessarily. She may have simply been reluctant to contribute to that deduction, even while believing him to be absolutely innocent. Still, she was very unwise to withhold a fact which was almost sure to come out. Now I'll see the boy — Jasper.'

7

Prout conducted Grant to the lounge, where Dorinda was sitting with Jasper. The boy had taken the tragedy badly. He was highly strung and easily overwhelmed by violence. He had refused dinner and was in such a state of nerves that his stepmother was trying hard to comfort him. Her eyes opened wide with joy and surprise when Grant was shown in.

'Did the Inspector send for you?' she asked.

'No. I read the news in the evening paper, and came along at once. But that Scotland Yard man wouldn't let me see you until he had put me on the rack.'

'Oh, Bob — I'm so sorry.'

'There's nothing to be sorry about — on my behalf. Hullo, Jasper! This is a nasty experience.'

Jasper gulped as he shook hands limply.

'He's all upset,' said Dorinda. 'We all are. The Professor and Mrs. Chatleigh are finishing their dinner. They were to have left this afternoon, but in the circumstances they had to stay on. It was good of you to come, Bob.'

Brook then made his appearance with the request that Jasper should go with him to be questioned. Jasper looked helplessly at his stepmother.

'You must go, Jasper,' she said.

'But I've already been questioned. Why don't they believe me?'

'They do,' said Dorinda. 'You see, Jasper — this case has been taken over by another official, and he wants first-hand evidence. All you have to do is tell the truth.'

Jasper looked ghastly as he accompanied Brook out of the room. The door closed and Dorinda turned to Grant.

'It's torture for him, poor boy. John is different — more self-reliant, but Jasper is imaginative. He fainted when he came home and was told that his father had been shot. It's all so horrible — so incredible.'

Grant took both her hands and held them tight.

'Tell me everything,' he said. 'The newspaper was so vague. Are you under suspicion — in danger?'

'No. I was here when it happened, with the Chatleighs and Prout. We all heard the shot.'

'Thank God for that! I feared they might make a case out of your miserable marriage.'

'I fear that danger isn't over,' she replied. 'Naturally they look for motives, and what

100

better motive than what this situation appears to provide? An unhappy wife married to a rich man, a friend close by — much younger than the husband. Can't you see how horrible it all is?'

'Yes. I was asked some very direct questions.'

Dorinda looked at him intently, and he was bold enough to continue.

'The Inspector wanted to know if I was in love with you.'

'How absurd!'

'Does it sound absurd?'

'I suppose not — from his point of view.'

'And from yours?'

'We've always been good friends, Bob,' she replied softly.

'I was a damned fool not to have kept in closer touch with you. I came down here on Saturday because I couldn't bear to be far away from you. You've had no kind of life — '

'I've been happy — in my own way.'

'Happy! With a man who consistently insulted you!'

'Bob!'

'All right. I'll leave him out of it. When McLean asked me that question, do you know what I said?'

She shook her head, but still continued to regard him intently.

'I told him I loved you.'

She made to rise from the couch, but he placed both hands on hers and restrained her.

'Why should I hide the truth?' he pleaded. 'I didn't realise it when I first came here, but since then it's been made clear enough to me. I don't care who knows it. Why should I?'

Dorinda was struggling with her emotions, and her eyes became round with terror as she began to get a real grip of the situation.

'You're trembling,' he said. 'Why are you trembling?'

'Bob, I want to ask you something. Did the Inspector question you about your coming to Eastbourne?'

'Naturally. He wanted to know when I saw you last — what communications I had had with you. You see, in a way I'm a suspect.'

'Did you tell him about the telephone call?' —

'Yes.'

'Oh, Bob, I gave him to understand that you had only come down for the day.'

Grant was surprised by this admission.

'Why did you do that?' he asked.

'I don't know. At first I didn't dream you could possibly come into this case, and then slowly I realised that all your movements were in question. Naturally I didn't want to say anything which might be prejudicial to you.'

'But, Dorinda, there was no sense in concealing anything. When I told you I had come down for the day I was serious — at the time. It was later when I telephoned you that I changed my mind. The police were bound to find out I was in Eastbourne during the time your husband was murdered.'

'Yes, of course. But I was bewildered. Bob, have you satisfied them — about your movements?'

'Unfortunately, no. Actually I was sitting on the beach at the time that shot was fired, but I can't prove it.'

'But you must,' she cried excitedly. 'There must be some means of proving it — some witness.'

'Don't worry,' he begged. 'Naturally there must be suspects. But it will take more than the lack of an alibi for them to bring anything against me. That inspector's no fool, and — '

They were interrupted by the Chatleighs, who halted on the threshold of the room when they saw the visitor. The Professor made a mumbled apology, and his wife looked a little uneasy. Mrs. Bosanquet introduced Grant as an old friend, and the Chatleighs sat down in an atmosphere that was noticeably tense.

'We have just dined,' said Mrs. Chatleigh. 'Such a pity you didn't feel like joining us, but I hope you're feeling a little better now.'

'Yes,' said Dorinda with a smile. 'I suppose you haven't yet seen the Inspector.'

'Not yet,' replied the Professor. 'What a waste of time it all seems — this duplicated evidence. I can't see how it helps poor Raymond, or you, my dear.'

'You say the most foolish things, Henry,' remonstrated his wife. 'Did you telephone Alice?'

'Yes. I told her we were unavoidably delayed, but that we might possibly be back late to-night.'

'It doesn't look much like it,' she complained. 'What are they doing now?'

'Questioning Jasper,' replied Dorinda. 'Poor boy! He feels the strain dreadfully. I hope they won't keep him long. After that perhaps they will take your evidence, and permit you to catch the last train — if you think that advisable. Otherwise you are perfectly — '

'Oh, no,' interrupted Mrs. Chatleigh. 'There are several reasons why we must get back to town tonight. Henry has a most important meeting quite early tomorrow morning. If I could help you, my dear, by staying over — '

'Thank you,' said Dorinda. 'But I shall be all right — now.'

Grant made an attempt to engage the Professor in conversation, but Chatleigh seemed to be sunk deep in reflection, and it was clear that both he and his wife were most anxious to be out of the house. So the party sat on engaging at odd moments in conversation which was clearly forced and unnatural.

8

Jasper's evidence had contributed nothing to the solution of the mystery. It was a repetition of what McLean had already heard — up to the time when Jasper had left the dining-room. He stated that he had not seen John after that, as John went upstairs to tidy himself, and he, Jasper, had gone to get his golf clubs. By catching a bus he had managed to get to the golf course at the appointed time, and had met his golfing opponent on the first tee at just after half-past two. He had been on the sixth hole when a message came from the clubhouse, informing him that he was required at home immediately. He had seen nobody in the garden when he passed through it.

'Scared stiff,' said Brook when the boy had been dismissed.

'Temperamental,' replied McLean. 'He answered up well enough, and I wasn't able to trip him up on any point. I have here a statement given to the police by the man he was playing golf with. It bears out his statement that he was on the first tee just after half-past two. He was rather breathless, but that would be the case if he hurried.'

'Wasn't he a bit vague and hesitant when you questioned him about the relationship which existed between his father and stepmother?'

'That, I think, was an attempt to whitewash his father — now that he's dead. You can't expect the boy to admit that his father was a bad-tempered, selfish man who made his wife's life a positive hell — which is the state of affairs as I interpret it.'

'But actually there was nothing to prevent his shooting his father as he passed the study window, and getting away before anyone saw him?'

'Nothing — given a strong enough motive, and a weapon. The facts, so far as we know them, point to someone who had worked out the details beforehand. The time chosen was that when Bosanquet was asleep in his chair. To render the investigation more difficult the ejected cartridge-case — presuming an automatic pistol was used — was retrieved by the murderer. This room is so situated that anyone shooting through the window could escape round the corner of the house very quickly, and be concealed from view in the main 'drive' which is fringed with evergreen plants, and slightly sunk. The obvious deduction is that the murder was deliberate, and the murderer someone who knew the habits of Bosanquet. It might have been some member of the family, or someone outside.'

'There's just one weakness,' pointed out Brook. 'The chauffeur-gardener was not far away. The murderer had to risk him.'

'That fact is agitating my mind at the moment. I'm keen to question Mr. Penny, but I think we should first dispose of the two guests, who, I believe, are anxious to go home.'

McLean saw the Chatleighs together, since there was no good reason to take their statements separately. They endorsed much which had already been told, but when it came to the various family relationships they were noticeably reserved. The Professor referred to his dead friend as a man of 'international reputation and high cultural ability' — a description which McLean found no fault with, but which was quite irrelevant to the points at issue. The Professor thought that the dead man had been moderately happy with his second wife, but that there was the possibility of her not quite appreciating her husband's point of view in matters affecting science.

Mrs. Chatleigh was not quite so academic. She said very bluntly that she had always liked the Bosanquets, and in her view the frequent friction was only what one would expect in a family where personalities were so strong. The sons had not their father's genius, but they were no less strongly individualised, as was Mrs. Bosanquet. Thus, she argued, one must expect to find disharmonies, but not of a kind which made for any real hate between one and another.

McLean didn't keep them long, and they were greatly relieved to know that they were free to go their way. After them came Penny the chauffeur-gardener. He was a curious type of man, and gave his evidence excitedly, as if for the first time in his life he knew, and appreciated, that he was in the limelight. His speech was bad, but quite impressive.

'The guv'nor gave me a spot of work in the garden,' he said. 'He wanted the big fishpond drained, and all the fish collected and put into a glass aquarium, so he could examine 'em. That took time, because the water had to be syphoned out — see? It was a quarter-past one before I got all the water out, leaving the fish in the sump at the bottom. I knocked off then, and went into the potting shed to have my dinner. I had a nice Cornish pasty, and a flask of tea, and I read the newspaper until a quarter-past two. Then I found the net so I could catch the fish, and was about to go back to the pond when I heard a kind of bang. I opens the door and sees Mr. Prout rush out on to the terrace. He waves his hand at me and I goes a bit nearer. Then he says something about a shot being fired, and asks me if I saw anyone. I tells him no, and he says something about the master, and tells me to run up the drive quickly, and stop any stranger I may see. Well, I did so, but there wasn't anybody there. I come back and told him, and then he tells me that the master has been shot at and killed.'

'Did you know that Mr. Bosanquet used to take a nap in the study after his lunch?'

'Yes. I've often seen him when I've been doing gardening along the terrace.'

'Did you hear any sound of a car engine when you ran up the drive?'

'No. Everything was very quiet.'

'Did you see Mister Jasper leave the house?'

'No.'

'Nor Mister John?'

'No.'

'Can you throw any light at all on this matter?'

'No. I wish I could.'

'How long have you been employed here?'

'Four years.'

'Were you satisfied with your job?'

'Yes. The master treated me fairly well.

110

Mind you, sometimes he would go off the deep end and tell me he was paying me too much, but forty-four bob isn't a lot, and I used to tell him so. Why, I save him quids doing repair work on the old car.'

They were interrupted by Superintendent Ball, who had had a good meal, and was bursting with food and information. At a gesture from him McLean got rid of Penny

'So you've made a start?' asked Ball.

'More than a start.'

'Well, here's something that may make matters clearer. Mr. Pole, who was Bosanquet's solicitor, got in touch with me. He didn't know you had taken over the case. He's outside now, and I think you ought to hear what he has to say.'

'Certainly. Will you ask him in?'

Mr. Pole entered with the timidity of a mouse. He was introduced to McLean, and after a nervous cough he made his statement in his own way.

'I didn't hear of this dreadful affair until an hour ago,' he said, 'as I have been out of town for the day. Last Thursday Mr. Bosanquet called on me on a matter of business. It was important business — in short, a new will.'

He paused to see the effect of his words, and McLean nodded and asked him to continue.

111

'There was a will in existence which was executed soon after his marriage — I mean his second marriage. It provided for trust funds for his two sons, some legacies to servants, and the residue to his wife unconditionally.'

'Did it leave a large residue?'

'Quite considerable — over two hundred thousand pounds, in fact.'

'And the new will?'

'I was surprised — I might even say shocked — by his requirements. The terms he laid down were so harsh I was compelled to plead with him, but he remained obdurate, and there was nothing I could do.'

'What were the new terms?'

'The trust fund for the boys was to stand, but to his wife he left the paltry sum of two hundred pounds a year, and stipulated that even this small annuity must cease if she remarried. He asked for a draft embodying the new details to be sent to him as soon as possible.'

'Did you send it?'

'Yes. It was posted to him on Friday evening. I have heard nothing from him since.'

'Was the draft will sent in the ordinary way? I mean was it registered?'

'No. I didn't think that was necessary. It

was enclosed in a strong blue envelope, which had the firm's name embossed on the back of it. I naturally assumed that Mr. Bosanquet had received it, but the Superintendent tells me that no such draft will has been found, nor my letter which accompanied it.'

'So the earlier will stands?'

'I'm afraid so. There is no one who would dispute the present will, as Bosanquet was preparing to endow some scholarships, with the residue of his estate. Even if a case could be made out — in view of my evidence — it could be argued in support of the existing will that Bosanquet might have changed his mind before he actually signed the new will. I have brought the earlier will with me.'

He handed this to McLean, who perused the terms for a few minutes in silence. He then pressed the bell, and asked the maid to tell Prout he was wanted. The imperturbable butler came in a few moments later.

'At what time does the first post arrive?' asked McLean.

'Usually about eight o'clock in the morning.'

'Who usually receives the letters?'

'I do, sir.'

'Can you recall Saturday morning?'

'I think so, sir.'

'Did you receive the letters that morning?'

113

'Yes, I'm sure I did.'

'Do you remember a long blue letter addressed to Mr. Bosanquet?'

'Yes. It was a fairly thick letter.'

'What did you do with it?'

'I laid it on the breakfast table with some other letters for Mr. Bosanquet. I remember that he was first down to breakfast that morning, and when I served the grapefruit I saw him opening the various letters.'

'Do you know if he posted any letters this morning?'

'I think not, sir. He went out fairly early in the car, and didn't go out again when he came home.'

'Thank you,' said McLean. 'That's all.'

Pole interjected that he had been to the office the first thing, and there had been no letter from Bosanquet. McLean called Dorinda, who stated that she knew nothing about any blue envelope, and nothing about a new will, and there the matter rested. Pole was shown out and McLean was left to wrestle with the facts.

'It looks very much as if that draft will is the cause of the whole thing,' pointed out Ball. 'And that points to a certain person. But we happen to know that that person was elsewhere when Bosanquet was shot. The two sons stood to lose nothing by the new will, but they loved their stepmother, and — well, there it is.'

'You really shouldn't, Ball,' said McLean, with a smile. 'Either boy could have shot his father, but so could Mr. Grant, who stayed at Eastbourne during the weekend, and saw Mrs. Bosanquet on Saturday morning, and is unable to prove an alibi.'

'What!' gasped Ball. 'I didn't know that.'

'He's in the house at this moment. Then there is Mr. Penny who was conveniently having his lunch when the murder took place. But he doesn't stand to lose anything under the new will. But he stood to gain by his employer's death — a sum equal to one year's wages. Can you imagine him murdering his employer for little over a hundred pounds?'

'No, but Grant is different. Bosanquet was jealous of him. He believed his wife was in love with Grant. If she knew that she was going to lose everything under a new will, and Grant — '

'Round we go in circles,' cut in McLean. 'I suggest that theories will knock each other down like ninepins, and that much more is required to get to the bottom of this business. I yet have to see Master John, and as its not likely he will be home before midnight I think Brook and I will follow your example and eat something.'

'Good idea,' said Ball. 'Well, I've got to get back to headquarters. See you tomorrow.'

McLean locked up the room, and he and Brook walked down to the Bay Hotel where they took a late meal and McLean engaged rooms. By the time they had finished the sun was setting, and the higher land on the eastern arm of the bay was radiant with soft roseate light which slowly deepened to subtle heliotropes and blues. There was now a complete absence of wind and the sea heaved in heavy fashion. The oppressive heat was conducive to bathing, and on the long fringe of shingle were many semi-nude forms. Then the distant piers sprang into light.

'Good beer they sell back there,' said Brook.

'You ought to have been a poet,' replied McLean, and left Brook to puzzle this out.

9

McLean and Brook waited at the house until long after the last train from London had arrived, and John made no appearance. Prout, who had been waiting up, came to McLean in a state of indecision.

'What am I to do, Inspector?' he asked. 'You told me I was to show Mister John straight into the study when he returned, but I don't see how it's possible for him to come back to-night. There's no train until the early morning.'

'You can go to bed, Prout,' said McLean. 'One of us will stay here.'

'Very good, sir. Shall I leave the hall light on?'

'Please. Has Mrs. Bosanquet retired?'

'She's in her bedroom, but I'm afraid she's very worried about Mister John. He didn't intend staying away the night.'

McLean nodded and Prout took his departure. Brook looked up at McLean.

'A bit significant, isn't it?' he asked.

'The boy's absence?'

'Yes. The news got through to the evening papers. That's how Grant got to know.

117

Surely the boy saw it.'

'It depends whether he bought an evening newspaper. There was only a very short paragraph. Brook, I think you had better stay here, and rest on the couch. If John comes home ring me at once. I don't want him to see anyone until I have questioned him. If I don't hear from you I'll come along very early in the morning, and you can go back to the hotel and get some real sleep.'

Brook didn't like the look of the leather couch, but his roving eye spotted a number of soft cushions, and he started to collect them. McLean took a pile of letters and documents which he had gathered together.

'I'll wade through some of these,' he said. 'If you want to improve your mind the bookcase is handy.'

'Who wants to read about fishes?' sniffed Brook. 'Well, see you later.'

McLean drove the car back to the hotel, with a view to using it to get back to the house if John Bosanquet turned up during the night — which now seemed highly improbable. Before retiring he went through all the letters and documents, but found nothing which was calculated to shed the slightest light on the murder. He was soon asleep, but was later awakened by a loud rattling of his window which he had left wide open. A wind had arisen since he went to sleep and was blowing the curtains inward. The wind was not unpleasant, for the temperature was fantastically high, but the rattling of the window made sleep impossible. He got out of bed and walked to the window. A half moon was slanting away in the west, shooting a broad beam of light across the sea. About a mile from the shore a small boat was just visible. It was slowly coming to the shore, a little to the right of the hotel, and he saw two human forms at the oars. Presuming they were returning from a belated fishing trip, he proceeded to pack the offending window frame with a folded envelope which he found in his pocket. The rattling ceased, and the oncoming boat now entered the bright patch of sea near the beach. On the dressing table was a pair of powerful night binoculars, which he had brought with him, and he took them up and focussed them on the two men, who were now dragging the boat out of reach of the tide. One of them was Penny. The other was a complete stranger to him.

He waited a while and saw them pass along the beach in front of him, and finally disappear behind some contraptions. Reflectively he put the binoculars away, and got back into bed. When he woke again the room was full of pale light, and his watch told him it was five o'clock. Already the shrimpers were at work, walking waist-deep in the sea and pushing their eight-foot shrimping nets before them, and at intervals transferring their catch into the wickerwork baskets strapped about their waists. McLean envied them their tasks as the sun came up and lent additional warmth to the scene. It seemed to him there was something immensely satisfactory in gathering the sea harvest. How much better and healthier than hunting murderers!

Having dressed he went down to the beach and took a look at the boat which Penny and his companion had drawn up on the shingle. It was a sturdy dinghy, with a locker at one end. On the side of it was painted a name, 'Nimrod.' One of the shrimpers was wading to transfer his creel of shrimps to a larger vessel which was lying beside his bicycle. McLean walked forward interestedly, and greeted the shrimper. Quite casually the man opened the lid of the larger basket and emptied an overflowing creel of transparent shrimps into it. They flicked about like squibs, until he closed the lid.

'That's a nice lot,' said McLean. 'I had no idea shrimps were so plentiful.'

'Oh, there's plenty here, but you have to catch 'em at the right time — just when the tide's making. But there are times when they don't come at all. There's no explaining 'em.'

'Do you come every day?'

'Only when the time suits me. This is a spare time job for me. I have to cycle over from Hailsham. Means getting up early these tides.'

McLean felt sure it did. He watched the man resume work and then drove the car towards Castle House. The views across the marshes were magnificent. It was yet far too early for the mass of holiday-makers to ruin everything, and he gulped in the salt-laden air through the open car window.

Brook opened the door to him. He looked sleepy and when McLean mentioned the matter he laid it down as a incontrovertible fact that the leather couch had never been slept on in its history.

'It simply can't be done,' he said. 'Chunks of horsehair rise up and hit you in the neck. No wonder Bosanquet preferred his high-backed chair. Well, anyway, the boy didn't come.'

'So I presume. I've brought the car. You'd better go and get some sleep. I'll join you at breakfast at nine o'clock, if the boy turns up by then. If not, I'll stay on.'

'Okay,' replied Brook, with a yawn. 'I've been reading the unfinished manuscript — or trying to. I don't believe it.'

'Don't believe what?'

'Bosanquet mentions a fish which breeds its young in its mouth. When they are hatched the little devils swim about outside, and when they spot an enemy mother opens her mouth and they pop inside. Sort of piscatorial A.R.P. Takes a bit of swallowing.'

'The fish or the statement?'

'Both.'

'I think it's true. I seem to remember having read it somewhere else.'

Brook yawned again and shook his head.

'Why am I so darned tired?' he asked.

'Fresh air. You're not used to it. There was nothing of value in those letters I took away.'

Brook left a few minutes later, and McLean went out into the very attractive garden, and made himself more familiar with its layout, for he had scarcely had a chance to see it since his arrival. Bosanquet had made the most of a rather unpromising site — from a gardener's point of view. There was no local stone, and hundreds of tons of water-worn Cumberland rock had been imported. Natural slopes had been used to give the effect of rock-outcrops, and this had been achieved with commendable skill — quite obviously by an expert. Water flowed from a hidden pipe under a boulder and was diverted down numerous channels, and through fish-pools, across bog gardens, until finally it flowed away into a drain. Behind a yew hedge, embellished with topiary work, was a stillwater pond, in which was a lovely assortment of fishes. Bosanquet had stocked it with oxygenating plants, water-snails, and such things as were necessary to complete the cycle of life. This was the pond which Penny had drained off just before Bosanquet had been shot. It was still empty save for the large deep sump where all the fishes had perforce collected. It was now a mass of fins and tails, and gaping mouths. McLean, despite his ignorance of fish-culture, felt that all was not right, and this conclusion was soon borne out by the arrival of Penny with a hose.

'Morning, Inspector,' he said. 'I remembered that this pond must be refilled at once, or the fish won't like it much. They're not used to them conditions. Excuse me!'

He put the hose over the side, and turned on the tap. Water gushed out into the concrete pond, and as soon as it was deep enough the smaller fishes escaped over the lip of the overfilled sump, and went careering round the pond, frisking near the place where the jet of water descended.

'Now they'll be all right,' said Penny.

'Do you feed them?' asked McLean.

'Now and again we give them daphnia

— water-lice, but it's not really necessary. You see, Mr. Bosanquet planned this pond on natural lines. It's what he called 'balanced.' We have to top it up with water to make good evaporation, but there's plenty of pond life for the fishes. Them plants give off oxygen — the snails eat up the muck, the fish eat the snails' eggs. Very much like our life — if you know what I mean, sir — everyone living by taking in the other fellow's washing.'

'Did you know anything about fishes before you came here?'

'Not a thing. I've learned it all from Mr. Bosanquet. Clever he was, too — cleverest man I ever knew. I always thought fish were stupid things. You call a man a 'poor fish' meaning he's got no gumption. Shows how much some of us know. You can't put anything over on them fish. When the sun's not out and they're skulking down below I can bring 'em all up in one place by ringing a bell. That means food to them — food without the trouble of catching it, and there's not one of 'em that won't eat out of my hand.'

'You mean that literally?'

'Honest to goodness. I'll show you when the water gets deeper. And they're all different in character — real individuals. Of course most of these are fancy fish, and you can tame them easily. Orfe and ide and rudd ain't so friendly. They prefer running water, and we keep 'em yonder.'

'Do they breed here?'

'Rather! But we take the small fry away early, and put 'em in a special pond, where we can watch 'em. But Mr. Bosanquet's interest wasn't commercial. Sometimes he would sell fish, but his main object was to study them, experiment with those that had disease. It's marvellous what he could do with a sick fish.'

'How do you know when they're sick?'

'Mr. Bosanquet always knew. Sometimes I can tell. Their scales go dull and dirty. Their dorsal fins collapse, and they get a list on when they're swimming. There are hundreds of different symptoms, but of course I only know the common ones. It's a very interesting study, sir.'

'Are you a fisherman — apart from breeding fish?' asked McLean.

'Me? Oh no.'

'You mean to tell me that with the sea just in front of you, you never yearn to throw out a line?'

'No. Maybe I've got to like fishes too much. But I do have a shot for a lobster now and then.'

'Not with a line?'

Penny laughed and shook his head.

'We — a pal and me — sometimes drop a couple of lobster pots, with some smelly fish as bait. Often we bring home some beauties. The more rotten the bait the better they seem to like it.'

McLean wandered on. Penny's remark about the lobster-pots appeared to explain his boating exploits of the previous night, but McLean was conscious of doubts in his mind. There was something decidedly sinister about Penny. His loquaciousness had a ring of insincerity about it. McLean felt that he was putting it on to cloak a quite different kind of personality.

In the sunken garden behind the tennis court he was surprised to see Dorinda. She was sitting in a semicircular stone seat gazing abstractedly at a family of blackbirds, the mother of which was giving her offspring first lessons in walking. They all scuttled as McLean approached. Mrs. Bosanquet turned her head, and McLean saw a pair of sad eyes regarding him.

'Good morning!' he said. 'I scarcely expected to find anyone about.'

'I slept badly,' she admitted. 'I'm terribly worried about John.'

'He may return on the first train this morning.'

'But one would have thought he would telephone if he missed the last train.'

'Young men are notoriously thoughtless.'

'Not John.'

'Have you no idea who the girl was he went to meet?'

'I only know that he met her in Oxford. She's in one of the women's colleges.'

'In that case one of his fellow-undergraduates may be able to say who she is.'

'Yes, that's true.'

'Do you know who his most intimate college friends are?'

'I've met two boys — he brought them home once. One is named Dalton, and the other Symonds. It was only last Easter. They stayed the night, and I think I may be able to find the letters they wrote to me afterwards.'

'That might help,' said McLean. 'Personally I think we shall soon see him, but in case we don't one of those boys may be able to help us.'

'Yes, but we must give him time. I don't want to raise enquiries which may have the effect of making him look foolish. Inspector — is there any news — any fresh information — But, of course, I shouldn't ask that question.'

'You can ask it, but I shouldn't answer it,' replied McLean, with a smile. 'But I'll go so far as to say the case is full of difficulties. These cases are much easier to solve when one is in possession of the weapon or implement used. So far the local police have failed to find the firearm used. All we have is the bullet.'

'And that's not much use without the weapon which fired it?'

'It may indicate the kind of weapon we have to look for.'

'In the meantime some of us are under suspicion?'

'Naturally.'

'But John's unexplained absence isn't against him, is it? I mean that John wouldn't — that there would be no sense in his staying away — even if — if — '

'If he shot his father.'

McLean finished the horrid sentence for her, and saw her mouth tremble.

'That's what I was trying to say,' she said. 'It's all so terrible — to know that such a possibility is even hinted at. John isn't that sort of boy. He's impulsive in some things, but not in anger.'

'So there was anger?' asked McLean sharply.

'Just the anger of a boy kept short of pocket money — refused the opportunity to meet and entertain a nice girl.'

'His father didn't approve?'

'I don't think the girl was mentioned to him. He didn't approve of John spending a day in London.'

'You say he refused to let him go — yet he did go.'

'I gave him some money. I wanted him to have a good time. It wasn't fair to him to keep him in such a penniless state. His father never seemed to realise that he was no longer a boy. John resented that outlook, but it never went deeper than a passive resentment.'

McLean saw in every word the deep desire to shield her stepson, and he could not blame her for this. In the meantime he kept an open mind on the matter.

'Has Penny ever possessed a firearm?' he asked.

'Penny! I really don't know. I don't see why he should.'

'Some chauffeurs do — for self-protection.'

'I'm not in a position to know. You see Penny doesn't sleep here. He lives at Wynne's Cottage in the village.'

'He appears to have been on quite good terms with your husband.'

'I think he was. He was here when I first came, and has in fact the longest service of anyone here.'

'Is it your intention to continue to employ him?'

'Oh yes. He's a very good worker — quite a handyman.'

'Do you think he would expect that?'

'How can I say? Certainly I've never given him reason to think that I should get rid of him in — in the event of my husband's death.'

McLean finally went back to the house by way of the rock garden, and entered the study through the French window which Brook had left open. It seemed to him that the more he probed the matter the more complex it became. Theorising was interesting enough, but what was vital was clues, and these were disappointingly few. For all he knew at the moment, the murder might have been committed by some outside person who had a private grudge against Bosanquet. Or it might have been done in collaboration with some person in the house, who was in a position to lend valuable aid by knowing all the habits of the family.

Dorinda came to him later with two letters, from the Oxford undergraduates who had been her guests. One lived in Yorkshire, but the other — Philip Dalton — lived at Haywards Heath, and the notepaper gave his telephone number. At ten o'clock Brook returned to the house having had three hours sleep plus what he called a 'man's breakfast.'

'Is he back?' was his first question.

'No.'

'Well, that does look a bit fishy to me.'

'Everything here is fishy. I want Master John's evidence, and I want it quickly. Here's a telephone number. Ask for Mr. Philip Dalton, and if you get him, put him through to me. If he's not at home find out where he is.'

Mr. Philip Dalton was at home, and judging from his voice, in excellent fettle. Moreover he had just read that Bosanquet had been shot, and said he was about to write to John and Mrs. Bosanquet and give expression to his sympathy. Brook cut him short and put him through to McLean.

'We are anxious to get in touch with John Bosanquet,' said McLean. 'He went to London yesterday to meet an old friend — a young lady he met at Oxford. Do you happen to know who this young lady might be?'

'Oxford bristles with 'em,' said Dalton.

'Well this one is believed to be in one of the lady's colleges.'

Dalton uttered a curious little laugh, and then said he was sorry.

'John wouldn't fall for a college bookworm,' he said. 'Oh no. I bet I know the girl.'

'Well, you would help his stepmother and me by telling me where we can find her.'

'You've clean bowled me there,' he said. 'I haven't a notion, but I do know that John went ga-ga over a girl who appeared in a musical show that played here in the spring. The show was called 'Take it Neat,' and the girl's name was Nancy du Park. I say, for the love of Mike don't reveal the source of your information. John wouldn't love me for it.'

'You can rely on me. Oh Mr. Dalton — one more question.'

'Go ahead.'

'John was a fairly good athlete, wasn't he?'

'Very good indeed. He was runner-up for the long-jump in the inter-Universities championships, and very nearly put up a record for the quarter mile. He was our college first choice in the relay race.'

'Keen on running?'

'Keen as mustard.'

'Thanks! That's all I want to know at the moment. I am most grateful to you.'

Brook was puzzled by these questions of McLean, which seemed to have no bearing at all on the case.

'Don't look so mystified, Brook,' said McLean.

'A lot of varsity men prominent in sport keep firearms for starting running races, bumping races and so forth. I was anxious to find if John Bosanquet came into that category. It looks as if he might.'

'Oh, I see. Dalton could have told you, couldn't he?'

'Yes, but I thought I had already asked Mr. Dalton quite enough. It's never wise to put too many questions to the same person, or he may deduce more than is good for your case.'

'Do you propose finding the girl?'

'Yes, but I'll give John another hour.'

Half an hour later Superintendent Ball called. McLean was busy examining Bosanquet's bedroom, and wasn't thrilled by the Superintendent's visit, because it knew it would mean a lot of useless questions and answers, which in view of the present position seemed a shocking waste of time. Actually McLean was in complete charge, but the Superintendent liked to think he was sharing the honours — such as they might be.

'So the boy hasn't returned?' he said.

'Not yet.'

'That looks bad.'

'Why?'

'Young men don't stay away all night for nothing.'

'A pretty girl isn't nothing.'

Ball gave him a sharp look.

'You don't think he's that sort of young

man, do you?' he asked.

'He might be any sort. When I see him I shall be in a better position to judge.'

McLean took out some books from a small case and turned over the pages.

'Expect to find anything here?' asked Ball.

'No. But at times things are where you least expect to find them. I should, for example, like to find that new will.'

'You won't,' said Ball. 'I'm convinced that that has a great deal to do with this case.'

'Yes, but what?'

'Ah, now you're asking something. But one can't help having theories. My mind is divided between two alternatives, and I shouldn't be surprised if yours is too.'

'What are these alternatives?'

'Grant and John Bosanquet.'

'Why do you single them out?'

'Grant is in love with Mrs. Bosanquet. The signing of that new will would have made a tremendous difference to Mrs. Bosanquet. The difference between two hundred pounds a year and a large fortune. Grant may have got to know about the new will.'

'From whom?'

'Mrs. Bosanquet. She swears she knew nothing about it, but I can scarcely credit that.'

'That makes her an accessory before the fact.'

'Well, why not? I believe her life with Bosanquet was a perfect hell. She made light of it because it suited her.'

'So Grant shoots Bosanquet, and he or she destroys the draft will. Mrs. Bosanquet is assured of her fortune under the existing will, and Grant is free to marry her when the case is over?'

'Doesn't that fit the facts?'

'I presume your alternative is much on the same lines. John having nothing to gain or lose under the new will does the job out of regard for his stepmother?'

'You've got it.'

McLean pursed his lips, and shook his head. It made the solution too easy. If Grant or John could have shot Bosanquet, so could Jasper or Penny, and in their cases also a motive could be built up. The Superintendent wasn't contributing anything to the solution by a gratuitous selection of two out of four suspects, leaving out of account outside persons, with unknown motives.

'I think we should be wise to wait a little, before we jump at any conclusions,' said McLean politely. 'I want our other chief witness, and more than that I want the firearm. You can help me materially by carrying out a more thorough search than you made before. You ought to get at least a dozen men, and go over every inch of the garden — not forgetting the fish-ponds, also hedges, ponds and bushes in the neighbourhood. You probably know from your experience how keen a murderer is to dispose of his weapon. He has no peace of mind while he is carrying it. Will you do that?'

'Certainly. As a matter of fact I was going to suggest the same thing. I'll get busy on that right away.'

When he had gone McLean decided to take some action in the matter of John Bosanquet, but he was still anxious that the boy should make a statement before he made contact with the members of his family.

'I'm going to London, Brook,' he said. 'Master John's whereabouts is now a pressing matter. But you had better stay here. If he should come home, don't let him have any conversation with anyone until he has answered these questions. I've written them down as a guide. Time he left home, how he got to Eastbourne station. The train he caught and his movements afterwards. I'll take that bullet with me, and see if I can get an opinion on it which will indicate the make of weapon used, or the probable make. If any reporters call, 'shoo' them off. I don't want too much in the newspapers. A lot is bound to come out at the inquest tomorrow, but that can't be helped.'

The train service to London was so bad that McLean took the car and beat the train by a quarter of an hour. He made a report at Scotland Yard to one of the high officials and left the bullet with the head of a department which specialised in firearms. Enquiries in a likely quarter produced immediate information about the musical show called 'Take it Neat.' It had made a twelve weeks tour of the Midlands and Home Counties in the spring, and had come off the road early in July. The name of the production manager was given him, and after several calls at private addresses and clubs this gentleman was found. His name was Sydney Rawlings, and he had travelled round with the company. At the theatrical club where McLean found him at last, he was apparently trying to talk another man into taking a financial share in another show, and there was much gesticulation, and mention of something being a 'wow' and a 'winner.' One look at Rawlings was enough to persuade McLean that any show produced by him might conceivably be a 'wow' or a 'winner,' but it would unquestionably be shocking.

When Rawlings saw the card which

McLean sent across to him he looked surprised, and then nervous. After a moment or two he came across to McLean, and smilingly asked him what he could do for him, adding that he hoped he wasn't going to be arrested.

'I hope so too,' said McLean. 'But you never know.'

'Well, I'll buy it, Inspector.'

'Did you take out a kind of musical revue called 'Take It Neat?' '

'I'm the guy. Did you see it?' asked Rawlings.

'No — I regret to say.'

'Pity. That was a nice show. To this day I can't understand why it flopped. It was well produced — catchy songs and dances, a pretty good troupe of show-girls. I picked 'em myself, and what I don't know about girls — '

'I'm coming to girls. Did you have in your cast a girl named Nancy du Park?'

'Nancy! I should say. Prettiest one of the whole gang. Gosh, that girl has the goods. Mind you, she can't sing, or dance, but can she walk?'

'Can she?' asked McLean, with an expression of innocence.

'She was a mannequin before she came to me. I said I'd make her a star, and so I would have done if the show hadn't flopped so badly. You see, there were a lot of nasty-minded people who said the show was too nood, and I had to put little frocks on all the show girls that hid the best part of their legs. Can't understand some of them town councillors. They come to the first night and squint at all my goils through opera glasses, and then go home pretending they're shocked. Shocked at a bit of noodity! What is there shocking about a pair of beautiful legs?'

'Do you remember playing at Oxford?' asked McLean.

'You bet. We had good houses there.'

'Do you know if Miss du Park met a young undergraduate named John Bosanquet?'

'No. Can't say I do. No manager can look after the private lives of his young ladies.'

'Can you tell me where I can find Miss du Park?'

'I believe I can. Wait a minute.'

He pulled out a fat, well-fingered black note-book from his inside pocket, and referred to it.

'Ah, here it is,' he said. Nancy du Park — 23, Cuthbert Mansions, Paddington. That's not far from the station.'

'Thanks!'

Rawlings put his reference book away, and peered at McLean.

139

'I say — she hasn't done anything, has she?'

'Oh no.'

'That's fine. I don't like my girls to get into any jam. Well, glad to be of service. Give my love to Nancy.'

Cuthbert Mansions was a very misleading description of the awful pile of bricks and mortar at which McLean eventually arrived. A narrow slot almost lost between a long row of very cheap shops gave entry to it. There was no lift and no list of tenants, but Rawlings had appeared to be sure of the number, and McLean plodded up two flights of stone stairs, and finally found a door numbered 23. He pushed a bell, and after waiting a minute or two, pushed it again. He then heard a shuffling inside. A light came on and the door latch was slipped. Facing him was a very lightly clad female, clutching a dressing gown about her, and smoking a cigarette. She looked as if she had just fallen out of bed, and she regarded McLean with a good deal of suspicion.

'Are you Miss du Park?' he asked.

'Sure!'

'Your friend Sydney Rawlings sent me here.'

'Oh! You a pal of Syd's?'

'Not exactly. But I should like a few words

140

with you in regard to a young man named John Bosanquet.'

'What about him?'

'A doorstep is not the best place to discuss the matter.'

'How do I know you're straight?'

McLean produced his warrant, and the hazel eyes regarded him a little anxiously, he thought.

'Something wrong?' she asked.

'Not necessarily.'

'Well, you'd better come inside.'

She glided along the narrow passage in a way which reminded McLean of lunch-time at Harrods, and waved him into a room that was cluttered up with stage magazines, and pictures of film stars. There were several ash-trays overflowing with ash and cigarette ends, and a smell of stale gin. So this was the girl from 'one of the women's colleges!'

'Take a pew,' she said, and pushed a cigarette box at him.

He declined the offer and gazed round the hopeless room.

'My woman didn't come to-day,' she said. 'So there's a bit of a muddle. What's all this about John Bosanquet — the dirty dog?'

'I'm anxious to know his whereabouts.'

'Well, I'm not. He can go to hell for all I care.'

'Weren't you with him last evening?'

'No, I wasn't.'

'He had an appointment with you, hadn't he?'

'Certainly he had, but he never showed up.'

'Where were you to meet him?'

'In the vestibule of the Café Royal at half-past seven. I waited there until nearly nine o'clock.'

'Did he plan that meeting when you saw him at Oxford?'

'Oh, no. It was much later. I gave him the tour list and he wrote to me about once a week. I had a letter from him about a week ago reminding me about the spot of dinner yesterday.'

'Have you got that letter?'

'I believe I have.'

'Please let me see it.'

She pushed her fingers through her untidy mop of reddish hair, presumably to revive her memory. Then she found her handbag, and removed a vast number of oddments.

'No,' she said. 'I didn't put it in my handbag, but I remember putting it somewhere. I'll take a look in my bedroom.'

She left him and again his gaze went round the room. In one corner was the portrait of Sydney Rawlings, with his pendulous lower lip and his very shifty eyes. Over a chair was hung a short embroidered evening coat, the hat to match which was lying on the floor. A pair of stockings were rolled up and reposing in a bowl. But what made the room so noxious was the overpowering smell of drink mingled with that of face-powder and nail polish. McLean could imagine the effect of this upon Mrs. Bosanquet, who had evidently believed that John was going to keep an appointment with a nice type of girl.

She came back to McLean with a letter in one hand and a small glass of what appeared to be gin in the other. Her dressing-gown had come undone, and her legs up to what McLean believed were termed 'scanties' were bare and visible. This fact quite evidently didn't embarrass her in the least.

'Got it,' she said. 'Dated twentieth August, from his home. I don't see why you should read it.'

'Why not?'

'Well, it's kind o' private. Still, he did the dirty on me, so why should I worry?'

McLean took the letter from her, and read the opening part of it. It bore out her statement that she was to meet John at the Café Royal on the previous evening, but what interested McLean more than the context was the paper on which the letter was written. It was quite common note-paper, torn out from a block, and on holding it up to the light he saw a water-mark, which convinced him that it was identical with the paper used by the writer of the anonymous letters.

'I should like to retain this,' he said.

'No!' she snapped. 'I don't want my private letters hawked about. Hand it over.'

She made a grab at the letter and knocked over the chair on which her evening coat was hanging.

'Now see what you've gone and done,' she complained. 'That stuff picks up every bit of dust. It'll cost me five bob to get it cleaned. Give me that letter.'

But McLean was gazing at the coat which she was dusting with her hand. In it was pinned a flower, a petal of which had come adrift. It was an uncommon flower, the name of which he did not know, but he remembered seeing similar flowers recently.

'Are you going to give me back my letter?' she asked, replacing the coat over the chair.

'I'll give you a receipt for it.'

'Oh, no, you won't. I don't believe you're a police officer at all. I'm going to telephone Scotland Yard and tell them what's happening.'

'There's no need,' replied McLean, 'because as a matter of fact I am going to take you there.'

'What!' she squealed.

'Get your clothes on.'

'I won't. You got nothing on me.'

'Then sit down, and answer some questions truthfully. If I'm satisfied, I may save you a journey. But no more lies.'

'What do you mean — lies? I don't tell lies.'

'You lied when you told me you didn't meet John Bosanquet last night.'

'Who says so?'

'I am saying so. You met him, and he gave you that flower.'

McLean pointed to the coat. The girl gave a glance at it and shook her head.

'Then where did you get it?'

'I bought it — in a flower-shop.'

'Which shop?'

'That big shop in Bond Street.'

'We'll go along there, and prove that statement,' said McLean. 'It is a most uncommon type of flower, and they are bound to remember it. Personally, I shall be surprised if they have, or have had, a single flower like that. Put on your clothes — at once.'

The girl glowered at him, grabbed her stockings and commenced to roll them up her shapely legs. Then she stopped.

'It wasn't in Bond Street,' she said. 'It was another shop, not far from Bond Street.'

'You'd better remember by the time you're dressed,' said McLean, 'because, if you don't, I shall hand you over to a lady who will see that you are safe until the morning.'

He could hear her swearing under her breath, using words which were usually restricted to infuriated taxi-drivers. Then she stopped and changed her attitude completely.

'He was a nice boy,' she said. 'I liked him a lot.'

'And you saw him last night?'

'Yes. We had dinner together, and then — then I took him to a place I know where we could dance.'

'Continue.'

'Then — then he vanished.'

'What do you mean?'

'I left him for a few minutes — to powder my nose. When I came back he had gone.'

'At what time was this?'

'Just after ten o'clock.'

'Didn't you take any steps to find out what had happened to him?'

'Of course. I asked one or two pals, and they told me they didn't know. They thought it wasn't the sort of place for a young man like him, and that he had taken the opportunity to slope.'

'You're lying. You're hiding something — or you would have told me that before.'

'Yes — I'm coming to it. You see, I really did think he had run out on me. Well, I danced with some other fellows and got home about three o'clock. Then I was rung up by a man who wouldn't give his name. He told me that if I wanted to keep out of trouble I'd say nothing about meeting John — if any questions should be asked.'

'What did you say to that?'

'I wanted to know why, and he said he wasn't answering any questions, but if I didn't keep my mouth shut he would know where to find me. I was scared — the way he said it. That's the truth. I don't know where that boy is.'

'But you know who it was who telephoned you, don't you?'

'No — honest I don't.'

'Where is the place to which you took Bosanquet?'

'The Crimson Poppy.'

McLean knew it. It was a properly licensed club, but its habitués were strange people. On two occasions arrests had been made there, but there had never been any proof that the place was improperly run, although McLean knew it was.

'Did anyone know who Bosanquet was?'

'No,' she replied hesitatingly.

'Didn't you tell anyone that you were going

to have dinner with an Oxford undergraduate, who was an admirer of yours?'

'Maybe I may have told a few girl friends.'

'In that club?'

'I don't think it was in the club.'

McLean decided not to put any more questions at the moment. He warned her not to change her address, and then hurried away. At headquarters he took swift action, and a raid was planned for midnight. It was successfully carried out, and two 'Black Marias' took from the club a number of people, including twenty odd members, the secretary and the manager.

Three of the members identified John by the description given them, but none of them had actually seen him leave the club. The secretary swore that he hadn't seen John at all — that he had been busy in his office over the period when John was known to have been at the club. The manager was seen last. Yes, he had seen Miss du Park enter the club with a tall, good-looking young man.

'Isn't it a rule of the club that members shall write down the names of visitors they may bring?'

'Certainly.'

'It didn't occur to you to find out if Miss du Park had done that?'

148

'No. I imagined she knew the rules.'

'Did you not see Bosanquet leave the club?'

'No.'

'Did you see him talking to any persons while he was there?'

'Only with Miss du Park. He danced a lot with her.'

McLean then surprised the manager by producing a small box in which were a number of capsules.

'Do you know what they contain?' he asked.

'No.'

'Cocaine — and they were found on the club premises.'

The manager waxed indignant, as he realised the seriousness of this discovery.

'I know nothing about it,' he pleaded. 'I have run the club on lawful lines for over ten years. My licence is worth more than a few quid gained by selling dope. This is a frame-up.'

'There's no frame-up, as you call it. This package was found on the person of a gentleman who gives his name as Fouquart.'

'Fouquart! He's quite a new member. I scarcely know him.'

'That makes little difference. We should be justified in assuming that his object in carrying so large a supply was to sell it. I think there would be grounds for withdrawing your licence, unless — '

'Unless — what?' asked the scared man, grasping at the straw which was plainly behind McLean's hiatus.

'Unless you are willing to help us in this other matter. Your voluntary help would convince us that you are as anxious to be on the side of law and order as you assert.'

'Of course I will do anything possible.'

'Then did you see Bosanquet talking to any member of the club whose motives you might reasonably question?'

The question, in view of McLean's promise, was a most embarrassing one.

'Answer!' said McLean.

'I did see him talking to a certain person. Mind you, I've nothing against this man. He has always behaved well in the club, but I thought that he and the young man were discussing something important.'

'Who was it?'

'A man named Letting.'

'Does Miss du Park know this man?'

The manager nodded his head.

'Very intimately?'

'So I understand.'

'Give me a description of him.'

'He's very dark, with a small moustache and long wavy hair. He would be about five feet ten inches tall, but broadly built. Age about thirty.'

'Can you give me his address?'

'If you will let me ring up the club I can get it.'

This he did, and gave McLean the address of a house in Coptic Street, near the British Museum. All the persons were then set free, with the exception of the dope-carrier, but McLean had a last word with the club manager before he left.

'The matter of your licence is under review,' he said. 'If Letting comes to the club again, telephone me here, and leave a message.'

'I will,' promised the unhappy man.

In the meantime a report on the revolver bullet was waiting in McLean's office. The expert stated that the bullet was .31 in diameter, and that it had been fired from a weapon with six grooves and a Leed of 16L, which meant that the weapon possessed grooves which went anti-clockwise, and that these grooves took sixteen inches to complete a full circle. The expert knew of only one firearm which corresponded to these details — a .32 Colt automatic. McLean put the report and the bullet into his pocket, and then attached the services of one of the men who had been employed in the raid. His name was Mitford, and he had come from the Police College. Mitford was the very antithesis of Sergeant Brook, who had had very little education, and was quite a snob in this respect. Mitford was young and very 'refeened,' and everyone at the Yard knew that he had only missed a title by a short head — his twin brother having opened his lungs to the world two hours before him.

'You can drive the car,' said McLean. 'I want to look up a man in Coptic Street. Do you know where that is?'

'Yes, sir. I used to buy Oriental books there.'

'Why?'

'I've always had a passion for probing the mind of the Orient. I submit, sir, that the great men of the East have forgotten more than we ever learned.'

'Indeed!'

'They weren't in all this hurry. No motor-cars, wireless, theatres. They had time to sit and ponder. They had patience, while we have none. Ask a western man to sit and do absolutely nothing for twenty minutes, and he goes nearly mad with boredom, but the Asiatics can sit still for days and make their minds complete blanks.'

'That's true,' replied McLean calmly. 'I remember hearing of such a case. A group of

Chinamen were waiting for a train at Canton. It was many hours overdue, but the Chinamen never worried about that. They just sat on and on, while the hours passed; and at last one of them was inspired to ask the station master if he had any idea when the train would arrive. He was told that the train came in and went out two hours before. I think you missed the turning. Better take the next left turning.'

Mitford coughed and apologised. After that he was a little less garrulous, and finally he brought the car to a standstill outside the house which McLean sought.

'Here we are, Inspector,' he said. 'Shall I stay with the car, or accompany you?'

'What would you prefer to do?' asked McLean.

'If there's any fun going I'd like to be in it.'

'When you've had as much service as I have you'll want to be as far away from the 'fun' as possible,' replied McLean. 'But come if you feel like it.'

By this time the street was absolutely deserted, and the house where Letting was alleged to have his abode was in darkness. It was above an empty shop, and access to it was up a side staircase, which had a dim light burning on the half-landing. McLean was about to go up the stairs when there came sounds of a person descending, and a moment later he saw a man turn the bend in the staircase. The light illuminated his face for a moment. McLean waited for him, and as the man reached the doorway McLean begged his pardon politely and asked if a Mrs. Crooke-Parker lived there.

'No, I'm sure there's no person of that name on the premises.'

'That's curious. This is the number I was given. Sorry to have troubled you. Charlie, we'd better leave it till tomorrow, and check up the address.'

Mitford, to whom the last remark was made, nodded his head, and the pair walked back to the car. As Mitford was using the self-starter McLean switched off the ignition, and the self-starter complained loudly.

'Do it again,' said McLean. 'I want to give him a moment or two.'

Again the engine, perforce, declined to start. Only when the walking man vanished round the corner into Great Russell Street did McLean turn the ignition key, and the engine fired at once. Mitford gazed at him questioningly.

'He's our man,' explained McLean. 'At least he's exactly like the description given me. Drive up to the corner, but don't turn it.'

Mitford did this, stopping short of the

154

corner. McLean got out and walked a few paces. He saw Letting getting into a saloon car which was parked by the kerb. It was headed in the other direction, and a moment later it moved forward. He hurried back to his own car.

'Get a move on,' he said. 'It's a grey saloon with two rear lights, only one of which is functioning. Don't overtake him — but don't lose him.'

10

The grey saloon car went eastward through the quiet streets, and the task of following it without arousing suspicion on the part of the driver was difficult. Mitford had to keep his distance, and whenever the leading car vanished round a turning it meant fearful acceleration on Mitford's part to avoid losing the quarry altogether. Eastward of the Tower Bridge they played a lovely game of cat-and-mouse, and once indeed they lost contact, but a half-drunken stevedore saved the situation. McLean stopped and asked him if he had seen a car with a grey body, and he waved a hand towards a turning and uttered something quite unintelligible.

'We'll take a chance,' said McLean to Mitford, who by this time was enjoying himself immensely.

The narrow street suddenly forked, and again came indecision as Mitford jammed on the brakes.

'Left,' said McLean. 'I believe they both go down to the water-front. Keep your eyes open for the car.'

The street led them to a wharf, and a

jumble of alleys and buildings, many of which appeared to be closed and waiting demolition. There were a few 'For Sale' boards on veritable junk-heaps. Anchored out in the river lay several tramp-steamers, apparently waiting to be unloaded and unable to get alongside the many vast wharfs lower down the river. But the grey car was not visible.

'Go up and turn right,' said McLean. 'We shall probably get back to the fork.'

Another narrow street was entered, and then, suddenly, off to the left McLean saw the car. It was parked by the side of a wall, on the right of which were several old houses in a state of great disrepair.

'There it is,' he said. 'Better park the car in that yard.'

Mitford swung the wheel over and managed to get the car off the street.

'Do I come?' he asked eagerly.

'Yes. Better take the ignition key, or we may lose the car.'

They walked to the grey car, and McLean tried to open the door with a view to obtaining the registration book, but all doors were locked. Having already noted the registration, he walked down by the wall which enclosed a concreted yard. In the section which ran parallel with the river there was an opening with some steps leading down to the water. The river was now washing over them. The house itself was in darkness, as were those on the farther side of it.

'Think he's inside?' asked Mitford.

'There seems to be little doubt. Climb over the wall and try that back door.'

Mitford mounted the wall with the ease of an athlete, and came back to report that the door was immovable. Other than that, there was only a small barred window very low down, which Mitford said gave ventilation to a cellar.

'We'll try the front of the house,' said McLean.

They walked up the long wall, turned the corner and came to a large front door with a huge knocker but no bell. McLean knocked softly, and then a light appeared and shone through the narrow fanlight. The door opened and a very small man, who blinked like an owl, surveyed the visitors.

'Is Mr. Letting inside?' asked McLean.

'Yes, sir. He's with Mr. Tice, who isn't very well.'

'Who else is here?'

'Only me, sir. I telephoned Mr. Letting to tell him that Mr. Tice was taken very bad. Shall I tell Mr. Letting — ?'

'Tell him that Chief Inspector McLean wishes to see him at once, and that — '

McLean had not been quite unprepared for trouble, and while he spoke his right hand rested on an automatic pistol in his pocket, but the trouble came much sooner than he expected, and by bad luck Mitford got in his way. Round the corner of the house came four men, who looked like stevedores. They were talking and laughing, and were level with the door when suddenly they fell upon McLean and Mitford. McLean tried in vain to use the pistol, but Mitford was pressed hard against him, just to the right of the door. He saw Mitford avoid a terrible blow from a piece of lead pipe and land a heavy punch on his assailant's jaw. But another man had better luck with a similar piece of pipe, and Mitford uttered a little groan and went down. McLean whipped out the pistol and shot at the legs of the man nearest him. Then another improvised truncheon struck his right forearm, paralysing it completely. The pistol dropped and one of the men gained possession of it and pushed the barrel into McLean's chest.

'Get back!' he growled.

McLean went staggering back into the wall. Mitford was dragged inside and the door was closed and bolted. From the top of the stairs someone threw a long coil of rope.

'Tie 'em up!' called a voice.

'All right, Mr. Letting,' said McLean. 'It's no use hiding yourself.'

'You shut up!' said one of the ruffians and pushed his fist into McLean's face.

The next moment he received an uppercut from McLean's left hand which he would undoubtedly remember for the rest of his life, and his mouth became red with blood. He went staggering backwards against an old grandfather clock, which crashed to the floor. One of the long brass weights became detached. The half-demented man seized it and prepared to batter out McLean's brains, but the man who now held the pistol stopped him.

'Obey orders!' he snarled. 'You asked for it.'

Five minutes later McLean suffered the ignominy of being dragged along the passage and down a flight of steps with his limbs tightly bound and his mouth gagged. He was finally flung through an open door, which was immediately closed and bolted behind him. A few minutes passed while he lay on the hard, gritty floor, and then the door was opened again and somebody else treated in similar manner to himself. He had no doubt that it was Mitford — the young detective who had so wanted to be in the fun — but there was no way of communicating with him, for the tight gag kept in place by a bandage rendered speech quite impossible.

He rolled over on the floor and finally came up against the wall. Here he managed to raise himself into a sitting position, and was thus able to rest his back. He listened intently, and heard the hard breathing of his subordinate. It appeared to come from his left, so he edged that way and ultimately touched a human form with his right side.

His eyes became accustomed to the darkness, and he could now see the barred window against the starlit sky. The arm where he had been struck set up a painful aching, made worse by the tight bonds. He blamed himself for this predicament. In the first place it had been a mistake to go to the house without sufficient help in case of emergency, and in the second place he called himself an idiot for having been caught off his guard. These people were certainly desperate characters, and there was no knowing what their next step would be. One thing was clear enough — they had plenty to conceal.

He moved his jaw as much as he could in the hope of moving the suffocating bandage, which was causing him the greatest discomfort, but all he did was hurt his jaw muscles. For a long time he sat there, watching the constellations pass slowly across the iron bars. He judged the time to be about three o'clock in the morning, which meant that a further two hours must pass before it was daylight. He tried to connect this adventure with the murder at Castle House, but was unable to see any logical connection. The plain facts suggested kidnapping. John Bosanquet had got himself mixed up with a desperate gang who doubtless intended making some money out of him, in view of the fact that he was the son of a wealthy parent. If there was anything in it beyond that, McLean wasn't able to see what it was. His thoughts were suddenly interrupted by a long sigh.

'Inspector!'

It was Mitford's voice speaking in a hoarse whisper. McLean's only possible response was to nudge his companion hard.

'I'll bet you're in the same plight as I was,' said Mitford. 'But I've had a bit of luck. I found a nail in the wall behind me and have been able to pull away my face bandage, and spit out a filthy rag which they shoved in my mouth. Oh, hell!'

It was half a groan, and McLean came to the conclusion that it was caused by the head injury. Mitford's next words proved the conclusion to be true.

'They sloshed me good and well,' he said.

'My head feels like two alarm clocks. But it's great to be able to breathe again. Listen, if you move in my direction, and feel the wall with the back of your napper, sooner or later you'll feel the nail-head. It did the trick with me, and I don't see why it shouldn't do the same for you.'

McLean felt Mitford moving away from him and, following the instructions, he soon found the nail. The operation recommended by Mitford was more than a little painful, for the bandage on the face side had to be forced up over his nose, and McLean's nose was one of his outstanding physical characteristics. In due course the bandage came off, and McLean forced the rag out of his mouth.

'Thank — God!' he gasped.

'That's fine,' whispered Mitford. 'Can you move your arms?'

'Not a fraction.'

'Nor can I. What's that?'

The sound came from above them. It was something being bumped along the floor, and the noises were accompanied by voices. The bumping grew more distant, and then ceased altogether. This was followed by other sounds, which appeared to come from the yard beyond the barred window.

'They're taking something down to the

river,' said McLean. 'I'm going across to the window.'

He had to roll himself across, and, having got there, he managed to peer through the narrowly set bars. Four men were carrying a big square crate towards the place where the steps went down to the tide. They were lighted by another man, who was soon joined by two others who came from the house after the slamming of a door.

'We're a bit early,' said one.

'It's a habit you might cultivate,' replied the other, whom McLean now recognised as Letting. 'We must get the case aboard as soon as the *Marietta* steams up. Better have it waiting on that large step half-way down.'

The whole party then disappeared, the last man closing the iron door behind him. Mitford had made his way across and his head was close to McLean's.

'What are they up to?' he asked.

'Unless I'm an idiot, in that packing-case is an important witness in a murder case, and unless some miracle happens we stand a very good chance of losing him.'

'Nerve those gangsters have got,' said Mitford. 'Treating police officers like this.'

They sat there for some minutes, and could hear at intervals the low drone of voices. Then someone said, in a louder voice, 'Here she

164

comes.' A little later there came the unmistakable sounds of oars creaking in rowlocks — then silence — and again the creaking, which finally ceased altogether.

'They've gone,' said McLean.

'Getting away down the river — to the continent?'

'I imagine so. Look behind me at my wrist — and see if my watch is visible. It has an illuminated dial.'

'Yes,' said Mitford. 'It says four o'clock.'

'Four o'clock and all's not well with the world,' said McLean. 'Detective Mitford, if we've any sense of pride, we've got to be out of this place within an hour.'

'We've got the use of our voices,' said Mitford.

'They won't help us, for I'm quite certain this row of houses are empty.'

'We could try,' said Mitford. 'I've a pretty penetrating sort of voice-box.'

'You'll need it if it's going to be heard anywhere outside this cellar.'

'Well, here goes!'

McLean could hear Mitford filling his lungs with air, and then a pitiful wail came from his throat, degenerating into a groan.

'Is that the best you can do?' asked McLean.

'It — was my napper,' gasped Mitford. 'It

seemed to split in two. Oh, Lord, there must be a crack in it.'

McLean sympathised with him, for he had witnessed the weight of the blow he had sustained.

'Don't bother,' he said. 'It's a waste of breath. There's a perfectly clear sky, so it ought to be daylight soon.'

His own position was very uncomfortable, for the rope cut into his bruised arm and set up acute and incessant pain. He sat and watched the sky, and very slowly it began to change from a star-spangled black vault to a lighter hue. The stars grew fainter and fainter, and at last disappeared altogether. The interior of the cellar was now dimly seen. It contained nothing but a heap of coal in one corner.

' 'And the dawn comes up like thunder out of China 'cross the bay,' ' murmured Mitford.

'I don't object to poetry in its right setting,' said McLean. 'But not this morning, please.'

'You know we might be here a week,' said Mitford, as if the thought had just struck him. 'After all, the house is empty, and the wall is pretty high. No one at headquarters knows we are here, and — '

'Why did you join the police?' asked McLean.

Mitford gave a painful grin.

'Because they wouldn't have me at the Foreign Office. Is there any blood on my face?'

'Quite a lot, but it appears to be dry.'

'Feels like it. It's like having my mug in a mould.'

McLean put his head closer and was able to see the wound in Mitford's scalp. The pale light showed a large bump and a cut, but the latter, fortunately, was not very wide, and it was no longer bleeding.

'You'll be all right,' he said. 'Turn your back to the window and I'll see what kind of knots those fellows tie.'

Mitford did this, and McLean peered at the two very tight knots. One appeared to be less impregnable than the other, so he set to work on this at once with his teeth. They were excellent tools and little by little he succeeded in unravelling it.

'What's happening?' asked Mitford, turning his head.

'Sit still!'

'Phew! Your mouth's all blood.'

'I've nearly finished. There!'

The last loop in the knot came free, and Mitford gave a little cry of joy as the rope which had bound his arms tightly behind him fell away, leaving only his legs bound.

'Eureka!' he ejaculated. 'I've got a knife somewhere. Gosh, that arm's gone dead!'

He rubbed the useless arm for a few seconds, and then produced a small penknife from his pocket and quickly cut away the rest of his bonds, also McLean's.

'You must have pulled nearly all your teeth out,' he said. 'Got a handkerchief?'

McLean nodded and wiped the blood away from his gums, while Mitford attempted to clean his own repulsive-looking face. He touched the bump on his head and winced.

'Leave it alone,' said McLean.

'What was it Coleridge said about — ?'

'I don't care what Coleridge said about anything at this moment. By some means I've got to stop that boat from getting out of the river, and there's no time to be lost.'

Mitford nodded and gripped the iron bars of the window with his two hands. He gave a lusty pull and then shook his head.

'Sandow couldn't do it,' he muttered. 'If we only had a lever of some kind — '

'Well, we haven't. The only alternative is to try the door.'

He went across to this, but found it was an iron one, locked or bolted on the farther side. Mitford whistled as he realised this fact.

'That's certainly torn it,' he said. 'What miracle can get us out of this mess?'

McLean walked to the barred window again. The wall ahead of him obstructed his view of the river, but he could now see the tops of ships' masts moving at different speeds. It was aggravating to the last degree to realise how close help was to them, and how helpless they were to announce their near existence and plight.

'Let's try our voices together,' suggested Mitford.

McLean nodded rather gloomily. He didn't think it would be the slightest use in view of the circumstances. They both put their heads near the bars and gave a wild yell, then another, and another. After waiting a minute or two they tried the same thing again, with painful effects upon Mitford. McLean shook his head and paced up and down impatiently.

'When I was at Harrow,' said Mitford, 'we had a fellow there named Gregory. He was an absolute genius for getting out of tight corners. On one occasion — '

McLean wasn't listening. He began to take off his coat, wincing as he used his right arm. Mitford imagined that McLean's object was to examine his injured arm, but when McLean's waistcoat followed his coat Mitford began to wonder if it had been McLean who had suffered the blow on the head, and not himself. Worse still was to follow, for McLean then removed his braces.

'Good Lord!' ejaculated Mitford.

McLean stretched the elastic braces in his hands and looked towards the heap of small coal. Even then Mitford remained in complete ignorance of the working of McLean's mind. But suddenly — a moment later — he was inspired.

'A catapult!'

'Exactly. But will it work?'

'Why, it's a marvellous idea. Now, why couldn't I have thought of that?'

McLean tied the two forward ends of the braces to two neighbouring bars, between which there was a space of about five inches. He then stretched the braces, and was quite pleased with the result.

'Get me a nice knob of coal,' he said. 'About two inches in diameter.'

Mitford brought up half a dozen such pieces. McLean chose one of them and held it in the loop formed by the two sides of the braces. Then, stretching them to the utmost, he aimed to project the piece of coal over the obstructing wall. It flew through the bars and they saw it fly clean over the wall, and then vanish from sight.

'Hooray!' cried Mitford. 'It works. Let me have a shot.'

McLean was glad to catch the top of his

sagging nether garment and hand over the artillery to Mitford.

'Just keep plugging away,' he said. 'If you manage to hit the skipper of a barge he may possibly take notice. Anyway, it seems to be our only hope.'

Mitford was like a small boy with his new toy, the braces slapped and slapped, and the coal supply began to vanish into the River Thames. But braces are fundamentally braces, and not catapults, and McLean's very soon began to show signs of wear and tear, until at last they were incapable of throwing the bullet over the top of the wall.

'You'd better have them back, sir,' said Mitford. 'I'll try my own.'

McLean looked ruefully at his ruined braces, but they were still capable of performing their normal function. In the meantime Mitford had renewed his battery. The first shot went off at terrific force.

'Beat yours into a cocked hat, sir, if I may say so,' he called out.

'Don't be such a cad,' retorted McLean.

'Here's a lovely lump,' said Mitford, and handled a piece of coal as big as his fist. 'What's the odds against it going over the wall?'

'I leave it to you,' said McLean.

'Four to one the field,' said Mitford. 'Five

171

to one bar one. Here she goes!'

McLean was quite sure the braces would snap, as Mitford stretched them enormously. Then off went the piece of coal. McLean saw it complete a very high parabolic curve, and knew it was short of the wall. But at that moment the gate in the wall opened and a man appeared. The big piece of coal missed him by about two yards, and broke into pieces against the wall.

' 'Ere — what the 'ell!' he shouted.

'We've done it!' shrieked Mitford. 'Hey, you — we're locked in here. Come closer.'

The big man in the blue sweater approached the iron bars much as one approaches the lion cages at the Zoo. Mitford's blood-smeared face appeared to disconcert him, for he switched his gaze, with a grimace, to McLean's visage.

'Wot's bin going on 'ere?' he asked.

'Who are you?' asked McLean.

'Me? I'm Joe Glaister — ferryman. I was rowing across to the Surrey side, not straight across, mind you, because the tide won't let you, when suddenly something went 'plop' into the water — missing me by abaht a yard. A minute later there was another 'plop' but I wasn't near it that time. Coming back with some cargo, blow me if it didn't 'appen agin. Well, I jest ships me oars and waits. Then I sees where the things comes from — bang over the garden wall. Nacherally I comes along to see who's monkeying abaht.'

'Naturally,' agreed McLean. 'Now listen, Mr. Glaister. My friend and I have been locked in here all night, and we're just a little tired of it. Will you go round to the front of the house and try to get in to us?'

'Suppose I'm seen — won't I be pinched?'

'You won't, because we are police officers. Here's a pound for your trouble, but please don't lose any time. Break a window if you can't enter by any other means.'

The ferryman took the note and went off. A few minutes later they heard his heavy boots descending the basement steps, and then two bolts were drawn and the ferryman looked in.

'What a 'ole!' he said. 'You bin 'ere all night?'

'Yes,' said Mitford.

'Blimey, your mug's like a ruddy murder. Who done it?'

'I fell down.'

'Nice place to fall on — I don't fink. And here's another fing — 'ow the 'ell did you chuck that coal so far?'

'Ah, that's a secret,' said Mitford. 'Well, we're much obliged to you.'

'Welcome, I'm sure.'

'One moment,' said McLean. 'Where is the nearest telephone?'

'Two hundred yards away, at the corner of Mason's Wharf. You turn left when you leave the 'ouse. You can't miss it.'

'Thanks!'

The ferryman went off whistling, and McLean and Mitford mounted the steps. Mitford found a toilet in the hall where the water was still running, and McLean hurried out to the car and came back with the first-aid outfit.

'Have a clean up,' he said. 'I'm going to telephone. Be back in a few minutes.'

When he returned Mitford looked a little less horrific. McLean got a piece of sticking plaster across the head wound, and Mitford swore he felt much better.

'What's the programme now, sir?' he asked.

'Mason's Wharf, where the telephone box is situated. I got on to the river police, and they are sending a fast launch. I think I've got time to look over the house.'

This he did, but apart from the grandfather clock which lay across the hall, and a few odd chairs and tables of no value, there was nothing else in the big house.

'All right,' said McLean. 'Let's get along.'

After waiting ten minutes at the wharf the

police launch arrived. McLean shook hands with the officer in charge, whom he knew, and he and Mitford went aboard immediately. Off went the launch at full speed down river.

★ ★ ★

Two hours later, after investigating a number of outgoing ships, a dirty looking little tramp was sighted off Canvey Island. The fast launch steamed up close to her, and McLean saw the painted name on her bows — 'Marietta.' The officer in charge of the launch picked up a megaphone, and his voice went ringing down the estuary.

'Ahoy there — *Marietta!*'

The man at the wheel saw the police launch and beckoned to someone aft. Apparently he was the officer of the watch for he gave the order to heave to. The engine was slowed and finally stopped. The launch, cleverly navigated, came closer and closer, and the tide was so flat that McLean was able to get a grip of the *Marietta's* iron ladder. Mitford followed him, and also the officer in charge of the launch.

'What's wrong?' asked the man in the peaked cap.

'Search warrant. Where's your captain?'

'In his cabin. Here he comes.'

The fat little captain came to the group. He spoke practically no English, being a Belgian, so McLean took control, speaking in French.

'What is your cargo?'

'Wireless sets.'

'Where bound?'

'Rouen.'

'Show me your clearance papers.'

These were brought, and appeared to be in order.

'I want every man aboard on deck at once,' said McLean.

The captain looked nettled, but there was no alternative but to carry out the order. The mate was sent down below, and soon men came scuttling up. Some of them were sleepy-eyed, others obviously came straight from the stokehold.

'Is this everyone?' asked McLean.

'Yes, sir.'

'Mitford, take a look below.'

Mitford was away a few minutes, but he finally returned alone, and said he hadn't seen anyone.

'H'm!' said McLean. 'These men can go, but I want to look at the cargo. Off with those hatches.'

The hatches were taken off the hold, and McLean peered down. There were about fifty large cases piled up at the end, but there was something else too — a big protuberance under a large waterproof sheet.

'What's under the tarpaulin?' he asked the captain.

The question was evidently embarrassing to the captain. He gulped, and hesitated.

'All right,' said McLean. 'You two men go down, and roll back the tarpaulin.'

The two seamen looked at their captain for corroboration, but he, poor man, looked sick unto death.

'Do as you're told,' snapped McLean.

The captain nodded wearily, and the two seamen went down the ladder. They removed the tarpaulin as if it were made of sheet lead, and there came to view all the people whom McLean had so recently seen at the house by the river, including Mr. Letting.

'Come up here!' he called. 'One at a time.'

As they reached the deck they were passed down to the launch, and at the tail end came Mr. Letting. McLean stopped him.

'Which case is it, Mr. Letting?' he asked. 'You may as well be helpful since you can't be harmful.'

Letting hesitated, took a look at the launch, and decided it was best to swim with the tide.

'Odd one — at the right end,' he muttered.

He was sent to join his confederates, and then McLean and Mitford went down into the hold. The case marked with the red cross had a strip of wood torn away, and through this could be seen straw packing. McLean guessed that the hole had been deliberately made to allow air to enter. Quickly the top boards were forced off, and under the packing reclined the bound and gagged body of a well-built young man. He had a black eye, and a scratch down the side of his face, but he was quite conscious. McLean cut the rope and tore away the gag. The victim was able to get out with some assistance, but he seemed momentarily stunned.

'Are you John Bosanquet?' asked McLean.

'Yes — but — '

'Better come up on deck.'

John was helped up the ladder, and when he reached the deck he stared out at the sunlit water.

'Where am I?' he asked.

'In the estuary of the Thames.'

'And who are you?'

'Chief Inspector McLean. For certain reasons the police have been searching for you.'

John saw the launch below and the long gaunt face of Letting staring up at him.

'That's the man,' he said. 'Here, let me — '

McLean restrained him by catching his arm.

'Have no fear about Mr. Letting,' he said. 'My colleagues will look after him and his friends. John Bosanquet, you're wanted at Pevensey, and you're wanted urgently. Come!'

11

Three hours later McLean and John were speeding towards Pevensey in the fierce noonday heat. Detective Mitford had been posted to other duties to his deep regret, for these were not always as exciting as his most recent experience.

'Moral — always buy good strong braces,' he said, when McLean finally left him. 'Hope you'll be needing me again, sir.'

The position was now a little embarrassing as between John and McLean. The young man thought, or appeared to think, that his return to Pevensey in McLean's car was exclusively connected with the attempt to kidnap him, and McLean for some time was content to let the conversation centre round that event.

'I'm sure she had nothing to do with it — Nancy, I mean,' said John.

'Didn't Letting come and tell you that she had suddenly been taken ill?'

'Yes, but she wasn't in the room when I got there, and he and his gang set about me, and got me away in a car. He could have found out about me without her help, couldn't he?'

'Perhaps — but he didn't.'

'But he didn't tell you that she was in the plot, did he?'

'No. But he has his reasons.'

'What reasons?'

McLean turned his head and looked into John's strained face.

'The girl was Letting's mistress,' he said. 'I didn't tell you that before, but you'd better know.'

'I — I can't believe it.'

'I'm afraid you must. Don't waste your sympathy on that girl. I'll admit Letting had an influence over her, but that doesn't exonerate her. We've enough evidence to put the whole gang away for a long time. The best thing you can do is to forget her. Letting's idea was to get you out of England and then suggest a nice substantial ransom from your father. He learnt all about kidnapping when he was in America. The girl would have got her share.'

John was breathing heavily. Slowly he was becoming to see that he had been deluded and made to look rather foolish.

'Did my father communicate with you?' he asked, after a long pause.

McLean considered it high time to come down to brute facts. The boy must know sooner or later, and presuming he was

181

innocent — which was yet in doubt — it was kinder to leave him in ignorance no longer.

'When I came to London to look for you,' said McLean. 'There was no suggestion of kidnapping.'

'I don't understand.'

'Your father died last Monday.'

John stared at him in a way which suggested complete astonishment, but McLean had to remember that time had passed since the murder — sufficient time for any murderer to be able to plan and rehearse his part — in the event of arrest or suspicion.

'But — but he wasn't ill,' said John.

'No — he wasn't even ill.'

'Then — oh, you can't mean that he met with an accident?'

'Not a normal accident. He was murdered.'

He never moved his head, but he could see John's reaction quite clearly. It was exactly what one would expect from a young man suddenly advised of a dreadful calamity. John was either innocent, or a very clever actor. He seemed to catch his breath — to be utterly incredulous.

'Murdered!' he gasped at last. 'Oh no — that's too ghastly.'

'Ghastly enough.'

'But — but why didn't you tell me before?'

'Surely it was better to postpone the bad

news as long as possible? I shall have to ask you some questions, but they must wait until we reach the house. It's necessary to have a record.'

'Where did it happen?' asked John in a shaky voice. 'At least you can tell me that.'

'In his study.'

'Good God!'

No more was said throughout the rest of the journey. John sat huddled up in a curious way in his seat. He smoked immoderately — cigarette after cigarette, and all the time his brow was wrinkled in thought. When they reached the 'drive' several persons moved away from the gates, as if ashamed of their tense interest in the tragedy. Prout opened the door to them, and gave John a polite greeting.

'How do, Prout!' said John, summoning a smile.

'Into the study,' said McLean.

But Dorinda had evidently been watching. She came into the hall from the dining-room, and gripped John's hands.

'Thank God!' she said. 'I've been so troubled.'

'I know,' said John. 'But cheer up.'

'What — what happened?'

'I have a few questions to put to him,' said McLean hastily. 'I won't keep him very long.'

She nodded sadly, and McLean hurried John away. In the study Brook was reading a book which he had taken from a shelf.

'Morning!' he said. 'The Superintendent and his helpers have just left. No luck, sir, I'm afraid.'

'This young gentleman is the elder son,' said McLean. 'I want answers to certain questions.'

John sat down, and as he did so his gaze went to the high-backed upholstered chair. On the seat was a dark stain, and at sight of this grim reminder of the tragedy so close at hand John's face lost what little colour was left.

'When did you go to London?' asked McLean.

'On Monday — after lunch.'

'What train did you catch?'

'The three-twenty — from Eastbourne.'

'Wasn't it your intention to catch the two-thirty?'

'Yes, but I missed the two-fifteen bus — only by a minute or two.'

'At what time did you leave this house?'

'I thought it was five minutes past two, but my watch was slow.'

'How long does it take you to the bus halt?'

'About six minutes.'

'How did you know the bus had gone?'

'Because there's an indicator which tells the time of the next bus. It gave the time as two-thirty five.'

'How did you fill in that time?'

'I walked along the street towards the castle. I passed the castle and finally caught the bus at Westham.'

'Did you see anyone you know during that walk?'

'No. I can't recall that I did.'

'Did you see anyone when you left this house?'

'No.'

'What about your brother?'

'I think he had gone to golf. I didn't see him anywhere.'

'Have you any means of proving that you were at the bus halt very shortly after two-fifteen?'

'No.'

'Do you possess a pistol?'

'No.'

'Have you ever possessed such a thing?'

'No.'

The significance of these questions were clear enough to the young man, and he answered them as one does who knows he is under suspicion and — illogically perhaps — resents it. McLean turned over some papers.

'Were you on good terms with your father?' he asked.

'I don't know what you mean by that,' said John slowly. 'I had every reason to be grateful to him, for sending me to the University. There were times when we didn't agree, but we never quarrelled.'

'Didn't he refuse to give you money to go to London?'

'Yes.'

'Who gave you the necessary money?'

'My stepmother.'

'You and she are on excellent terms, I believe?'

'Yes — she's been splendid both to me and my brother.'

'And to your father?'

'Yes — to him, too. She's been as loyal as anyone could be.'

'But she wasn't very happy here, was she?'

'How do I know? I've been away from home for three years.'

'The terms at the University are short — eight weeks, I believe. Three terms of eight weeks are less than half the year. You have had ample opportunity to know if your stepmother was happy.'

'If you're trying to impute a motive to — '

'All I want is the truth regarding the various relationships here. You must have observed that your stepmother grew increasingly unhappy.'

'Well, what of it?'

'So you admit it?'

'Yes — if you force me.'

'Did you ever remonstrate with your father in regard to his treatment of your stepmother?'

'Certainly not. He wouldn't have tolerated such a thing.'

McLean detached a sheet of paper from a clip. It was the letter which he had taken from Nancy du Park's flat.

'Did you write that?' he asked.

'Yes,' replied John.

McLean then produced the three anonymous letters, and handed them to John.

'Did you write any of these?' he asked.

John perused the letters, and glared at McLean.

'No,' he said. 'Any fool can see they're not written by the same hand.'

'But they are written on the same type of paper,' said McLean. 'It is not notepaper such as is normally used in this house. Where did you get that sheet of paper?'

'I can't remember,' replied John slowly. 'It was days ago. I was in a hurry and grabbed the first sheet of notepaper which I saw.'

'It was torn from a pad.'

'Yes — I can see that. It must have been in the house.'

'The house has been searched. No such writing-paper has been found here.'

'But it must have been here. I've never bought a writing block like that. At college I use the college-notepaper, and here there's usually plenty of our own embossed paper.'

'The person who used this paper naturally had a definite reason for doing so.'

'You mean the person who wrote these notes is the murderer of my father,' said John, in a hoarse voice. 'You think it might have been me — '

'Please!' begged McLean. 'I had rather you merely answered my questions.'

'Then here's an answer to all of them,' said John passionately. 'I never shot my father, and have never entertained such a ghastly idea. He was harsh to us, cruel perhaps to my stepmother, but he was my father. I've always remembered that. Now can I go? I'm starving, and lunch — '

'One moment,' said McLean. 'Did you know that your father was about to execute a new will shortly before he — died?'

'No.'

'Did you know of the existence of a will at all?'

'No. But I took it for granted there must be one.'

McLean nodded and allowed John to go. Brook finished his shorthand notes, and closed the book.

'Bit high-spirited,' he said. 'Can he be trusted?'

'I wish I knew,' replied McLean. 'He lied to his stepmother about the girl he went to meet. She wasn't by any means a fellow student, but a show girl.'

'Phew!'

McLean told him briefly what had happened, but omitted the means employed by himself to secure his release from the coal-cellar. Brook's music-hall type of humour were better not encouraged.

'Then there's no connection between the kidnapping and the murder?' asked Brook.

'I think not.'

'But why did they go on with it, when they must have read about the murder?'

'That didn't affect their purpose. The money was still there. Well, the inquest opens at three o'clock, so there's no time to do anything else. One thing is established — the pistol used was a thirty-two Colt automatic.

Until we find that we shall probably continue going round and round in circles.'

'That's what Ball said. I can tell you he's mighty pleased he handed us this Chinese puzzle. They're searching further afield this afternoon, and tomorrow.'

12

The inquest didn't take long. With suicide ruled out completely by the circumstances, murder by some person or persons unknown was the inevitable verdict. Such facts as emerged were seized upon by the many representatives of the press, and that evening the Bosanquet murder became — in Brook's phrase — 'front page bilge.'

The interment followed, and the family watched in tense silence the lowering of the coffin into the grave. The Professor and Mrs. Chatleigh had come down from London for the occasion, and afterwards they all went back to Castle House, and had a meal. With the party was Grant, who had stayed on at the Eastbourne hotel, and was by no means reluctant to display by words and actions his deep regard for the widow. The Professor and his wife were absolutely loyal to their dead friend, and at first had shown a slight resentment towards Grant, but Grant accepted the situation with quite commendable tolerance.

'Listen, Professor,' he said. 'This is a bad business for Dorinda. You and your wife are very old friends of Bosanquet, and I appreciate your loyalty to him. In return you should appreciate my loyalty to Dorinda. I knew her long before Bosanquet did. She's a fine girl and this unhappy business is breaking her down. Thank God, the circumstances rule her out as the culprit, but it doesn't rule her out as an accomplice. I believe that nothing can prevent her inheriting close on a quarter of a million pounds, and that fact alone is apt to start horrible rumours — about her and me. But because you are — or were — Bosanquet's friends, I want you to understand that never at any time has Dorinda been willing to consider me as anything more than a friend. But from the moment I set foot in this house Bosanquet regarded me as an enemy. He set the police on me, because there had been anonymous letters sent to him. He made her life hell because he couldn't believe that a woman could have a man friend after her marriage without being unfaithful.'

'Oh, no,' said the Professor. 'Bosanquet wasn't like that. He loved her, and — '

'He never loved her. He believed he possessed her, and that's a very different matter.'

'*De mortuis . . .* ' quoted Mrs. Chatleigh.

'De nothing. Let's rid ourselves of all that

humbug. Bosanquet was a brilliant writer and scientist. His family was not so brilliant, and instead of accepting that unalterable fact he treated them with contempt.'

'I think that's a slight exaggeration,' protested the Professor.

Mrs. Bosanquet and some friends came from the garden and put an end to a conversation which the Professor and his wife found very discomfiting. They all trooped into the lounge where Prout and one of the girls were serving refreshments. With the police still in possession of the study it was a curiously tense gathering. A few people had the temerity to recall some incident relative to the dead man, but the majority steered a very wide course of the subject, and talked about the weather, and the chances of a break in the very trying heat.

'Where's Jasper?' asked Grant of Dorinda.

'He wouldn't come,' she replied. 'He seems to think there's something indecent in eating and drinking at such a time. Perhaps there is, too.'

'Convention dies hard. Jasper's very upset, isn't he?'

'Yes. He's a curious boy — not like John.'

John came across to his stepmother with a plate of thin sandwiches. He looked very different and most uncomfortable in his funeral garb. Dorinda shook her head with a smile.

'Just a little one,' begged John. 'I've been watching you. You haven't eaten a thing. And that, after missing your breakfast. Mr. Grant, tell her she must.'

Dorinda gave way under the double attack, and John took away the sandwich-plate. Her gaze followed him.

'He suffered a disillusion,' she said. 'A girl as usual. She appears to have been nothing but a little crook, mixed up with a gang of blackmailers or kidnappers. But I think I told you about that.'

'Yes. Dorinda — how do the boys come off? I mean — has their father provided for their future?'

'Yes. There is a trust fund. They will receive a thousand pounds a year each.'

'And you?'

The Professor came forward. He and his wife had to get back to London. They said their farewells, and John went with them to make sure that Penny had the car ready to drive them to the railway station. Soon afterwards the party broke up completely, all the guests leaving except Grant.

'Well, that's over,' he said. 'You're not looking well, Dorinda.'

'I'm all right. Tell me about yourself. How

long are you staying down here?'

'Until this matter is cleared up.'

He turned his head as John entered the room after a brief absence. He had changed into shorts and tennis shoes.

'I envy you, John,' said Grant, and thrust his fingers down his stiff collar.

'Has the kid been in?' asked John.

'Jasper? No,' replied Mrs. Bosanquet.

'I'll go and collar him. What an ass he's making of himself over this.'

'Be careful, John,' begged his stepmother.

He nodded, and went out to the terrace. Prout cleared up the debris and stole away in his usual silent fashion. A moment later John came back closely followed by Jasper, who wore a dark suit and a black tie, against which his face appeared to be dead white.

'Here he is,' said John. 'I found him crying into the fishpond.'

'That's not true,' retorted Jasper angrily. 'I wasn't thirsty and I wasn't hungry, and I didn't want to meet all those people.'

'But why not?' asked Mrs. Bosanquet.

'Because — ' He hesitated for a long time, while they all looked at him. 'Because father was murdered, and it might be one of us — who did it.'

'Jasper!' cried his stepmother.

John seized the boy by the arm.

'You madman!' he said furiously.

'If I'm mad, then the police are mad, too. Don't you realise they're watching us all the time? Yes, Mr. Grant, too — he's in it because he's a friend of Dorinda's — and father hated him. Somebody shot father dead in his study — and there'll be a hanging for it. It's terrible to think about it — a dead man in a chair — someone who did it — very near to us — the police out there, watching us all the time, never leaving us. They've been to my bedroom, all our bedrooms. To-day they went to Penny's cottage to search it. There'll be no peace for us now. People keep stopping at the gate — looking up at the house. I can see them whispering to each other. I know what they're saying too — about us — '

The boy's voice was getting shriller and shriller. Every word he uttered seemed like a blow to Dorinda. Grant saw her mental agony, and took Jasper firmly by the arm, right out into the garden.

'Let me go,' said Jasper. 'What are you doing?'

Grant turned him round and faced him.

'It's what you're doing, Jasper,' he said. 'You've got to get a firm grip of yourself. He was your father, but it isn't you who has to bear the full brunt of it. If this mystery is never solved there will be tongues wagging for years afterwards — wild speculation, subtle innuendo, not so much against you or your brother, but against Dorinda.'

'But she — she wasn't near him when it happened.'

'No — thank God! But what about me?'

'You?'

'If I committed such a crime there could be only one motive. Love of Dorinda, and the desire to free her from a very unhappy marriage.'

Jasper shrank back, with horrified eyes.

'Come,' said Grant. 'I only wanted you to look at things the way the police are bound to look at them — the way the world may look at them. Your job is to help Dorinda, and being hysterical isn't calculated to do that. She needs all the help and love we can give her. Your brother is old enough and wise enough to realise that.'

Jasper's expression changed. Grant had touched just the right note, and the boy looked just a little ashamed of himself.

'You're right,' he said. 'I've been letting it get me down. I'll go back to them.'

Grant let him go, and wandered through the water gardens, stopping at intervals to look at the fishes in the pools. Penny, who was wearing a black tie to mark the occasion, was kneeling over one of the pools, scattering

197

something from a box which he carried under his arm. He touched his hat as Grant approached him.

'Meal time?' asked Grant.

'I give them a feed every other day. I vary it as much as possible. This stuff is dried daphnia.'

'Water fleas?'

'That's right, sir. Millions of 'em. Sometimes I give 'em ants' eggs, and some powdered shrimp. Pretty, aren't they?'

Dozens of beautifully tinted fish had risen to the surface and were gulping at the floating food, and then suddenly a pair of strange blue eyes and a cavernous mouth appeared on the water-line.

'What a monster!' ejaculated Grant.

'That's old George — the king carp. He's quite a pet. Doesn't think much of daphnia, do you, George? What he's after is a biscuit — a sweet one. He won't look at an ordinary biscuit. All right, George, I know — I know.'

He put down the box and produced a round biscuit from his pocket. Breaking off a piece of this he offered it to George with his fingers — just below the water-line. George came up at once and took the piece of biscuit with a loud sucking of his lips, upon which he took a dive and created a tremendous commotion of the water, but the next moment he was up again waiting for the next contribution.

'Can't swallow without a dive,' ruminated Penny. 'Mr. Bosanquet told me he was older than I am, and I'm thirty-two. Now, George — no diving this time.'

But George had his own ideas about that, and repeated his former performance, coming up for more, until the last piece of biscuit had been consumed. Penny glanced towards the terrace and saw McLean walking up and down. He turned his gaze to Grant.

'Bad time for the family, sir,' he said.

'Very bad indeed.'

'This morning the Inspector and the Sergeant searched my cottage. I call that a bit thick, after the way I've worked for Mr. Bosanquet. What did they expect to find there?'

'They're looking for a pistol.'

'But if I was a murderer, would I take home the pistol that I did the murder with?'

'I can't answer questions like that,' replied Grant, with a smile. 'The fact is, Mr. Bosanquet was shot and somebody is guilty. If the police embarrass you, you mustn't blame them. They've got a tough enough job solving the mystery.'

'Mystery it is,' muttered Penny. 'Bold, too, I call it — shooting a poor man in broad daylight, and in his own study; with me so close at hand, too. What's to become of all the fish? The mistress won't want to keep them.'

John had left the house and was sauntering across the garden. Grant left Penny and joined John by the big cedar tree which gave a wide area of shade. He sat down on the seat and lighted a cigarette. Grant declined the proffered cigarette-case.

'Did you give him a dressing down, sir?' asked John. 'I mean my kid brother.'

'Oh, no. But I think I got him to realise he wasn't helping much by his behaviour.'

'He's curious about violence. Makes him absolutely ill, and yet once he wanted to go into the Army. Just a box of contradictions. I think he ought to have been born a girl. Wonder when the police will leave us in peace?'

'Not just yet. They have scarcely commenced.'

'Funny business,' said John reflectively. 'Even now I can't believe it really happened — that father isn't in the study writing hard. And those letters which the Inspector showed me — who the devil would want to write them?'

'They may have no connection with the murder.'

'The police evidently think they have. Oh, I

don't want to think about it. I'd like to go to sleep for six months until mother has forgotten all the horror of it. I want to see her happy and safe. I want to forget that father could have been so mean as to contemplate leaving her practically penniless.'

'Who told you that?' asked Grant.

'The solicitor. He said it was against his advice, and he seemed glad that the new will was never actually completed. That's another strange fact — the absence of the draft will. Where did it vanish to? What part does it play in this rotten business?'

'I wonder if it has occurred to the police that your father may have changed his mind and destroyed it?'

'That's an idea,' said John. 'It's more reasonable than that someone should have killed father in order to stop mother from being disinherited.'

'But he was still murdered.'

'Yes, but in that case it could have been some outside person, who perhaps had a private grievance, in which case it's more than likely the police will never find him. Oh, let's drop the subject. What about some tennis? Mother told me you're staying on at Eastbourne. Why not come over tomorrow and have a whack? We can fix you up with shoes and a racket of sorts. If I don't hit something hard I shall go mad.'

'All right. I'll come at ten o'clock tomorrow morning — unless it rains.'

'It can't rain. It's never going to rain again. I'll get the court nicely marked, and we'll have a blood match. May the best man win.'

13

That evening McLean went to London to attend a private meeting at which were present the Chief Constable, Superintendent Ball, and two high officials of the C.I.D. He took with him all the available evidence in the case, and these documents were passed round the table and perused by the several persons present. Afterwards McLean made a brief but concise summary of the situation.

'There is no doubt that Bosanquet was shot dead with a thirty-two Colt automatic pistol last Monday at approximately two-fifteen,' he said. 'The shot was heard by seven different persons. These included Mrs. Bosanquet, Professor and Mrs. Chatleigh, Prout — the butler, and two maidservants, all who were in the house at the time, also by Penny the gardener-chauffeur, who, according to him, was in a potting shed in the garden. The first four persons were in the drawing-room when the shot was heard. There is every reason to believe that the two maidservants were in the kitchen. I have had drawings made of the exact angle of the shot-wound, and there seems to be no doubt that it was fired from the direction of the right casement window, which was open at the time, and this would suggest that the murderer entered by the terrace, and afterwards made his escape round the end of the house. Unfortunately, the weapon used has so far not been found, and the search is still going on. Nor can it be proved that any person connected with the family has ever owned any such weapon. The two sons of the murdered man left the dining-room at about two o'clock, one to keep a golfing appointment and the other to catch a train to London. In both cases there are gaps in the time-table which cannot be filled in, in view of lack of evidence. The only outside person who, so far, comes under suspicion is Mr. Grant. He is a friend of Mrs. Bosanquet, and on his own evidence is in love with her. Bosanquet was so suspicious of Grant's relations with his wife that prior to his death he saw Superintendent Ball, and placed in his hands certain anonymous letters which he had received, and which he believed were written by Grant. I must admit that so far there is no evidence that this was the case. But it is noteworthy that Grant came to Eastbourne for the weekend, and actually met Mrs. Bosanquet on the Saturday morning prior to the murder. I questioned him about his movements at the time of the murder, and he made a statement which he is unable to prove. Now as to motive — there appears to be but one. The murder was committed at a time when Bosanquet was about to sign a new will, which would almost completely disinherit his wife. The draft of that will is missing. Thus, by the sudden death of her husband, Mrs. Bosanquet will inherit nearly a quarter of a million pounds under the existing will. It is only natural to deduce that some person, in possession of the facts, took steps to safeguard Mrs. Bosanquet's interest under the old will. That person could have been either of her two stepsons, who undoubtedly love her, or alternatively Mr. Grant, who knew her before she married Bosanquet. None of these three can provide alibis. The only other person connected with the household, who had the opportunity, but against whom we can impute no reasonable motive, is Mr. Penny. If none of these persons is guilty the murder must have been the work of some quite unknown person who harboured a grievance against Bosanquet, of which, at the moment, we know nothing. That, gentlemen, is the present position.'

The chairman thanked McLean for his clear exposition, and asked the Superintendent if he agreed with McLean.

'Yes, sir, absolutely,' said Ball. 'I questioned certain members of the family before Inspector McLean arrived. The impression I got was that Mrs. Bosanquet had won completely the love and devotion of her stepsons. The servants emphasised that view. The 'master' was dictatorial and disliked by all of them, but Mrs. Bosanquet was spoken of almost with reverence.'

'There could not, I presume, be anything in the nature of a conspiracy between the persons who have stated that they were in the lounge when they all heard the shot fired?' asked the Chief Constable, addressing the question to McLean.

'No, sir. Professor and Mrs. Chatleigh were on the closest terms of friendship with Bosanquet. Without disrespect to them I feel sure they would side with him rather than Mrs. Bosanquet if any prejudice existed. There is no doubt that the shot was fired while Prout was serving coffee to the three persons.'

'So there's an impasse?'

'I shouldn't call it an impasse,' said McLean. 'But more evidence is required before we shall make much progress. The recovery of the weapon used would doubtless expedite a solution, but failing that there may be other methods of arriving at the truth. Mr.

Grant, I believe, is due to sail in about a week. I submit we can't let him go until it is established beyond all doubt that he is innocent.'

'I agree,' said Ball. 'If any person had a motive he has. No one can upset that old will, under which Mrs. Bosanquet will inherit her big fortune. In my opinion Grant is the man to be watched.'

'He shows no desire to escape observation,' said McLean. 'His present actions are those of a completely honest and fearless man, but that, of course, may be a bold pose.'

'Is it your opinion that the person who sent the letters and the person who committed the murder are the same?'

'There's no evidence either way,' replied McLean. 'The two things may not be related at all.'

'Then what's the next move?'

'Nothing very definite, except for the continued hunt for the pistol. I propose to carry on the investigation, with emphasis on the psychological side. Someone may make a slip sooner or later. I shall need more help for observation purposes. There may perhaps be unexpected contacts between the persons closely connected with the deceased and others who are at present in the dark.'

'You mean there may have been collusion from outside?'

'It's possible.'

'Well, select what extra help you want. A tremendous lot of publicity is being given to the case in the press, and I sincerely hope it isn't going to beat us. I propose we meet again in a week's time. Is that convenient to everyone?'

All nodded their agreement, and the meeting broke up. McLean selected two very highly trained detectives to watch the two boys in case either, or both, of them should go away, and then looked round for a third man. At this juncture he ran into young Mitford.

'Good day, Inspector,' he said with a grin. 'I had no idea you were in London.'

'How's the head?' asked McLean.

'Completely better, thanks. That was a great event for me — better than my present rotten job.'

'What is it that's getting you down?'

'Night clubs. I visit the lousiest places imaginable to see they're being properly conducted. If there's a more boring place than a night club, I'd be glad to know where it is.'

'How would you like a spot of work near the sea?'

'You don't mean — at Pevensey?' asked Mitford with eager eyes.

'Not exactly at Pevensey, but close by. Eastbourne to be exact. I'm interested in a gentleman named Robert Grant, who is staying at a nice hotel along the front. I want some unobtrusive person to note all his actions, from the time he gets up to the time he goes to bed. If he should go to Castle House, Pevensey, you needn't bother to break in — as I shall be on the spot. Just wait for him and observe his movements. But don't expect anything half so exciting as that other affair.'

'Right up my street,' said Mitford. 'When do I make a start?'

'I'll run you down to Eastbourne in an hour's time. Stevens and Young will come with us, but they'll drop off at Pevensey.'

The party reached the coast rather late that evening. Mitford was able to engage a room at Grant's hotel, and the other two detectives got lodgings in an inn not very far from Castle House. On reaching the house McLean found Brook looking very bored. Nothing had happened so far as he was concerned, except that a few minutes before Mr. Pole, the solicitor, had called to see Mrs. Bosanquet.

'He's with her now,' said Brook. 'I suppose that's in order?'

'Quite. Oh, Brook, I've had to get more help. Stevens and Young are at the North Star. They'll look after the two boys for us. And Mitford is covering Grant — at Eastbourne.'

'Mitford,' ejaculated Brook.

'Don't snarl like that. What's the matter with Mitford?'

'Police College,' sniffed Brook. 'Reads poetry and knits jumpers.'

'Both very innocent and commendable occupations,' said McLean.

'All right up west among the playboys,' grumbled Brook.

'As a matter of fact, he's just the man for Grant. They should be bosom friends in a day or two. Headquarters are anxious for results, and we've got to produce something.'

'Mighty like a guessing competition to me,' said Brook. 'Fact is, I'm getting to like this family.'

'Your job is not to like anyone — too much,' retorted McLean.

14

Mr. Pole had waited in the morning-room for Dorinda, who was finishing dinner with her stepsons. He had telephoned to say he was coming, but had been unavoidably delayed. When she came in he apologised for this.

'That's quite all right,' she said. 'Is it a family matter, or do you want to see me alone?'

'It really concerns the family.'

Thus the two boys were brought into the discussion. Mr. Pole produced a batch of papers and put on his reading glasses.

'Just a few documents that need signing,' he said. 'I think I've tabulated all the assets, with the exception of the valuation of this house and its contents, which should be in my hands tomorrow. Everything is so straightforward that we should be able to get probate very quickly. You may like to know how the estate stands. In all I make the assets £330,000, the better part of which is invested in Government loans and insurance shares. The trust fund for your two stepsons will take about sixty thousand pounds, and when the other small legacies have been paid you Mrs.

Bosanquet, will inherit the residue — '

'Wait!' interrupted Mrs. Bosanquet.

Mr. Pole gazed at her blandly, and saw that her face was pale and her jaw set hard.

'I've been thinking about it all,' she said in a low voice. 'My husband never intended me to inherit that very large sum.'

'But the will provides for it.'

'Yes, an old will dating back to a time just after my marriage. But, you know — we all know — there was another will in process of being executed. I want the estate administered on the basis of that new will.'

Mr. Pole adjusted his glasses. He was clearly amazed by this request, as were the two boys, who gazed at Dorinda with obvious incredulity.

'Mrs. Bosanquet,' said Pole, 'I assure you there will be no trouble regarding the will. The mere drawing up of a later draft will does not invalidate the will signed by your husband. It would not even be true to say that any of us knew your husband's last wishes regarding the distribution of his estate. I have taken advice on the matter and — '

'I appreciate what you say,' said Mrs. Bosanquet. 'But I know that my husband would have signed the new will had he lived long enough. He wished me to receive an income of two hundred pounds a year, so long as I remain unmarried. It is my intention to accept that decision. I want you to draw up the necessary document, which, I presume, will entitle his sons to the whole estate, less my annuity and the legacies mentioned.'

'My dear Mrs. Bosanquet, if you insist — '

'No,' said John. 'It isn't fair. If father liked to vent his spite on mother, I and Jasper won't be a party to it, will we, Jasper?'

'Definitely no,' said Jasper. 'Mother's got every right to that money, and she's going to have it.'

Dorinda put out her hand and laid it on Jasper's, but at the same time she shook her head.

'I'd never be happy with it,' she said. 'How could I handle a large sum of money like that, knowing that only by a terrible accident I had come into possession of it. Boys, it's nice to know what your feelings are in this painful matter, but my mind is made up. I'll not take a penny more than he wanted me to have. That, Mr. Pole, is absolutely final.'

'But, mother — '

'No more, boys. Please excuse me — all of you.'

She left the room, and John hit the table with his clenched fist.

'How could the old man be so ghastly?' he

said. 'Why isn't Mr. Grant here? He'd make her see reason. Mr. Pole, don't do anything yet. Mr. Grant is coming tomorrow to play tennis. He has known her a very long time. I'll talk to him, and perhaps he can persuade her to change her mind.'

Mr. Pole sighed. It was indeed hard to be patient with a client who was prepared to throw away a quarter of a million pounds for what she believed to be a principle. Mr. Pole knew quite a lot of people who would find it convenient to forget principles in such a situation.

'If your stepmother should change her mind, let me know immediately,' he said. 'Otherwise I have no option but to carry out her wishes, and that would be a pity — a very great pity.'

In the hall on his way out he met McLean, and after a moment's reflection he drew McLean away to the study, and told him of his dilemma.

'You really think she means that?' asked McLean.

'Undoubtedly. John thinks that Grant may induce her to take a more sensible view, but personally I doubt it.'

'Why Mr. Grant?'

'He's an old friend, with her interest at heart. Did you ever hear of such a foolish sacrifice? For years she has been kept outrageously short of money, and now when the chance comes for her to have a good time she declines to take advantage of it because she feels that it wasn't her husband's wish that she should benefit.'

'Aren't there such things as principles, Mr. Pole?'

'You wouldn't think so if you had been in practice as long as I have, Inspector. Well, I hope Mr. Grant will persuade her that her present intentions are silly.'

When Brook heard the news he cocked a sly eye at McLean, the meaning of which was fairly clear.

'Evidently you suspect her motives?' said McLean.

'Don't you?' retorted Brook. 'It would create a bit of impression on everyone if Mrs. Bosanquet caused it to be known that she was opposed to benefiting under the will of her rich husband. Remove a lot of nasty suspicion, wouldn't it?'

'Also remove the fortune,' pointed out McLean.

'Oh, no. That's where Mr. Grant comes in. He brings the full weight of his influence to bear on her, and finally she gives way.'

'And if she doesn't give way?'

'Then it will look as if the money wasn't

the motive, and that she and Grant can be ruled out.'

McLean smiled and shook his head.

'Your conclusions are not very sound,' he said. 'Grant loves her, and if he were guilty the question of money mightn't have come into it at all.'

'What about the missing will! Doesn't that prove that money was a motive?'

'It would seem so, but Mrs. Bosanquet's final refusal to accept any large sum of money doesn't necessarily rule her out as an accessory, nor Grant, nor either of the boys.'

'Why not? If the intention was merely to get rid of Bosanquet because he was an obstacle, or made for unhappiness, why take steps to prevent the new will from being signed?'

'We seem to be at cross purposes. Mrs. Bosanquet may not have been an accessory before the fact, but she may have been one after the fact.'

'You mean by covering someone?'

'That would account for her refusal to take full advantage of the situation. Suppose she knew — or even suspected — who really shot Bosanquet, I think her refusal to benefit from a brutal murder is quite logical.'

'Yes, I see that,' replied Brook thoughtfully. 'But if that is the case, wouldn't you expect her to show some resentment towards the person she suspected?'

'Yes, and that's where I'm mystified, for so far as I can see she bears no animus towards anyone who might conceivably be the culprit.'

Later McLean and Brook walked back to the hotel, by the footpath across the marshes. It was longer than the walk by the road, but much pleasanter. In the bright moonlight every detail of the scenery was perfectly clear, and from the sea came a light, cool breeze which was a pleasant relief from the heat of the day. McLean was very silent, for his mind was entirely occupied with the case, the complexities of which seemed to increase rather than diminish. When at last they entered the hotel the crowd in the saloon bar was dispersing. McLean saw Penny emerge from the doorway, in close conversation with a grizzled type of man, and he was sure that this was the person he had seen recently in Penny's company — his fishing companion. Penny passed by without seeing him.

'Wasn't that the gardener at Castle House?' asked Brook.

'Yes.'

They had a late meal alone, after which McLean made a point of having a word with the landlord.

'I noticed a nice little boat along the

beach,' he said. 'It was called *Nimrod*. D'you know it?'

'Oh, yes. It belongs to Amos Brown.'

'Not for sale by any chance?'

'I shouldn't think so. Old Amos thinks a great deal of the boat. He bought it from Mr. Mangus last year. Uses it for fishing.'

'But it never seems to go out.'

'Amos is keen on lobsters. He usually puts down some pots overnight, and picks them up early in the morning.'

'Isn't he a friend of Mr. Penny?'

'Yes. I think there's a business arrangement. They're pretty good at lobsters, and I often buy some from them. Of course it's only a side-line with them. Penny's a gardener — but, of course, you know that. Amos had a bit of money left him by his father, and adds to his small income by catching lobsters. They make a good price in Eastbourne and Hastings.'

'They don't appear to have much competition,' said McLean with a laugh.

'That's true. As a matter of fact, most of the fishermen about here don't favour this spot, but Amos says they don't know their business, and I'm inclined to agree with him. All the lobsters I've had from him have been first class.'

'Perhaps it's all a matter of bait,' said McLean.

'Well, there's something in that.'

Brook wondered why McLean should display the slightest interest in the boat, but McLean didn't enlighten him, and a little later they went to bed. McLean slept badly, for he was disappointed with the small progress he was making. Three or four times during the night he went to the window and looked out at the sea. It was at the first blush of dawn — while he was still sitting by the window — that he saw a figure cross the beach in the direction of Brown's boat. He reached for his binoculars and was able to recognise Brown himself. On reaching the boat Brown sat down on it and lighted a pipe. A few moments later Penny came into view, walking in sprightly fashion towards the sitting man. After which, the pair pulled the flimsy boat down to the sea and quickly got it afloat. Penny rowed while Brown smoked away in the stern. The boat went out a long distance, and in the gathering light McLean was now able to see two dark spots on the surface of the sea. They were undoubtedly the cork floats of the lobster pots.

He slipped on a pair of trousers, a tennis shirt and some rubber-soled shoes, seized a towel and bathing costume, and left the hotel. By the time he reached the beach near the spot where the boat was usually kept the two fishermen were on their way back. McLean disrobed, donned the bathing costume and dived into the sea from the sloping beach. He swam out for some distance, and then sported about. The rowing boat came closer and closer to him. Brown was now rowing and Penny seated by two large lobster pots.

'Why, it's the Inspector!' said Penny. 'Morning, Inspector!'

'Good morning!' gasped McLean. 'Any luck?'

Brown stopped rowing and McLean got a grip on the side of the boat. Penny pointed to the two wickerwork contraptions. There was a large lobster in each of them.

'Beauties,' said Penny. 'That one's the biggest we've caught this season. You're out a long way, aren't you?'

'Just a bit.'

'Hang on, and we'll tow you in.'

McLean nodded, and Brown put all his weight on the oars. He was a man of about sixty, but still very powerful. His arms were nut-brown and bulging with muscle.

'Nothing like the early morning,' said Penny, stretching his arms. 'No visitors to spoil everything. I hate this place when the visitors are about.'

Brown made no comment of any kind, and went on rowing like an automaton. Finally the boat's keel grounded on the shingle, and McLean waded ashore, and proceeded to rub himself down and dress. The two fishermen took some time to haul their craft to a safe spot, and then they removed the oars and the lobster-pots.

'What are you going to do with the catch?' asked McLean as he got into his nether garments.

'Sell 'em at the hotel — I hope,' said Penny. 'Place is full up just now. Big demand for fresh lobster. Look at that chap!'

He poked through the cage at the larger lobster with a short stick, and the beast grabbed ferociously at the stick with its enormous claws.

'Nice little chap to put in someone's bed,' said Penny. 'Well, Amos — ready?'

Brown nodded. He shouldered the two oars and one of the lobster-pots. Penny took the other one.

'Good morning, Inspector!' he said.

McLean nodded and the pair went off. By the time he got back to the hotel the landlord was up and in possession of the two lobsters.

'Can I tempt you — for lunch?' he asked. 'I can put up a nice mayonnaise.'

'They're booked,' said McLean. 'Where does Brown live?'

'Along the beach — right at the end of the bungalows towards Cooden. He's got a tumbledown shack there. Painted blue and called 'Pantiles.' Just a couple of rooms, and no comfort, but he makes do with it.'

During breakfast McLean reflected on the incident. So far as he could see, it was innocent enough. There was nothing remarkable in Penny wishing to add to his wages at the expense of his sleep. It didn't interfere with his normal work, and he had appeared to enjoy the change of occupation. What was noteworthy was the fact that nobody else appeared to trouble about lobsters, which could obviously be captured with little trouble. There seemed to be no connection whatever between this matter and the death of Bosanquet, with the exception that Penny was related to both events by reason of his vocations. But McLean never missed any opportunity to gather up even the slenderest threads, and later, on his way to Castle House, he called on Detective Stevens at his lodging.

'There's a man named Amos Brown, who

lives at a blue shack towards Cooden — beyond that horrible line of bungalows,' he said. 'The hut is called 'Pantiles.' Keep an eye on him and report his movements to me.'

15

Grant arrived at Castle House dead on time, to find John ready for the fray. The tennis court had been newly marked and, despite the burnt grass and the occasional bare patches, it was in fair condition.

'I've done the dirty on you, John,' he said. 'I've bought a new racket.'

John took the racket and gave a low whistle as he hit the strings with his knuckles.

'Hard as a board,' he said.

'I'll probably hit the ball clean out of the court. I ought to see Dorinda before we start.'

'Yes, do,' replied John. 'She knows you are coming. Oh, there she is.'

He indicated Dorinda, who was gathering flowers for the house in the lower garden, and Grant walked across to her and greeted her with a handshake.

'It was good of you to come and give John a game,' she said. 'He's like a lost soul unless he's playing some game.'

'You know it's always a pleasure to come. Dorinda, are there any fresh developments?'

'I don't think so, but I'm really not in a position to know. The police are still in the house, looking through everything. I've a good mind to take the boys away somewhere.'

'Would they let you?'

'Why not?'

'It might inconvenience them in their investigations — if you weren't on hand to answer any more questions they may ask.'

'But they can't actually prevent us leaving, can they?'

'I really don't know. A solicitor is the best man to answer that question. You're a little pale this morning.'

'Perhaps I've laid the powder on too thickly. There's John dying to start playing. Come in later for a drink.'

'I certainly will.'

A few minutes later Grant and John were engaged in a terrific battle. The ground was hard and fast, and Grant's fierce left-hand drives kept the younger man performing athletics on the back line, until Grant changed his tactics, chopping the ball short and dexterously working John out of position, finally to win the point with a lightning passing shot. Every game, however, went to 'deuce' many times, and with the sun pouring down heat the two players were soon reduced to playing with their bodies bare to the waist. The first set was won at ten-eight by Grant, after which they rested for a few minutes on the rustic seat at the end of the court, which lay in the shade of a tall elm tree.

'That was great,' said John.

'You'd have won if you were as good on back-hand half-volleys as you are in your general play,' said Grant.

'I'm not so bad as a rule, but that topped drive of yours gets me rattled. How do you do it?'

Grant illustrated the stroke, and then gave a little advice against his own interest.

'Don't try to hit it back,' he said. 'Simply put your racket down to it very early. You'll find it as easy as pie.'

'I doubt it,' said John. 'Anyway, I'll try. Come on — revenge!'

During the next set he adopted Grant's advice, and was jubilant to find it worked admirably. But Grant seemed to be improving the whole time, mixing his game in the most bewildering way. John, with all his youth and agility, couldn't do better than lose at five-seven.

'You're too good,' he said. 'And that's the awful truth.'

'I've had a few more years' experience — that's all. In two years' time I won't be able to look at you.'

'Thanks,' said John. 'But I can't accept that. Oh, Mr. Grant, there's something I want to talk to you about.'

'Well — here we are.'

'It's about mother. Last night the solicitor called about father's estate. Under the old will there's a tremendous lot of money to come to mother, but she refused to accept it.'

'What!'

'She argued that father was about to sign a new will, and she wants the estate administered just as if that will had been properly signed.'

'But that's silly.'

'I know it is. Father may never have signed the new will at all. He was inclined to be impulsive. I don't believe he really meant to leave mother practically nothing. Jasper and I are quite satisfied with our legacies, and we want mother to have what she's entitled to, but she's hurt, and won't look at it sensibly. That's where you come in.'

'How?'

'You've known her a long time. She may listen to you. We want you to persuade her to change her mind.'

'To accept the money?'

'Yes.'

'Do you realise that you are asking her to take a great sum of money which, in the present state of affairs, might go to you and your brother?'

'Yes, but we're already well provided for. Mother's a right to the residue. You've no idea how decent she's been to us — how much she had to endure from — no, I don't want to refer to that. The plain fact is that she mustn't be allowed to make a martyr of herself. You will speak to her, won't you?'

Grant was silent for a few moments, but finally he nodded his head.

'That's fine,' said John. 'What about a final set?'

'What a glutton you are. All right.'

While they raced about in the heat, Superintendent Ball decided to call on McLean. There was nothing that he wished to discuss in particular, but with time on his hands a chat with an expert sleuth-hound was always pleasant. He left his car outside the gate and meandered up the drive, stopping at intervals to peer into one of the numerous pools and admire the fish and aquatic plants. From the direction of the tennis court came the resounding bang of balls hit very hard. Soon the players came to view, and the Superintendent lingered a little and watched the game. Both the men were too engrossed even to notice his presence, to say nothing of the gleam in his eyes when, finally, he went on his way. Prout let him in, and left him while he went to announce him.

'Show him in,' said McLean with a sigh.

'Hope I'm not disturbing you,' said Ball as he entered. 'I had to go to Hastings and practically pass the door. Nothing fresh, I suppose?'

'Nothing of any importance.'

'I notice that Grant is here again.'

'Yes. He's playing tennis with John.'

'I saw them,' replied Ball with a lift of his eyebrows. 'I keep my eyes skinned, as you might say, and I noticed something just a little significant.'

'What was it?'

Ball took him to the right-hand window, from which it was just possible to see the tennis court and the players at intervals.

'Wait a minute,' he said. 'Grant's out of sight. You'll probably see him . . . Here he comes, after that ball. Watch him! There, did you see that?'

'I did,' replied McLean. 'A very neat return shot.'

'Yes, and played with his left hand. That's the whole point.'

'That he's left-handed — at tennis?'

'We don't know that his left-handedness is restricted to tennis. Expert opinion was that those anonymous letters were written with a left hand. We haven't solved that part of the business yet, and when you suddenly find a man closely connected with the case exhibiting that peculiarity — well, I ask you.'

'I saw them when they started to play,' said McLean. 'There may be something in it, and there may not. He is being closely watched, as are several other persons. By the way, do you know a man named Amos Brown, who lives at a hut near the beach?'

'Everybody knows him.'

'Respectable?'

'So far as I know. He's never been charged with any offence. But he's a curious man.'

'In what way?'

'Dumb as an oyster. Doesn't seem to have any conversation, and occasionally drinks heavily. His father used to live at Hastings and was a highly respected citizen there. Amos went to a good public school, and afterwards he went abroad. Some people say he was kicked out because the old man hated drinking. Three or four years ago old Brown died, and Amos came home. I think he expected to handle a lot of money, but his father apparently knew his weakness, for he left him only just enough to live in a very modest way. Why do you ask about him?'

'Just curiosity.'

The Superintendent didn't stay much longer. McLean made it quite clear that he had a lot of detail work to attend to, and finally Ball left.

'He's tickled to death,' said Brook.

'Why should he be?'

'He handed us a real dud, and doesn't he know it? Thought he'd done something marvellous in discovering that Grant played left-handed tennis. I wish he'd leave us alone.'

McLean noted that Grant stayed to lunch, and immediately afterwards he and Mrs. Bosanquet went into the garden and were together for a long time. When finally Grant left, McLean saw Detective Mitford appear in the road on a motor-cycle and ride after the vanishing car.

'Mitford is enjoying himself,' he said to Brook.

Brook curled his lip, to express his incurable disrespect of the young man from the police college. Later in the evening Detective Stevens telephoned McLean, and arranged a rendezvous. McLean met him on the path across the marshes.

'I was lucky, sir,' said Stevens. 'I went to the shack you mentioned, and saw the man — Brown. It's a queer sort of place that he inhabits — worth about ninepence. I walked past it and a few minutes later Brown left the shack and walked to Cooden. He's got a car garaged there, and he drove into Hastings. To keep on his trail I had to hire a vehicle. Well, I managed to get in touch with him before he reached Hastings. He left the car in a side-street, and walked to a bank. I went inside and made an enquiry about a new share issue which I knew was on the market. The clerk wasn't able to tell me much, and had to fetch the assistant manager. That gave me time to see what Brown's business was. He paid in some money. It was all in notes. I tried to see the amount on the paying-in slip, but can't be sure whether it was a hundred or a hundred and fifty pounds. There were certainly three figures in the pounds column. I couldn't wait to see the assistant manager, or I should have lost Brown. He did a bit of shopping — '

'What kind of shopping?'

'Some fruit, a book of stamps, and a couple of lobsters.'

'Lobsters!'

'Yes. He got them from a fisherman in the old town. Not a shop, but a hut near the harbour. All alive and kicking too.'

'What happened then?' asked McLean interestedly.

'He went back to the car and drove home. On this occasion he left the car on a patch of shingle near his shack. I hung about for two hours but he didn't venture out again.'

This information was amazing in view of the fact that Brown posed as a man attempting to live on a pittance, and to supplement that pittance went lobster fishing. Why should a man engaged in such an occupation buy lobsters from another? These facts combined with his close association with Penny rendered an investigation necessary. That night McLean took precautions to ensure his getting up very early. He awoke just before sunrise, and walked to the beach. The small boat was still there, and there was no sign of either Penny or Brown. McLean walked on the edge of the tide eastwards, past the hideous line of modern bungalows which completely spoiled what had been a lovely piece of coast. Finally he scrambled over the stones and came out by one of the Martello towers, beyond which he could see what he believed was Brown's shack. On approaching it he saw the name painted most inartistically on the side. The place was not conveniently situated for the keeping of a boat, and he presumed that was the reason why Brown's boat was beached further along the bay. Around the shack was a wire fence enclosing about a quarter of an acre of land, all of which was shingle, from which sprouted several varieties of natural plants. At the rear was a large water tank, which appeared to collect the rain from the roof, and this and a number of old motor tyres scattered about the shingle added to the general ugliness. Brown was not on view; this, considering the early hour, was not remarkable if, as McLean believed, Brown had not been out fishing. He walked round the place twice, and finally entered the gate and peered through a window. It was partly curtained, but he was able to see a very untidy diminutive sitting room, with a paraffin stove in one corner, and numerous articles of broken-down furniture. The second window was that of a bedroom. McLean could see a bunk-bed, a wash-hand stand, and a couple of prints pinned on the opposite wall. The bunk had evidently not been slept in, and he was driven to the conclusion that Brown had not been home the previous night. He wandered round to the door at the back, but on trying it he found it locked. Quite close to the door was the large cistern. It was provided with two taps — close to the bottom of it, and on opposite ends. To find out the reason for this McLean raised the heavy lid. He discovered that the tank was divided into two compartments, and that the rain water was conducted to the right one only, until it overflowed a partition and then was able to fill the second. He was about to lower the lid when he saw something below the surface of the water in the left compartment. On letting in more illumination he could clearly see the tops of two lobster-pots. He dipped his finger into the water and touched his tongue with them. It was salt!

He hoisted one of the lobster pots out, and found it very heavy. This weight was partly accounted for by a metal sinker, and partly by the presence of a huge live lobster! The second pot was identical as regards its contents. McLean sat and surveyed the two lively crustaceans. Could it be doubted that they were the lobsters purchased only yesterday by Brown?

Were they to be the 'fake' catch of tomorrow, or the next day? If so it was obvious that Brown and Penny were engaged in activities a good deal outside the law. On what other supposition could one explain these facts?

Ultimately he undid the bottom of one of the traps and after avoiding the attacks of its prisoner, and thwarting its attempts to escape he managed to extract the sinker. It was an oblong metal block, with a ring on the longer end, but heavy as it was it was by no means heavy enough to be solid. McLean suspected the ring, and brought force to bear on it. It turned comparatively easily, and the screw stopper to which it was attached came out. A tightly fitting washer showed that care had been taken to render the canister watertight. He shook it and turned it upside down, but nothing came out. The second canister was the same in every respect. McLean managed to get them both back into the lobster-pots, and the pots themselves into the tank, after which he made his way back to the hotel for breakfast.

16

'Dope running?' asked Brook, when McLean related what he had discovered.

'It looks like it. That would account for Mr Brown paying into his bank large sums of money. It would also account for Mr. Penny's eagerness to work overtime.'

'But how is it worked?'

'I imagine a ship comes up the channel, and under cover of night the lobster pots are raised, and the dope secreted in the hollow canisters. Penny and Brown go out early in the morning and pick up their catch. It must be dope, to be contained in so small a space.'

'And the murder — is there any connection?'

'That remains to be seen. It may prove to be quite unrelated — just as the kidnapping of John Bosanquet was.'

'But in what way could it be related?'

'Only one way, I think. If Bosanquet by some means discovered the truth, and had to be dealt with before he could report the matter. What weighs with me is the fact that Superintendent Ball called at the house shortly before the murder. It's conceivable that Penny might become suspicious, and tell Brown. We have to realise that Penny was in a position to commit the murder, and alternatively to be an accessory. But it's all theory so far. One could formulate half a dozen different and quite reasonable theories in this peculiar case — and none of them may be the right one.'

'Anyway, what's the next move?'

'To catch Penny and Brown in the act. Stevens and Young must stay up all night in turn, and warn us when the next lobster expedition takes place. Whether it helps our case or not we'll clear up that matter. I can't think it will be long before those lobsters are brought into use.'

They took the usual pleasant walk across the marshes to Castle House, and McLean found himself intrigued as ever by the many varieties of butterflies which were already busy plundering the summer flowers. The two neighbouring churches shimmered in the heat mist, and the peaceful atmosphere was a pleasant contrast to the underlying drama.

'This place suits me down to the ground,' said Brook. 'Never had such an appetite in my life.'

'That's saying a lot,' commented McLean.

Brook made a wild swoop at a magnificent Red Admiral which had zoomed lazily in the neighbourhood of his face.

'Missed him,' he muttered.

'What a Sadist you are,' remonstrated McLean.

'A what?'

'Forget it.'

On reaching the house McLean failed to see Penny in the garden, and the doors of the garage were closed. The family were having breakfast on the terrace, Prout serving them by means of the lounge window. They smiled as McLean and Brook raised their hats, and Brook sniffed when Prout passed him carrying an enormous tray. Outside the front door were two golf-bags full of clubs, from which McLean deduced that the two boys were contemplating a trip to the neighbouring links. The younger maidservant was polishing the letter-box and door-knob. She flirted with Brook, who was not slow to respond.

'Didn't know you played golf,' he said.

'No such luck. The two young gentlemen are starting early, but Penny's late this morning. He's supposed to put them clubs into the car.'

They passed on and finally opened up the study. McLean then unlatched the French window, and let in some fresh air. He heard John say, 'It's high time Penny showed up. I wonder if he's ill?'

'He was all right last evening,' replied Jasper. 'We'd better drive ourselves and look in at his cottage on the way.'

McLean re-entered the study in a reflective mood. Had Penny's lateness anything to do with Brown's absence from home? It was certainly an interesting coincidence in view of his recent discovery.

'Ring up Stevens,' he said to Brook. 'I'd like to talk to him.'

Detective Stevens was soon speaking to McLean, who gave him detailed instructions for that day and the following night. He had scarcely hung up the receiver when there came a rapping on the door and John Bosanquet entered without waiting to be invited. He was gasping for breath, and clearly deeply moved.

'Penny — !' he gulped.

'Well?'

'Penny's been murdered.'

'What!' ejaculated Brook.

'I went to the garage to get out the car, and I found Penny lying on the floor, with blood all round him.'

'Have you telephoned for the doctor?'

'Not yet.'

'You'd better do so at once. I'll go out to the garage.'

McLean and Brook found Penny lying far back in the garage, with terrible wounds in his head. A few feet away, lying in a pool of partly congealed blood was a crowbar. McLean leaned over the battered victim, and felt his pulse.

'I believe he's alive,' he said. 'Pass me that mirror.'

The small framed mirror became slightly clouded when it was held before Penny's nose and mouth.

'Just alive, and no more,' said McLean.

'We must keep him alive,' said Brook excitedly. 'What about some brandy?'

'No. We must wait for the doctor. His condition is too serious for us to deal with.'

John entered the garage, in breathless haste.

'I was lucky,' he said. 'Doctor Galbraith was just about to go out. He was actually in his car when he heard the telephone. He should be here — ' He stopped as he heard the sound of a car in the drive. 'That must be he.'

'Get the car outside,' said McLean. 'We need more room here.'

The car was backed out just as Galbraith arrived. He nodded to McLean and at once got down to work.

'It's hopeless,' he said to McLean after a

241

few minutes. 'A blood tranfusion might have saved him an hour or two ago, but not now. A horribly savage attack. He was struck at least twice, with tremendous force. I'm surprised he has survived so long.'

'You don't propose to move him?'

'No. It would be useless. He would almost certainly die at once whereas now there is a small chance that he may recover consciousness before he passes out. I have known that happen in such cases.'

'Can you tell by the blood on the floor about what time the attack took place?'

'Not with any accuracy. Undoubtedly the bleeding occurred some time ago. That blood against the wall, which obviously was spilled when he was struck is at least six hours old, and may be older. I'll be able to deal with that later.'

Again he tested the respiration and pulse of the fatally injured man, and shook his head. Penny never moved an eyelid, but the doctor soon detected a subtle change in his expression, and made another test at once.

'He's gone,' he said.

McLean shrugged his shoulders. A mere word from Penny might have made all the difference in the world to the case, but luck was against him.

'Better get the ambulance,' he said to

Brook. 'I'll go through his pockets now.'

Penny's clothing contained nothing out of the ordinary, but the significant thing in that respect was that he wore no part of his uniform or working clothes. He was wearing a pair of grey trousers, a thin pullover and a light tweed coat. The watch on his wrist had suffered no damage and was still going. In his trousers pocket was a purse, and this contained rather a large sum of money for a chauffeur to carry — over twenty pounds mostly in one-pound notes. Pending the arrival of the ambulance McLean locked up the garage, and took some evidence. The last person in the house to have seen Penny alive was the maidservant — Violet.

'He came into the kitchen at half-past five,' she said, 'and filled the coal scuttle — I mean the one we keep the anthracite in for the stove. Cook was out.'

'Was that his last job for the day?'

'Yes. He told me he thought of going to the pictures at Eastbourne. I gave him a cup of tea before he left.'

'Where was Mr. Prout?'

'He went out after lunch, and came back at half-past six.'

'And you never saw Penny again, after he left the kitchen?'

'No, sir.'

None of the family was able to give any information. Mrs. Bosanquet said that Penny's time for leaving off work was half-past five. She knew that he was in the habit of taking a cup of tea with the maid and cook, and had never had any objection to it. The car had not been used after tea, and neither she nor the two boys had had occasion to go to the garage that evening.

Superintendent Ball, having heard of the new development, arrived at the house, and was present while McLean was questioning the two boys.

'Well,' he said, when McLean had finished. 'This is a pretty kettle of fish, isn't it?'

'It's certainly something we didn't expect. No one here appears to have seen Penny after six o'clock yesterday. He evidently went home, changed his clothes, and came back here at some later hour. The circumstances seem to indicate that it was a very late hour, or he would have been seen. I should like to know just why he came back and went to the garage.'

'There's a connexion, of course, between this crime and the shooting of Bosanquet?'

'I think there must be, but at the moment I can't see where the connexion lies. One thing I have discovered, and that is that Penny and Amos Brown were engaged in smuggling.'

'What!'

'I was making plans to catch them in the act when this happened.'

'But what were they smuggling?'

'Dope, I think. The lobster-pots played a part in the business.

'But are you quite sure?'

'Yes. But unfortunately I have no proof — yet. It may be that I never shall have — now.'

'Why not?'

'Because Brown, with his confederate dead, may drop the whole thing.'

The Superintendent was thinking hard.

'Mightn't Brown be responsible for this?' he asked. 'If he had the slightest suspicion that he and Penny were being observed, mightn't he take steps to silence the one witness who could give him away?'

'He might, but I can't imagine him doing it the way it was done. There were many other safer ways. Besides, I'm not sure that the motive is good enough. If my suspicions are correct Penny had as much to fear as Brown.'

'There may have been a quarrel about the proceeds of the contraband.'

'All these things will have to be taken into consideration. I happen to know that Brown didn't sleep at his shack last night. You can save time by getting a search warrant for his shack, and we'll pick up Brown himself at the first opportunity. If he isn't back to-day we'll circulate a description of him. I have the number of his car, and that may aid us.'

'Car! You mean to tell me he runs a car?'

'I do. I think that's the ambulance. Like to have a look at the dead man?'

Ball nodded and went out with McLean. He saw Penny while he was being laid on the stretcher.

'Phew!' he said. 'He certainly got it in the neck!'

McLean picked up the crowbar, avoided the blood on it. He had already looked for finger-prints, but had found none. The handle-end had, in fact, fallen into a pool of blood, and the only clean part was about half-way down the implement.

'Does it belong here?' asked Ball.

'Yes.'

'No footprints?'

'None.'

'Well, if it wasn't Brown, who was it?'

McLean couldn't help smiling at the naïve question.

'The most likely person is the one who shot Bosanquet,' he said. 'Why Penny had to go isn't at all clear. If it was half our work would be over, but, as I see it, Penny was a threat to the murderer of Bosanquet.'

'But did you get the impression that Penny knew more than he was willing to admit when you questioned him?'

'No, but that doesn't invalidate the theory. Mr. Penny may have been cleverer than we imagined, or, alternatively, he may have discovered something quite recently. Now, if you'll get me that search-warrant we'll pay another visit to Brown's place, and see if that helps in any way.'

Ball went off, leaving McLean and Brook together. The car was searched, and a little later McLean took a key which he had found in Penny's pocket, and went with Brook to Penny's small, old-world cottage.

It was a most attractive dwelling — one of a row of about half a dozen similar Tudor cottages, each of which had a well-kept garden. They were all in a poor state of repair, but not so bad that a little money spent on them would not have made them almost perfect specimens of their type. Inside there were many quaint corners, and fine old oak beams. For a man who looked after himself Penny deserved praise. The little sitting-room was clean and tidy, and nowhere in the cottage was a thing out of place. The bedroom which he had occupied was plain, but it contained a good modern single bed, and some books by the bedside.

The bed was now made, but there was no means of telling whether it had been occupied for part of the previous night. McLean hoped to get some definite proof that Penny had been engaged in illicit traffic with Brown, and perhaps establish some connection between them and the Bosanquet murder, but the cottage yielded nothing but some documents locked up in a box which in themselves were interesting, but not incriminating.

'A hundred Woolworth shares. A hundred International Nickel. Fifty U.S. Steel. Five hundred pounds in the Post Office Savings Bank. Not so bad for a chauffeur-gardener,' he said.

'It spells dirty work to me,' said Brook.

By this time the neighbours had heard the news, and were discussing the tragedy with bated breath over garden fences. Brook went out and brought in the next-door neighbour. She was a Mrs. Lake, and she had known Penny for many years. According to her, Penny had arrived home on the previous evening at about a quarter-past six, and had gone out again soon after seven o'clock. She had not seen him since then. He often used to go out at unusual hours, but she knew he was interested in fishing, and shared a boat with Brown.

'Did Brown come here often?' asked McLean.

'Oh, yes — quite often.'

'When did you last see him here?'

'About three days ago — in the evening.'

Other neighbours were seen, and one of them stated that he had seen Penny in a local inn soon after six o'clock the previous evening. This was in keeping with the other evidence. No one had seen Penny after he had left his cottage soon after seven o'clock.

'That's as much as we can do here,' said McLean. 'We'd better go back to Castle House and wait for Ball.'

Ball got his search warrant through quickly, and handed it to McLean. They motored to Brown's cottage, but found the place still locked up.

'Do we enter?' asked Ball.

'Yes.'

A small window was broken, and a latch slipped. Brook went through and opened the back door to McLean and the Superintendent. The shack consisted of a sitting-room, bedroom, and wash-up. It's only form of lighting were oil lamps, and for cooking purposes there was an oil-cooker. Brown could not boast of the tidiness of Penny. The whole place was filthy, and the sitting-room was still littered with dirty crocks and glasses.

As there were two dirty glasses of the same size, with whisky in the bottoms of them, McLean suspected a recent visitor. On the floor near the fireplace were two cigarette ends. He picked them up and examined them. Both were hand-made, and the paper was watermarked with a zig-zag pattern. It was significant that he had taken a book of similar papers, and a pouch of fine tobacco from Penny's pocket.

'Looks as if Penny came here,' said Brook.

'Yes, but there are no means of telling when he was last here. Open that cupboard.'

The small cupboard was full of oddments — gum-boots, fishing-tackle, lead weights, and cork floats. By the side of these was a metal box with a padlock on it.

'Lift it up here,' said McLean.

Brook lifted the metal box on to the table. 'It's locked,' he said. 'Shall I break it open?'

'He's here!' interjected Ball. 'Brown, I mean.'

McLean went to the window and saw Brown getting out of a car. He was evidently suspicious of the other car which had been parked on a hard patch of shingle near his own, for he went to it and looked through the side window.

'Maybe he won't come — ' commenced Brook.

'You're wrong,' said McLean.

Brown turned away from the police car and came walking towards his shack. He disappeared from view for a moment and then they heard a key being used in the front door lock. The three intruders had taken up positions out of sight of the window, and when Brown entered he was taken aback by the sight of the three men.

'What are you doing here?' he snarled.

'Have no fear, Mr. Brown,' said McLean. 'We are police officers — not burglars.'

Brown directed his gaze on the Superintendent, whom he appeared to recognise.

'Pity you couldn't wait until I was at home,' he grunted. 'What's the trouble?'

'Simply a search warrant,' replied McLean. 'Have you the key to this box?'

'Yes.'

'I should like the loan of it, please.'

'What business — ?'

'The key — please!'

He searched in his pocket and finally produced the key, which he handed to McLean with a scowl. McLean removed the padlock and opened the box. It was full of documents which on inspection proved to be share certificates, property deeds, and bearer bonds. There was also a cheque book and a recent bank statement. The statement was most interesting, for it showed that large sums of money were paid into the bank at regular intervals, apart from smaller amounts which might have been dividends on the shares he held.

'What is the origin of these large cash payments?' asked McLean.

'Bets.'

'But aren't winning bets paid by cheque? These sums are in cash.'

'Yes — I won it all on the course.'

'Are you sure it wasn't on the sea?' asked McLean.

'What do you mean?'

'When did you last see Mr. Penny?'

'Last evening. He called here about half-past seven.'

His ready reply astonished McLean in view of what had taken place.

'How long did he stay?' he asked.

'About half an hour. We had a couple of drinks, and then he left.'

'What did you do then?'

'I went to see a friend — in Hastings.'

'His name and address?'

'He doesn't live there. I had a card from him telling me he was at Hastings, and that he could meet me on the pier at half-past eight.'

'At what time did you get back?'

'About midnight.'

'Did you then go to bed?'

'Yes.'

'What is your friend's name, and where can I find him?'

'His name is Reynolds, but I don't know where he's living just now. He's a commercial traveller, and — '

'Stop!' said McLean sternly. 'I warn you, Mr. Brown, that lying may put you into a very dangerous position. You never slept here last night, and I am certain that the man Reynolds is an invention. I may as well tell you that Penny was murdered last night, and that I propose to detain you until you can furnish a satisfactory alibi.'

He watched Brown's reaction. It was that of a man completely surprised. This expression slowly changed to one of deep and unmistakable anxiety.

'You don't imagine that I had anything to do with it?' he asked.

'That remains to be proved.'

'But — but why should I want to kill Penny?'

'Were you not engaged in a certain business enterprise with him?'

'You mean — fishing?'

'I think you know well what I mean. I have had the opportunity of examining your lobster-pots, and their contents, including the hollow weights. I can imagine circumstances which might induce one partner of an illegal business enterprise to silence the other partner. Much depends upon your proved movements of last night.'

Brown's mouth twitched as Brook moved close to him, and then he was escorted to the waiting police car. Before he was driven away McLean searched his car, but found nothing in it. But at police headquarters when Brown was personally searched, the sum of two hundred pounds was taken from his wallet. When asked how he came in possession of the money he said it was part of his recent winnings at Goodwood. 'What do you make of him, McLean?' asked Ball, when they were alone.

'Innocent of murder.'

'Then why doesn't he prove an alibi?'

'Because he's in a mess. Up to a point he told the truth — about meeting Penny and having a drink with him. Also I think he left Penny after a short period. But I don't think he went to Hastings. That plea was to put us off the scent. My own opinion is that he went to London with a consignment of dope — hence the large sum of money found on him. If he wants to free himself of a murder charge he must give away the man, or gang, who act as distributors of the dope. That is what is disturbing him now.'

'By jove — you're right,' said Ball. 'We've got him by the short hairs, and perhaps his associates, too.'

'Yes, but only if he feels we have a case against him. Make him believe that.'

'You bet I will. But it will be a bit of a disappointment in regard to the murders, won't it?'

'One more disappointment more or less won't make a world of difference,' replied McLean. 'This case is just a long series of disappointments. Let me know if he talks.'

A few hours of solitary confinement, during which Ball paid the prisoner two short visits, were sufficient to bring about the expected result. Brown, without revealing his reason for going to London, gave Ball the address of a man he had stayed the night with, and this information was telephoned to McLean. McLean immediately communicated with Scotland Yard.

An hour later McLean was told over the telephone that a most successful raid had taken place, in which large supplies of dope had been confiscated. So far as the murder of Penny was concerned Brown had a perfect alibi, but there was abundant proof of his participation in the drug smuggling, and he could be charged on that score.

'So it leaves us just where we were,' said Brook, making a sour face.

'Yes. We fish for whales and bring up a stray tiddler,' said McLean with a yawn.

17

In the meantime Detective Mitford had been enjoying himself immensely. The hotel at which he was staying was a comfortable one, and he had managed to secure a particularly good room, looking out to sea. He had not been long in making the acquaintanceship of Grant, and a round of golf together formed a solid basis for friendship. But Grant was not willing to lay bare his heart to anyone, and none of Mitford's leading questions got him any further regarding Grant's intentions. When not in Grant's company he became Grant's shadow, and he flattered himself he did this very well. Twice Grant had gone to Castle House, and stayed for a long time, and once he had met Mrs. Bosanquet in Eastbourne. They had done some shopping together, and Mitford recorded every detail faithfully, and passed the details on to McLean.

He came to like Grant, despite Grant's occasional chilliness when Mitford tried more or less subtly to introduce ladies into the conversation, and he himself had to lie nobly when Grant in his turn attempted to probe his mode of existence.

'What would you think?' he replied.

'Civil Service.'

'No.'

'Independent.'

'Not far wrong.'

'So you've a fond relative who hands you money when you need it, thus making it unnecessary for you either to toil or spin?'

'Would that disgust you?'

'Frankly — yes. But I don't believe you.'

'Why not?'

'You don't look that sort of parasite.'

'Thanks for the compliment. I'll buy you a drink in token of my gratitude.'

He called for the drinks, and then watched Grant gazing into his glass reflectively.

'What's the matter?' he asked. 'A fly?'

'Several,' replied Grant, and drank.

'What about a game of billiards?'

'I don't play billiards. But I play good poker.'

'Not for me.'

'Aren't you playing it now?'

'Gad, you do say some queer things!'

At that moment a boy entered the bar, and looked towards the two lone occupants.

'You're wanted on the telephone, Mr. Mitford,' he said.

'Coming,' replied Mitford. 'Excuse me,' he

said to Grant. 'I'll be back in a few minutes.'

When he returned to the bar he found Grant playing with one of the numerous gambling machines.

'Nothing of any importance,' he said. 'Now where did I leave that drink?'

'You finished it before you left. Have another.'

'Thanks, but I always know when I've left a drink unfinished. Leaves you with a kind of vacuum at the back of your throat. Oh, there it is!'

He found the drink and, having finished it, went across to Grant who was firing his last ball in the automatic machine. It bumped off a number of electrified knobs, and at each collision the lighted number at the back of the machine increased in value.

'Six hundred and twenty,' said Mitford. 'Bet you I can beat that. I've got a penny somewhere.'

'And how was Inspector McLean?' asked Grant quietly.

Mitford was so astonished he forgot all about the needed penny, and stared hard at Grant.

'I don't get that,' he said.

'You will,' replied Grant, with a smile. 'You see, Mr. Mitford, some of my young life has been spent in wild parts, in places where it's highly necessary to keep one's eyes wide open. I do the same here from sheer force of habit. That motorcycle of yours is rather outstanding.'

'Look here, what is all this?' blustered Mitford.

'Have another drink.'

He pressed the bell and the barman came to view. After serving the two cocktails he vanished again.

'Here's mud in your eye, Detective Mitford,' said Grant.

Mitford nearly choked as he gulped down his own drink. The situation to him was most embarrassing.

'Let's get this clear,' he said.

'Don't let's waste any words, Sonny Boy. Inspector McLean has doubts about me, and being otherwise engaged he dumps you here to report on my movements. All a matter of routine, of course — but a shocking waste of time, and public money.'

'Suppose I tell you that you are completely deluded — that I don't know who Inspector McLean is, and — '

'Don't!' begged Grant, holding out his hand. 'I can tolerate a sleuth-hound, but not a liar. I thought you ought to know that I'm perfectly wise to what is taking place, but don't let it interfere with your work. Have a good time, and let's forget it.'

'You're a cool customer,' said Mitford. 'It's no use my denying everything — '

'Not a bit. But you needn't tell McLean.'

'I've got to,' moaned Mitford. 'You're a nice sort of fellow to mess up things like this.'

'Sorry. Are you looking for a penny for this machine?'

'Damn the machine!' said Mitford. 'I've got to go out.'

'Well, give my love to McLean,' said Grant. 'You can assure him that I've no immediate intention of running away — even if he gives me the chance. In fact, I propose calling at Castle House tomorrow to see the Bosanquet family. That information will save him the trouble of having me followed.'

★   ★   ★

Half an hour later Mitford arrived at Castle House. McLean wasn't there, but Sergeant Brook was. He greeted Mitford with quite unnecessary effusiveness.

'Where's the Inspector?' asked Mitford.

'Out on the case. Didn't he ring you up about Grant?'

'Yes, but something happened immediately afterwards, and I don't quite know where I stand.'

261

'Anything important?' asked Brook, raising his eyebrows.

'Yes. Grant knows of my connection with McLean.'

Brook's heavy shoulders began to shake with laughter. It was all the more annoying to Mitford because it was silent.

'Don't do that — you big blancmange!' he said.

'Eh?' ejaculated Brook, looking aggressive. 'What the blazes is there to laugh at?'

'Police College,' said Brook. 'McLean's always telling me I ought to take a special course. Look what I've missed. First lessons in sleuthery. How to look like a turnip without being suspected. So you don't know where you stand? Well, I'll tell you. You don't stand anywhere, my lad. You're out — and taking the count.'

'You mean I'll be sent back to head-quarters?'

'What else? Murder investigations call for a pretty high standard of efficiency. For all we know, Mr. Grant may have done this job — both jobs in fact — and you let him lead you on a wild goose chase round the country. You know, you'd really be better on traffic duty.'

'That's an idea,' said Mitford. 'But you aren't so bright yourself if you think that

Grant's the nigger in the woodpile.'

'Oh, so you've got opinions?'

'Naturally — and they are based on good psychological principles.'

'Psychology! That's what the cat died of.'

'You're wrong. It died from kindness. Can I take a pew?'

'No, you can't,' replied Brook. 'Nothing in this room is allowed to be touched. Apart from this small table and these two chairs, everything is exactly as it was when Bosanquet was shot.'

'Where was he shot?'

'In the heart.'

'No! I mean where was he when he was shot?'

'In that high-backed chair. Please don't ask me any more questions. I'm busy.'

'Really!' said Mitford in an astonished tone.

The goldfish in the various tanks drew his attention, as did the little air-pumps which worked off the electric mains and provided the two larger aquaria with oxygen.

'Why are the fishes in the round bowl denied oxygen?' asked Mitford. 'Haven't they earned it, or can they exist on carbon-dioxide?'

'Give over,' begged Brook. 'Look it up in the *Encyclopædia*.'

Mitford went to the book-case and took out a book or two. Most of them were highly technical, but finally he found one containing a large number of beautiful coloured plates illustrating tropical fishes. He was looking at the illustrations when McLean arrived.

'Hullo, Mitford!' he said. 'Did you get those details?'

'Yes, sir. I had them already. There's no evidence that Grant left the hotel on the night when Penny was murdered. I have his programme up to one a.m. He and I and two other men played bridge until that time. I know he never took his car out after that time, and it would have taken him over an hour to walk here. That doesn't seem probable, does it?'

'No. Penny was attacked before one a.m.'

'There's something else,' said Mitford hesitatingly.

'Well?'

'Grant knows all about me. Honestly, sir, I did my best not to be seen by him, but it didn't work. He seems to have known from the very beginning.'

'Hm!' grunted McLean. 'He's evidently a very observant person.'

'He is indeed. He told me he had no intention of trying to run away, and I must say that he gives me the impression of being

264

absolutely innocent.'

McLean was gazing at the pictorial wrapper of the thick volume which Mitford had been reading. It was called 'Malayan Waters,' and its author was Professor Chatleigh. He picked up the book and turned over the preliminary pages. It was dedicated to 'Raymond Bosanquet, with acknowledgments of his invaluable help.' Under this was inscribed in handwriting, *'This is an understatement, as you well know. Henry Chatleigh.'* The date was appended, August 18th.

'Must have arrived during the weekend,' said McLean. 'Probably Chatleigh brought it down with him.'

'As I was saying — ' resumed Mitford.

'Oh, yes, about Grant. It certainly seems useless for you to follow him about if he is well aware you are doing it. I think, in the circumstances, I had better return you to headquarters.'

'That's what I thought,' muttered Mitford. 'Sorry I've been so useless.'

'I'm not sure that you have,' said McLean. 'Where did you find this book?'

'In the book-case.'

'Show me the place.'

Mitford went across to the book-case to the right of the window, and indicated a gap in a long row of books on the bottom shelf.

'I looked at some of the others,' he said. 'They all seemed pretty dull to me.'

'Yes, I suppose they would. Well, you had better get back to town, but there's no frantic hurry. I'll write to-night and announce your arrival tomorrow.'

'Thank you, sir,' said Mitford, and left the room.

'Poor devil!' said Brook. 'He thought it was all as easy as falling off a log, and now he knows different.'

'I didn't think he'd learn anything from watching Grant. He had a bang on the head and I wanted to give him a change of air. As a matter of fact, I may have been wrong.'

'In giving him an unofficial holiday?'

'No. In the assumption that he wouldn't be able to help us.'

'How has he helped the case?'

'That remains to be seen. But I'm interested in this book. It is dated the eighteenth — that is the day before Chatleigh came down here. So Chatleigh either posted it or brought it with him. I think we had better be clear on that point. Find Mrs. Bosanquet and asked her to come in here.'

Brook was absent for some time, as Dorinda was in the garden, on a search for flowers which were getting more and more scarce in view of the unending drought. When she did come her hands were full of flowers, most of them looking far from their best. The strange occurrences of the past week had laid their mark on her. She looked pale, but had obviously tried to counter this by extra make-up, which was far from achieving her purpose.

'I'm sorry to bother you again, Mrs. Bosanquet,' said McLean, 'but I'm interested to know when this book came into your husband's hands.'

He showed her the back of the book.

'It was on the Saturday, or Sunday, before — before my husband met his death,' she said. 'But I can't remember which of the two days it was. We were in the lounge, and the Professor went upstairs and brought the book down. He presented it to my husband.'

'Who else was present?'

'Mrs. Chatleigh.'

'No one else?'

'Yes. Prout came in to serve cocktails. I think he must have seen the Professor hand the book to my husband.'

'Then he may remember which day it was.'

'Yes. He is almost sure to.'

McLean pressed the bell once, and Prout entered the room almost immediately. McLean showed him the book.

'Do you remember seeing Professor Chatleigh hand this book to Mr. Bosanquet?' he asked.

'Yes, Inspector.'

'When was it?'

'On the Sunday evening after he arrived here. It was about seven o'clock in the evening.'

'Have you seen the volume since then?'

'No, sir.'

'That's all, thank you.'

When Prout had gone McLean turned to Mrs. Bosanquet.

'Can you recall what happened to the book after your husband received it?'

'No. I don't think it was in the lounge on the Monday morning, because I always go round the lounge myself, to make sure it has been properly dusted and tidied. But my husband may have brought it in here early that morning.'

Still dissatisfied, McLean had the two boys brought in. They both denied having seen the book at all. On the night in question they had both been late for dinner, and had gone straight to the dining-room. They had no idea that the Professor had given Bosanquet a book of any kind. The servants made similar denials.

'Is it important?' asked Brook, who was

quite unable to appreciate McLean's keen interest in the book.

'It may be. The fact is I'm reduced to the consideration of trifles. Look at the wrapper of the book. Do you see anything strange about it?'

'Only that someone has apparently laid a cigarette end on it and burnt the wrapper a little.'

'That's true — or appears to be true. But so far as I know the only two members of the family who smoke cigarettes are the two boys, both of whom swear they have never seen the book. Prout also swears he hasn't seen the book since it was given to Bosanquet. If Prout himself had laid a cigarette end on the book and burnt the wrapper there would be no real reason why he shouldn't admit it — now. That also applies to the other servants. Now if, as Mrs. Bosanquet thinks, her husband brought the book into this room early the next morning — the morning when he was shot — how comes it that it was in the book-case removed from the table where he worked? Why should he deliberately take this book so recently given him by a friend, and hide it at the bottom of a shelf? There is plenty of room in the book-case close to his hand.'

'That's a point,' said Brook. 'But I can't

think where it would fit in to any theory.'

'That's not the real point. Something a little strange has happened, and I want to know why. See if you can get Chatleigh on the telephone.'

The Professor spoke a little later. He stated positively that there had been no burn on the paper jacket of his book, when he had handed it to Bosanquet, and he added the important information that on the following morning he had seen the book on Bosanquet's desk in perfect condition. Bosanquet had remarked that it was his intention to read the work at once, and he felt sure this was no insincere compliment.

'Just where does that get us?' asked Brook.

'Who knows? It's a fact we must take into consideration.'

There was a rap on the door and Prout entered to inform McLean that Mr. Pole had called, and would like to see him. McLean nodded and Mr. Pole entered the study, carefully closing the door behind him as he did so.

'I thought you would like to know the upshot of the controversy over the will,' he said.

'Well, what is it?'

'Mrs. Bosanquet is absolutely adamant. She will accept nothing but what she believes her husband intended she should have. I had shelved the matter for a few days hoping she would change her mind, but now I must go ahead.'

'That means that the two boys might inherit practically everything between them?'

'Yes. That is her intention.'

'Do they know?'

'Yes. They think their stepmother is being unnecessarily quixotic — as I do.'

'Wasn't Mr. Grant to make an attempt to dissuade her from signing away her interest?'

'Yes, but he was unsuccessful.'

'Do you think he mentioned the matter?'

'I know he did. I have seen him, and he told me that he had done his best, but failed. It seems deplorable to me, but one mustn't overlook the other side of the matter.'

'What other side?'

'It will clear Mrs. Bosanquet of any suspicion. Naturally the newspapers have seized upon the matter of the missing draft of the new will. The murder, following so swiftly, provides the gossips with a nice story, but when the chief person involved voluntarily relinquishes a great sum of money the scandal has the bottom knocked clean out of it.'

'That's true. Have you any idea what Mrs.

271

Bosanquet's programme is for the immediate future?'

'I believe she and her two stepsons are planning to go on a world cruise once probate is got, and the whole matter cleared up.'

'I hope she realises that the whole matter can't be cleared up until the murderer of Bosanquet is found?' said McLean.

'Will he ever be found?'

'That sounds rather like a challenge,' replied McLean, with a short laugh.

'If you succeed you will have achieved the incredible.'

'What makes you so pessimistic, Mr. Pole?'

'The character of the person involved. I can't believe that any member of the family is the guilty person. I'm equally doubtful about Grant, despite the fact that he has no alibi for the time when the murder was done. Penny is dead, and whatever he might have known about the matter is a closed book.'

'But Penny himself was murdered — most brutally.'

'Yes, and that only reinforces my opinion. Shooting a man requires a cold-bloodedness not inherent in normal individuals, but battering a man lifeless with a crowbar calls for a state of mind which I fail to find in any of the persons that have come into this case — so far as I am aware. Forgive me for holding strong opinions on something really outside my province.'

'Almost every person in England is holding an opinion of some sort, Mr. Pole. Even I have an opinion.'

Mr. Pole smiled at the retort, and then bade McLean 'good morning' and went on his way.

'He seems to have the idea that nobody did it,' scoffed Brook. 'What does he know about murderers, anyway? Most of the people who look as if they could disembowel you without winking an eye are incapable of wringing a chicken's neck, and more than one pitiless murderer has looked as meek and docile as a parson. Still, I will say that Mrs. Bosanquet appears in a more favourable light.'

18

Grant carried out his programme and came to Castle House again armed with a tennis racket. On this occasion no begoggled motor-cyclist followed his car, and he mentioned this fact to Dorinda.

'But have you been followed?' she asked.

'Yes. I forgot to mention it, but it started on the day that a Mr. Mitford arrived at my hotel. He was quite a charming young man, and a good golfer. I should have been flattered by the attentions he paid me, but in the circumstances I thought he was just a little too nice. I discovered he was a C.I.D. man — acting on behalf of our old friend Inspector McLean.'

Dorinda expressed her surprise, for it was the first time that Grant had ever mentioned the matter.

'Why didn't you tell me before?' she asked.

'I thought you had quite enough troubles. Where's John?'

'Having a bath before he engages in battle with you.'

'Dorinda, did you see Mr. Pole again?'

'Yes. That matter is all arranged. It had to be that way, Bob.'

'You mean complete renunciation?'

'If you like to call it that.'

'What other word is there for it? I admire your pride, but it doesn't seem fair. How can you live on two hundred pounds a year?'

'Quite easily. Millions of women manage to live on less.'

'John was telling me something about a cruise — in the near future. Is that definitely fixed?'

'It was John's idea. He has always wanted to see the world. Jasper doesn't want to go to the University, and we are all free agents — or shall be very soon, when the police have given us a clean bill. I shall be glad to get away from here.'

'You haven't been very happy here, have you?'

'I've had moments of great happiness. But the place must go. Neither of the boys want to keep it. We must all start new lives. Everything is in a mess, and perhaps the cruise will give us time to find out what we all want to do.'

Grant looked at her keenly, and he noticed that she found some difficulty in meeting his gaze.

'Let's go into the garden,' she begged.

'No — not yet. Dorinda — there's something I must ask you. I'm due to leave England in a fortnight. In normal circumstances I shouldn't ask you the question I want to ask now, but things aren't a bit normal. You've been through hell and — '

John burst into the room, clad in shorts and tennis shoes. He had made an attempt to comb his rebellious hair, but the result wasn't very satisfactory, for it was almost visibly rising from his scalp.

'How do, sir!' he said. 'I saw you arrive from the bathroom. Believe it or not, I've been working on the court in company with the early worm, trying to make one blade of grass look like two, and using tons of water. It simply seeps away through the cracks. Am I interrupting a *tête-à-tête*?'

'Oh, no, John,' replied Dorinda. 'I've got to go into the village. Be sure you beat him this time.'

She rose and vanished with quite unexpected rapidity, and John's gaze followed her.

'I've got to get her away — quickly,' he said.

'What do you mean?'

'She's in a terrible state of nerves.'

'I didn't notice it.'

'You would — if you were here long enough. She can't bear any more — the

276

gossip, the newspapers, the telephone calls begging for interviews. Yesterday I had to chuck a newspaper reporter clean out of the grounds. He was trying to get a photograph of her in the garden — the swine!'

Grant looked very disturbed, for John's face expressed his very deep concern, and Grant took him to be the sort of man who would not exaggerate any set of conditions.

'Isn't she sleeping well?' he asked.

'I don't think she sleeps at all. During the night I've seen a thin ray of light under her door, and I've heard her walking about. There is a board which creaks, and in the silence it seems to yell out.'

'If she's not sleeping, she should have medical advice. I thought she wasn't looking quite herself.'

'Why must she suffer like this? What has she done to have all this trouble on her shoulders? Why must the police come here daily and continue to ask questions?'

'What questions are they asking now?'

'Mostly old ones — all over again — trying to trap us, I suppose. I wrote a letter to a girl on a sheet of notepaper I picked up somewhere. That sheet of notepaper seems to stick in McLean's gills. He's always saying, 'If only you could recall just where you found that sheet of paper it might help' — my God!'

Grant winced at the sudden ejaculation, and stared into John's tense face.

'Isn't that amazing?' said John in a hoarse voice. 'I've racked my brains a hundred times to recall where I got that sheet of notepaper, and it came to me when I was scarcely thinking about it.'

'That often happens,' replied Grant. 'Where did you get the sheet of paper that so intrigues Inspector McLean?'

'You gave it to me.'

'I!'

'Yes. It was just after I came down from Oxford. The first time you came here. You stayed the night, and on the following morning I played you a game of tennis. You mentioned a book to me — it was a travel book.'

'I remember that. It was by Keyserling.'

'That's right. It was a very expensive book, but you said you knew a shop where I might be able to get a second-hand copy. After you had changed you gave me a sheet of notepaper. It contained the name of the book, and also the name of a second-hand bookseller in Charing Cross Road. Later I discovered that behind the sheet of paper was a blank sheet. I realised you must have torn out two pages from a writing-block without knowing it. Funds were low, so I didn't try to get the book, but the blank sheet of notepaper got into the blotting-pad in my bedroom. When I wrote to that awful girl I was too lazy to go downstairs and get a sheet of our own notepaper, and used the blank sheet. I'm positive it was the same sheet.'

Grant was silent for a moment or two, and John fidgeted with the strings of his tennis racket.

'You do remember, don't you?' asked John.

'I remember writing an address on a sheet of notepaper. Have you got the letter you wrote to the girl?'

'No. McLean has that. He took it from her.'

'And he has other letters, written on identical paper, eh?'

'Yes. One of them read like a threat — to my father. I can understand his desire to find the writer — '

'And you think it might be me?'

John declined to answer for a few moments. A situation was developing such as he had not dreamed of, and it looked ugly on the face of it.

'Out with it,' said Grant. 'Be frank.'

'You love Dorinda, don't you?'

'Yes.'

'Do you know that my father suspected you from the moment you came here, and when the letters began to arrive he had little doubt that you —

'Oh, God, it's horrible. I can't believe it.'

'You needn't,' said Grant. 'I never wrote a single letter to your father, nor had I any intention of smashing up your home.'

John seemed slightly relieved by this statement. His gaze swept Grant's grave face, and the quiet eyes never winced.

'What became of the rest of that writing-pad?' asked John.

'I don't know. I bought it in Cairo, and used it there and in several other places. When I came here it was in the small suit-case which contains my toilet things. But I can't remember using the last few sheets.'

'Could you have left it here?'

'It's possible, but I can't swear I did.'

'Why did I have to remember that?' said John. 'I don't want to drag up the past — '

'Yes — you must. Dorinda will never be happy until this mystery is solved.'

'No good can come of my making matters even more complicated — dragging more people into the area of suspicion.'

'You mean, you want to keep this quiet?'

'Yes.'

'And become an accessory after the fact?'

'Only you and I know this fact. If McLean

were to know everything would boil up again. Wouldn't the police seize upon it as proof that you and Dorinda were conspirators — you writing the anonymous letters and Dorinda — '

'Dorinda signing away the property which came to her as a result of the conspiracy — and murder.'

'Oh, but there's more than that in it. There's the love motive. That would still count. If I believed that either you or she had really done that dreadful thing I'd go — '

'We're going now,' cut in Grant. 'Two men have been done to death and neither you nor I are going to keep anything back. Come on — let's go to the study.'

'You really — want that?'

'Yes.'

'But oughtn't Dorinda to be told? We can't leave her in the dark — about this. We all ought to stick together, oughtn't we?'

Grant reflected for a moment, and then agreed that Dorinda should be told of their intention. John said he would go and find her, and left the room for a few minutes. When he returned Mrs. Bosanquet was with him.

'I thought you two were playing tennis,' she said with a wan smile. 'What is John so mysterious about?'

'You tell her,' said John.

Grant seemed to find his task difficult. He opened badly, but after a little incoherence he succeeded in putting the new situation neatly and correctly. All the while Dorinda grew more and more excited.

'And there it is,' said Grant finally. 'As we are all keen to get the matter cleared up, I propose to place the police in possession of these facts. If McLean has the letters I shall doubtless recognise the notepaper when I see it.'

'No,' said Dorinda. 'It wouldn't do any good. Bob, you mustn't do that.'

'Why not?' asked Grant.

'Because — oh, can't you realise how dangerous it would be for you to admit such a thing? You are suspect. I know it's foolish — unwarranted, but you have no alibi, and more than one innocent man has suffered because of wrongly interpreted evidence. I've spent hours and hours thinking about this horrible business. The police are baffled, and are in the mood to take some drastic step if only they could find the slenderest evidence against some person closely connected with the case. They might even put you under arrest.'

'I must take that risk.'

'But the thing looks bad — worse perhaps than you imagine. I can't bear to think of you, in prison, charged with a crime you couldn't have committed.'

'Two crimes,' said Grant grimly. 'Penny's murder is not unfavourable to me. The man who murdered Bosanquet also murdered Penny.'

'Oh, please — please!'

She had risen from her seat and was in such a state of emotion that John hurried to her and put an arm about her shoulder.

'It's all right, mother,' he said consolingly. 'We wanted to talk to you first. If you feel that way about it we'll say nothing, and let the police do their own work. That's so — isn't it, Mr. Grant?'

But Grant gave no assent to this declaration. He walked slowly to the window and stared out at the burnt lawns and the blue, clear-cut watery horizon beyond marshland. When at last he turned his head Mrs. Bosanquet had gone and John was closing the door behind her.

'You can't do it,' said John definitely. 'She's hurt enough already. Let's play tennis — and forget it.'

★ ★ ★

For the remainder of the morning they played dull tennis. There was none of the dash and brilliancy of their former games, and the ball went out of court and into the net with quite aggravating regularity.

'Can't seem to get going,' grumbled John. 'What's the matter with us?'

'The weather maybe. It's as hot as Hades. Well, that's game and set to me, although I don't deserve it.'

Such as the match was, Grant won it, and they adjourned to the table under the sun-awning on the terrace, where they came under the observant eye of Prout, who sensed that in the circumstances drinks were indicated, and swiftly conveyed a tray and glasses and sundry bottles to the two thirsty men.

'Thanks, Prout. You're a wizard,' said John. 'Ice, too. I thought the refrigerator wasn't working.'

'I managed to get it going, sir. More soda, sir?'

'Right up to the top. That's fine.'

Prout went back into the house, and a moment later Jasper came and collapsed into a chair.

'How did the tennis go?' he asked as he helped himself to a bottle of beer off the ice.

'Horribly.'

'That means you lost.'

'We both played terrible stuff,' said Grant.

'Neither of us could concentrate. I suppose it's the heat.'

'It's a record to-day,' said Jasper. 'It's got mother down. She asked me to apologise for her if she wasn't down to lunch.'

John displayed anxiety at this information, and Grant looked very uncomfortable. When Prout ultimately announced that lunch was ready Dorinda was not visible.

'I think I'll go up and see how she is,' said John.

'I shouldn't,' said Jasper. 'I think she is trying to get to sleep. It was clear she didn't want to be disturbed.'

The meal was very cheerless, and after a rest the three men went for a bathe. For a long time afterwards they reclined on the steep shingle beach and added yet another shade of brown to their sunburned bodies and limbs. Then Jasper remembered that he had a tea appointment and rode off on his cycle. Grant had been singularly silent since lunch, and was now throwing stones rather aimlessly at other stones.

'Bad luck, Dorinda crocking up,' said John. 'Do you think it is the heat?'

John's head came round. He saw Grant regarding him intently.

'Worry, too, I imagine.'

'Yes — worry, and nothing else. The sooner

these murders are cleared up the better. That brings me to the point we were discussing this morning. I'm going to talk to McLean.'

'About the origin of that writing block?'

'Yes.'

'But Dorinda — '

'She's anxious on my behalf. She thinks that my position will be made worse by telling McLean the truth. Whether it is or not, I'm certain that no fact should be withheld from the police. How can we expect them to solve this mystery if we deliberately obstruct them? I shall see McLean as soon as we get back.'

John winced, but made no further objection. A little later they walked back across the marshes in the heavy evening heat. At intervals there came to them ominous rumbling, and by the time they had reached the main road the sun was partly enveloped in a strange blue haze.

'Storm coming up,' said John. 'We are going to get our rain at last. By gosh, and we need it.'

They were actually entering the drive of the house when the edge of the storm reached them. The sky had become a deep electric blue, and suddenly a blinding flash of lightning split the whole vault. Deafening thunder followed, and then the rain.

'We'll have to run,' shouted John. 'Come on!'

They were half-way up the drive when Prout came running towards them carrying a large garden sunshade.

'Good man!' said John.

'This sort of rain can be very unpleasant, sir.'

'Unpleasant! Why, haven't we been praying for it?'

'Not this kind, sir.'

They raced into the hall as the drive became a raging torrent, and the thunder threatened to split the house in twain.

19

McLean and Brook had been out all the afternoon, but had returned to the house just in time to miss the storm, which was now in full swing. From the window McLean had seen Jasper arrive on his cycle and leave again after changing. He had also seen John and Grant reach the shelter of Prout's sunshade and finally disappear round the end of the terrace.

'I should like to feel that they were innocent,' he said.

'The family?'

'Yes. And that includes Grant.'

'If they're all innocent, who's guilty?'

'Someone we've never had cause to suspect.'

'Well, there are two thousand million people in the world,' said Brook. 'What do you make of Mrs. Bosanquet being unwell?'

'I have known even you to be unwell.'

A terrific flash of lightning, and thunder which was like an artillery battle intervened. A breeze created by the conditions brought rain into the study through the open window.

'Better close it,' said McLean.

Brook closed and latched the window, and then came back to the table. He was about to sit down when there came a rap on the door.

'Come in!' he called.

To his surprise, Grant came to view, closing the door behind him.

'I should like a word with you, Inspector,' said Grant, staring at McLean.

'Certainly. What is it?'

'Believe it or not, I am as anxious as you are to solve the mystery of Bosanquet's death — and that includes Penny.'

'It's nice to hear you say so.'

'That sounds as if you doubt my sincerity. As a matter of fact, I may be able to contribute something to the evidence you already possess.'

'Every scrap of evidence is of importance.'

'Isn't it a fact that before he was shot Bosanquet received a number of anonymous letters?'

'Quite true.'

'I believe that one of those letters contained a paragraph which might be construed as a threat.'

'It might.'

'May I see the actual letters?'

McLean hesitated for a moment, and then nodded his head. Brook went through a pile of documents, and finally found three letters received by Bosanquet, and also the letter written by John to his girl friend. McLean took them and handed them to Grant. Grant read them and nodded his head.

'I believe that all these letters were written on sheets from a writing-block once in my possession,' he said. 'This letter written by John to the girl in London was written on a spare sheet of the paper which I left here when I first called. It was only to-day that he recalled how he had come into possession of that sheet of paper.'

'Please tell me the circumstances.'

Grant did so very briefly.

'So you cannot remember what happened to the rest of that writing-block, after you left this house?'

'No. I'm certain I never used it again.'

'It might have been left here?'

'Yes. That is possible.'

'And you insist that you did not write any of these letters?'

'I did not.'

McLean took back the letters, and handed them to Brook who was putting them into a file when suddenly there came a vivid flash of lightning, and a nerve wracking crash of thunder. This was mingled with a smashing of glass, and a loud exclamation from Brook.

'The fishes!' cried Grant.

McLean suddenly realised that the large circular fish-bowl on the table near the window had been broken, and that the water and a number of fishes were on the carpet. The colourful fishes were flopping about in agony.

'Ring the bell,' said McLean. 'We shall need a pail.'

Brook rung the bell, and then saw McLean go to the window. In one of the panes was a neat round hole. McLean looked toward the spot where the fish bowl had rested, and then went to some panelling close to the fireplace. Embedded in the wood was a bullet. It must have missed him by about a foot. Prout entered the room, and stared at the mess.

'A bucket of water,' said Brook.

'Oh, the goldfish!' ejaculated Prout. 'Poor little things!'

McLean opened the terrace window and went outside. The heavy rain had lifted for a moment, but the sky was still extremely dark. He took the shortest cut to the gate, and on reaching it he looked up and down the road. The back of a motor cycle was vanishing from view. It was too far away for the number plate to be read, and was gone the next instant. He went back through the garden, investigated the garage and potting-shed en route, and finally reached the terrace again.

Another ear-splitting clap of thunder brought a resumption of the rain. On entering the study he found Brook and Prout busily engaged in rescuing suffocating goldfish from the carpet and putting them into a bucket of water.

'Eight,' said Prout. 'That's the lot. What happened? Was it the lightning?'

'Funny sort of lightning,' grunted Brook, and glanced at the perforated window.

Prout saw the hole in the glass as he was picking up the pail.

'Good gracious!' he ejaculated. 'This is terrible. I'll put the fish into one of the garden ponds, and come back and tidy up.'

'I'll ring for you,' said McLean grimly. 'Mr. Grant, I'm grateful for your information.'

Grant interpreted the remark as a polite dismissal, and followed Prout into the hall.

'Did someone try to shoot the Inspector?' asked Prout.

'It certainly looked like it.'

'What's that?' asked John, coming from the stairs.

'Didn't you hear?'

'I heard something like glass breaking — just as the thunder crashed.'

'A shot was fired from the terrace. It went clean through the window pane, broke the round fish bowl and must have narrowly missed the Inspector. I saw him extract the bullet from some woodwork close to the fireplace.'

'But didn't he make any attempt to catch the culprit?'

'We were all taken completely by surprise. The shot wasn't heard at all. It was drowned by the thunderclap. When the fish bowl was shattered my own first impression was that it had been struck by the lightning.'

'Queer business,' ruminated John, as they went into the lounge. 'But at any rate it will have one good result.'

'What is that?'

'It clears you. It must mean that the person responsible for these incidents is outside the house. Unless you are the world's greatest magician you couldn't have fired that shot, could you?'

'What was there to prevent my arranging it, with the assistance of a confederate — just to throw dust in the eyes of McLean?'

'Don't!' begged John. 'My brain is already tottering.'

★   ★   ★

In the meantime McLean had gathered up all the many fragments of the broken fish bowl, and Brook had borrowed a swab and basin from the kitchen.

'Looks a bit better!' said Brook. 'I must say this case is getting me dithery. Who was meant to be the victim that time?'

'That would be interesting to discover. Where do you think I was standing when the shot was fired?'

'Where you are now,' replied Brook. 'Within an inch or two I should think.'

'Then stand here while I take a line from the hole in the window pane.'

Brook did this and McLean went outside the window and peered through the hole in the glass. He could see the scar in the panelling opposite, but a straight line to the scar was some distance from the base of the fish bowl which still rested on the table; and Brook's broad chest was only a few inches from the bullet's final resting place.

'The bullet was deflected by the rounded side of the bowl,' he said. 'If it was aimed at me it was a very wide shot. It might just as easily have been Grant who was to my right.'

'You would surely be the more likely target,' argued Brook.

'I can't see why. The evidence which we have is on record. What sense would there be in shooting me?'

Brook shook his head, and as the rain was easing off again they both went out on the terrace and looked for the empty cartridge case — presuming a pistol had been used. It was found lying close to the short wall, near a flight of steps which went down to the lower garden. McLean took it inside and placed beside it the damaged nickel-coated bullet which he had taken from the panelling.

'It's mighty like the one which killed Bosanquet,' said Brook.

'Exactly. Have we the other bullet here?'

'Yes.'

Brook produced the first bullet, and the two were compared as closely as was possible within the limits of a pocket magnifying glass. McLean could see no difference at all, but it would require a much more powerful instrument to prove the point beyond doubt.

'We'll get a quick report on that,' said McLean. 'If the same pistol is being used there's little wonder that we failed to find it.'

'The fellow's bold enough, to come and take a shot at you like that.'

'That's what puzzles me. He ran a tremendous risk without sufficient justification.'

'He was clever enough to use the thunder to cover the sound of the pistol. Must have been lurking outside waiting for the crash. Shall I get rid of the broken glass?'

'No. Pack it all up together. The base too.'

Half an hour later Superintendent Ball called, just to see if there were any further developments. McLean wasn't overwhelmed with joy for matters had reached a stage when some really hard thinking was necessary, and Ball's presence was not contributory to such.

'Hell of a storm!' he said. 'I simply couldn't drive through it. Had to stop the car and wait. Well, how are things?'

'Far from stagnant,' relied McLean. 'Take a look at that window.'

Ball went to the window indicated and gave a low whistle of surprise.

'What's been happening?' he asked.

'A little pistol practice, fortunately with no very serious results.'

'You mean you were shot at?'

'Brook seems to think so, but I'm not so sure. Anyway, no one was hurt, and we have two more exhibits. These.'

He showed Ball the empty cartridge case and the damaged bullet, and Ball became intensely interested.

'The same gun — for a million!' he said excitedly.

'It looks rather like it.'

'Damned cheek!'

'It was rather bold.'

'But didn't you get a sight of him?'

McLean shook his head, and declined to go

into details. As Ball was on his way to headquarters he suggested he should take the bullet and cartridge case with him, and ascertain for certain whether the same weapon had been used.

'I'll telephone you the result,' he said. 'Will you be here or at the hotel?'

'The hotel. I'm going to give the case a rest for an hour or two.'

'That's right,' said Ball. 'Must be getting on your nerves. Just one damned complication after another. Well, I'll be going before the next storm arrives. We seemed to be ringed round with them. Floods everywhere. Cheerio!'

20

Grant was persuaded by John to stay to dinner and Dorinda came downstairs just before the meal was served.

'Is Jasper back?' she asked.

'Yes,' replied John. 'He was wet through and is changing. How are you feeling now?'

'Much better,' she said with a smile. 'I think the storm cleared the air a bit. I'm glad you stayed, Bob. What a poor sort of hostess I've been.'

'Glad to hear you're better,' replied Grant. 'As a matter of fact John has been an excellent deputy. We had some tennis, and a bathe. Didn't the thunder alarm you?'

'No. I've always enjoyed thunderstorms. But was something broken? I thought I heard glass breaking.'

Grant glanced at John, and was quite unable to decide from John's expression whether he favoured a relation of what had recently taken place.

'Don't you think I had better know?' asked Mrs. Bosanquet. 'John never could hide anything from me.'

'That's true,' said John. 'The fact is that

someone fired a shot at the Inspector, at least we presume it was the Inspector who was the intended target. Fortunately it missed him.'

'Oh!' she gasped. 'Did he catch the man?'

'No.'

'Doesn't he know who it was?'

'I don't think so. But there can be little doubt that it's the same person who is responsible for the other crimes. It seems a crazy thing for him to do.'

'Horrible!' she said, with a shudder. 'When shall we be free of all this?'

Prout came in to announce the meal, just as Jasper appeared, looking fresh from a bath.

'Don't mention the shooting during dinner John,' whispered Dorinda. 'Jasper is so sensitive, and it can't serve any purpose.'

As they passed the study John noticed that the door was padlocked.

'Cheers,' he said. 'The police have gone — at least for the nonce. I wonder they don't sleep here, and put an end to the last scrap of our privacy.'

Prout waited at table alone, reminding Mrs. Bosanquet that the two girls were out, and that cook had left as she always did immediately her job was done.

'I had forgotten,' said Dorinda. 'The girls won't stay unless they can go out together. It's very inconvenient, but one has to knuckle down to hard facts.'

'Why not sack 'em both, and get another man, like Prout?' asked Jasper, while Prout was out of the room. 'He's worth ten girls.'

'What's it matter?' put in John. 'With any luck we'll all be on the high seas in a few weeks, with stewards galore to look after us. Lord, I'm looking forward to that, aren't you, mother?'

Mrs. Bosanquet sighed and remarked that she couldn't believe it would ever happen. After dinner the two boys decided to go to a cinema, and left Grant with Dorinda, as that appeared to be Grant's desire.

★ ★ ★

Shortly before eleven o'clock that evening McLean was rung up by the Superintendent to be told that the bullet which had been fired that afternoon had been fired by the same weapon as that which had killed Bosanquet.

'That settles that,' said Brook. 'And what are we going to do about it?'

'Find the man who fired it.'

'Sounds good to me,' said Brook. 'But I'd like to know just where we start.'

'Go to bed,' said McLean. 'We've already started.'

At seven o'clock the next morning McLean

was called to the telephone to hear John's voice at the other end.

'Can I see you at once, sir?' he asked. 'Something most mysterious has happened.'

'What is it?'

'Mother went out last evening, and hasn't come back. We're worried to death. Please come.'

'I'll be with you in a quarter of an hour,' said McLean.

Brook was unceremoniously jerked from his slumbers, and informed of the telephone message.

'Well I'll be — !' he ejaculated. 'If this isn't the blue limit! Kind of 'who goes next?' game. Do we have breakfast first?'

'We do not. We don't even shave ourselves. Be downstairs in five minutes. This may be serious.'

The storm of the previous night had cleared the air to some extent, but not yet was the thirsty earth satisfied, and there was now very little evidence of the recent deluge, except in those places where the flood water had swept debris into piles and scoured deep holes in the gutters. Though the air was less heavy the sun blazed no less fiercely even at that early hour.

At Castle House everyone was in a state of great excitement. John Bosanquet looked as if he had not slept at all, and Jasper's face was as bloodless as an egg. The two boys took McLean into the lounge, and there John related what had happened.

'After dinner last night Jasper and I went to a cinema in Eastbourne,' he said. 'Mother didn't feel like coming, so we left her with Mr. Grant, who stayed to dinner. We arrived home soon after eleven o'clock. Prout was up and he told us that mother had apparently gone out for a walk — — .'

'Why apparently?'

'Prout himself went out after Grant had left, but was back at eleven o'clock. He found no one in the house. The maids came home a few minutes later. They had been out since the afternoon, so of course knew nothing. We all waited up, and at midnight Jasper and I took the car out, and went over all the roads — and along the beach. It was no use. We came back and found she was still absent. Prout then suggested we should telephone Grant. We did so and woke him out of a sleep. He sounded amazed, and said he had left mother at a quarter to nine — just after Prout had gone out. We didn't know what to do. Perhaps we should have rung you earlier, but we were hoping all the time that mother would come back and explain everything. She didn't leave a note, but we can't find the handbag she was using yesterday, and a red waterproof of hers is missing.'

Prout was then called. He looked very grave — more perturbed than McLean had ever seen him. Although he had had very little sleep he was freshly shaved and as neat as always.

'Tell me what you know, Mr. Prout,' said McLean.

'It's little enough, I'm afraid. After the young gentlemen had left for the cinema, Mr. Grant stayed on with the mistress. I served some coffee, and at about a quarter to nine I asked Mrs. Bosanquet if I might walk into the village. She said I might.'

'Had you any particular reason to go to the village?' asked McLean.

'No — except that I hadn't been out of the house for days, and it was a beautiful evening — after the storm. I walked to the bay and took the road which goes to Eastbourne — the old road. Near the spot where they dig for shingle I cut off into the fields and finally found the footpath which leads to Westham. The church clock was striking eleven as I entered the drive. I was rather surprised to see no lights in the house. When I entered the hall I switched on the light, and rapped on the lounge door. I quickly discovered that Mrs. Bosanquet was not in the house. I wasn't anxious because it was natural enough for her to go for a walk. But when the young gentlemen came back, and Mrs. Bosanquet was still absent, we all became anxious, and the young gentlemen took out the car.'

'Had Mr. Grant left the house when you asked Mrs. Bosanquet if you might go out?'

'Yes — he had just left.'

'That was at a quarter to nine?'

'Yes. I was actually in the hall, when he left. Immediately afterwards I went into the lounge, and got permission to go out.'

The other servants, when questioned, corroborated Prout's statement about the time of their return, but they had no idea of what had happened until that morning, when they learned that Mrs. Bosanquet had not been home all night. McLean was still questioning them about the clothing which Dorinda might have worn, when Grant arrived. McLean kept him waiting for a few minutes, and then had him shown in. Grant was clearly greatly agitated. He declined the proferred chair, and stood with clenched hands staring hard at McLean.

'Haven't you any questions to ask me?' he rasped.

'Quite a lot,' replied McLean calmly. 'At what time did you leave this house last night.'

'At a quarter to nine. I remember that I

reached my hotel just before nine o'clock.'

'Up to that time Mrs. Bosanquet was with you — alone, wasn't she?'

'Yes — after the two boys had gone to the cinema.'

'A period of something like an hour?'

'Less than that. I think the boys left at eight o'clock.'

'During that time did Mrs. Bosanquet say anything which might have led you to believe that she intended to go out later?'

'No.'

'Was there any suggestion from her that she wished to be left alone?'

'No — none at all. As a matter of fact, she seemed quite disappointed when I said I must go.'

'Why had you to leave?'

'Well, I had been here most of the day.'

'But you have already admitted being in love with her.'

'Does that necessitate my spending every minute of my time here? As a matter of fact, I was tired. On the previous night I went to bed, very, very late.'

'Was there any telephone message for her during the evening?'

'Yes, there was. Prout came in at half-past eight to tell her that she was wanted on the telephone. There is no extension in the lounge, so she went out to the hall.'

'Do you know who the caller was?'

'Yes — Mr. Pole, the solicitor.'

'Have you any idea what the object of his call was?'

'Yes. It was to tell her that a certain document was ready for signing — '

'The transfer of the property back to her stepsons?'

'Yes.'

'Was she still of the same mind?'

'Yes. She arranged to call at Pole's office this morning at eleven o'clock, to sign the transfer.'

'Mr. Grant, have you any idea at all where Mrs. Bosanquet may have gone last night? Are you, for some reason which you may consider justifiable, keeping anything back from me?'

'No. Listen, Inspector. Throughout this strange business I've been absolutely frank. I told you from the start that I loved her, despite the fact that such a confession was apt to put me under suspicion. That applies, too, to my recent admission that the anonymous letters were written on notepaper which originally belonged to me. I did that against her wishes — '

'Indeed! That's something I didn't know,' interrupted McLean sharply.

'She was against my telling you because she believed it would be prejudicial to me. But I don't care a damn what view you may take about that. I'm certain that she's in great danger. During the past few days I've noticed a change in her.'

'What sort of a change?'

'She's anxious — fearful of something. When I talk to her, her attention wanders. Last night I tried to get something definitely fixed, regarding the future — as it concerns her and me, but it all fell flat. She hedged me off, and I had to drop the subject. It isn't a natural development of the circumstances. I got the impression that there's some fresh factor which she won't talk about — that it was wearing her down. Now she's gone, and I'm worried out of my life. What are you going to do about it?'

He put the question almost fiercely, as if he resented McLean's calm acceptance of such a calamity as was now facing him.

'I wish I could produce her out of the proverbial hat,' said McLean. 'But rest assured that everything possible will be done.'

Brook let Grant out and came back to the table. McLean had sat down and was resting his chin on his hands in an attitude of deep reflection.

'Quite annoyed with us,' commented

Brook. 'What a case! Every day it gets worse. D'you know what I think?'

'Yes. You think that Mrs. Bosanquet was got out of the way so that she couldn't possibly sign the transfer.'

'Phew! You're a bit uncanny at times.'

'There's nothing uncanny in a perfectly natural conclusion. Moreover, the chances are you're right. Get me the hotel — Grant's hotel.'

A few minutes on the telephone were enough to convince McLean that Grant had told the truth regarding the time at which he returned to the hotel. Afterwards he had taken a bath and gone to bed early.

'We'd better take a look round,' said McLean.

He left the study and walked into the lounge, followed by Brook who sniffed and sighed at the delicious aroma of frying breakfast which was wafted into the hall from the direction of the kitchen. The pretty housemaid was about to enter the lounge armed with a hoover, but McLean stopped her.

'Not this room, nor Mrs. Bosanquet's bedroom,' he said.

The lounge was fairly tidy, but it yet carried the smell of yesterday's cigarette smoke. McLean opened the windows, and drew back the curtains. On a low table was an ash-tray full of cigarette ends, and various newspapers were scattered about the room. One of these lay on the couch. It was folded in such a way as to bring a crossword puzzle to full view. This had been started, and about a dozen words had been pencilled in. The pencil itself lay on the couch beside the newspaper.

'It looks as if Mrs. Bosanquet commenced the crossword puzzle after Grant left,' said McLean. 'If so, she seems to have been interrupted, for here's a word half written. Was it a caller, or the telephone bell?'

The lounge yielded nothing more in the nature of a clue, so McLean went upstairs to the bedroom which the missing woman had occupied. Here there were signs of a hasty departure. On the floor was a pair of evening shoes, which appeared to have been kicked off in a hurry, and on the bed were a pair of silk stockings, which McLean associated with the shoes.

'So she came here from the lounge and changed her footgear,' he said. 'That would be necessitated by the prospects of a walk, and we know she took a red waterproof. Question — why was it necessary for her to take that walk in such a hurry?'

The telephone supplied the answer a few

minutes later. McLean went to the instrument in the hall, and found beside it a memorandum pad and a sharp pencil secured to a hook by a piece of string. The memorandum pad was blank, but its sheets were thin, and on the uppermost blank sheet were some faint impressions. He tore it off and went into the study with it.

'Undoubtedly Mrs. Bosanquet's writing,' he said. 'She made some notes on the sheet which she tore off, and a few impressions have come through the thin paper.'

The small sheet of paper was closely examined. The first few broken words were not difficult to interpret.

Battle road. Turn right at one mile . . .
W.T. . . .

'Is it W.T.?' asked Brook, peering at the impressions.

'It looks like it.'

There was a rap on the door and Prout entered.

'Sorry to interrupt,' he said. 'But Mr. John thought you might not have had breakfast, and wishes to know whether I shall serve you some breakfast?'

McLean took one look at Brook's eager face, and nodded.

'Shall I bring it here?' asked Prout. 'Or would — '

'Here, please.'

'Very good. Coffee or tea, gentlemen?'

'Coffee,' replied McLean.

'Me, too,' said Brook.

Prout bowed, and went out, leaving Brook very much happier, for Brook in his knowledge of McLean had dreaded that he would start out on some long quest without even remembering the fact that neither of them had eaten anything for twelve hours. McLean had turned again to the sheet of paper.

'Not another single complete word,' he complained. 'Here's N.D.M. together with long blanks either side, and further on IDGE, which might easily be 'bridge.' I don't think we shall get any further. Find the road map. It must be in the car.'

While Brook was hunting for the large scale road map, Prout brought in an excellent breakfast, and laid the tray on the table at which Brook had been working.

'Will you ring for anything you may need?' he asked.

'Thank you, Prout.'

Brook came back with the map, and all but smacked his lips at the sight of the things on the tray. He lifted the top of one of the silver hot dishes, and brought to view a lovely array of eggs, bacon and kidneys.

'You really should take care of that appetite of yours,' remonstrated McLean.

'That's exactly what I'm going to do. Three cheers for Mr. Prout! Oh; here's the map.'

While McLean examined the map, Brook made a start on the food, after making a remark to the effect that it would be a shame to let it get cold. Finally McLean sat down and poured out a cup of coffee absent-mindedly.

'If she turned right one mile along the Battle road she would face miles of marshland,' he ruminated. 'Why should she want to go there?'

'Why should she want to go anywhere?' asked Brook, with his mouth half full. 'Gosh, these kidneys!'

McLean put aside the map and gazed at Brook with troubled eyes. Then he shook his head and took a piece of toast.

'Say it,' challenged Brook.

'I will. One of these days I shall be called to investigate your sudden demise, and I shall be in no difficulty about it.'

'Loss of breath,' retorted Brook. 'I'd rather lose all my breath than half my appetite. Some people don't eat half enough. Thank God, Nature gave me a good appetite, a good thirst and a good constitution.'

'It's a shame to put the blame on Nature,' said McLean. 'Well, you've just ten minutes to complete the ruin of your digestion.'

'Oh, have a heart,' begged Brook.

21

The road to Battle ran through the most verdant and beautiful part of the marshland. The dykes on either side were fringed with tall reeds, which in places rose to the height of a man. There were long vistas of unique beauty — a delicious commingling of earth and sky, with grazing herds in the middle distance, and an occasional dwelling, which with its trees formed a striking oasis in this alluring green desert.

'Lots of people hate flat country,' said Brook. 'But I must say this looks pretty good to me.'

'Probably you like to see your steak running about,' said McLean unkindly.

'That's a good one,' said Brook, quite good-naturedly.

'I'm sorry, Brook. It looks as if I'm in a bad temper. You're right. It gets into one's blood — the peace and beauty of it. The fly in the ointment is the business which brings us here. For days we've chased spectres, and every time we set out for an objective, it seems to move away with us at about the same speed as our approach, and yet I feel that there's a simple solution to this riddle.'

'Simple!'

'Something that really efficient investigators would have seized on at the start.'

'Blimey, ain't you modest!' exclaimed Brook, with a deliberate lapse into the vernacular. 'Oh, look, we've just done a mile. Can't see any sort of turning on the right.'

'Slow up. I'm sure we haven't passed a turning.'

The car was soon moving at little more than walking pace, and suddenly McLean saw a break in the tall reeds on his right. Across the dyke in this gap a simple wooden bridge had been thrown, and beyond this McLean could see a vast flat expanse, broken in places by some long undulations, and backed in the far distance by sunlit hills. There was no place to park the car but on the road itself, so McLean told Brook to drive it as closely as possible to the uneven narrow grass verge.

'Do you think this is the place?' asked Brook.

'It doesn't seem to lead anywhere — except miles and miles of just nothing.'

'That's consistent with most of our clues,' said McLean. 'But let's go and look.'

They crossed the road and approached the bridge which was nothing more elaborate than a pair of nine-inch oak planks, placed side by side. On the near side the grass verge led directly to the planks, but on the further side the ground was bare of grass and wet from the storm of the previous evening. On this were registered some quite good footprints. There were but two sets — both going in the same direction, and it was clear that both had been made after the rain had ceased.

'We'd better take patterns of these before they are spoiled,' said McLean. 'Get some paper from the car, and a pair of scissors.'

The smaller imprints showed shoes equipped with rubber soles, with a zig-zag pattern. The larger were quite plain, and in one of them was a defect near the toe, which registered quite clearly.

'A woman and a man,' said Brook.

'It looks like it. Oh, that's interesting.'

The open view disclosed a concrete column in the distance. It was erected on a mound, and partly obscured by trees.

'What is it?' asked Brook.

'An old water tower. I think that must be the object indicated as W.T. on the memorandum pad.'

'That's an idea!' said Brook. 'It was probably given as a landmark. Perhaps the incomplete word which you took to be 'bridge' had reference to the water tower, and did not mean this bridge.'

'That may be so. This track seems to go in that direction.'

They walked on, and McLean kept his eyes open for more footprints, but these failed to materialise, for the track was only just visible on the grass.

'Probably only used by shepherds and cowherds,' he said. 'There's no habitation in that direction.'

A little further on the track met a deep dyke, and ran by the side of it. Unusual water-plants grew on the margins and in the rank water itself. Lazy butterflies rose from innumerable wild flowers and frogs 'plopped' back into the water at intervals. From the direction of the sea came a steady breeze which salted their lips and invigorated them.

'Wouldn't mind a small shack here, and half a dozen cows,' mused Brook. 'What's the matter?'

'S-sh!'

McLean had stopped dead but a moment later he went forward cautiously, in a bent position. Then again he stopped and beckoned Brook, finger on lip. Brook expected to find at least a couple of corpses with the murderer leaning over them, but instead of this McLean, with excited eyes, pointed to something in the tall grass to his right. It was the neck and head of a great bird, as still as if it were carved in stone. Its marvellous colouring was enhanced by contrast with the green grass, and its eyes were like living gems.

'Well!' said Brook, 'I thought — '

The statue became alive. There was a heavy beat of wings and away went the bird.

'You would do that,' said McLean disgustedly. 'I show you a sight you may never see again, and all you do is burble.'

'What was it?'

'A bittern. I've never been so close to one in my life.'

Brook swallowed the rebuke. It was like McLean momentarily to forget the pressing needs when brought face to face with something of rare natural beauty.

'What about Mrs. Bosanquet?' mumbled Brook.

'Even Mrs. Bosanquet isn't the whole of life. Ah, that must be the bridge.'

The structure was but fifty yards ahead. In this case it was of concrete, and provided with a handrail. It went across the dyke at its narrowest place, and seemed to lead simply nowhere. McLean stopped and looked down into the brackish water.

'Water tower and bridge,' he said. 'The

connection is obvious.'

'No chance of footprints here,' said Brook. 'I wonder what she did next — if she really got as far as this.'

McLean crossed over the bridge and went to the water-tower. It was nothing more than a ruin, and incapable of concealing anything. The whole place looked like a dead end, for there was no sign of a beaten track. For miles in every direction the marshes rolled like a bright carpet, except to the north-east where the land rose in a wooded islet. McLean consulted the map which he had brought with him. The country round about was intersected by numerous dykes, and footpaths were almost absent.

'We might wander round here all day quite uselessly,' he said. 'I believe that Mrs. Bosanquet actually came to this point. Whether this was the rendezvous is doubtful.'

'You mean there may have been further instructions?'

'Yes.'

'There were two sets of footprints at the first bridge.'

'It doesn't follow they were made at the same time.'

'That's true. What do we do now?'

'Go back and get in touch with Ball. He'll

probably know where we can get some trained bloodhounds. They may save us a lot of time.'

They walked back to the car, and Brook drove McLean to police headquarters. Ball had just arrived, and was amazed to hear of the latest development.

'This is going to cause some excitement,' he said. 'Bloodhounds? Yes, we've used them before. Captain Mallory has a good pair of trained hounds. I'll telephone him.'

The captain said his hounds were available, and it was arranged that they should be picked up half an hour later. The Superintendent was not to be robbed of a bit of unusual excitement, and went along with McLean in his own car. On reaching Mallory's house McLean was introduced to the two hounds. They were magnificent beasts, trained to the last degree and highly intelligent and obedient. Mallory put them on leash, and he and his hounds occupied the rear part of the Superintendent's car.

'Castle House,' said McLean. 'I want to pick up a pair of stockings.'

The cars waited outside while McLean went into the house and got Mrs. Bosanquet's discarded stockings. John came to him as he was leaving.

'Any news, Inspector?' he asked.

'Nothing worth mentioning, but we may have some soon.'

John's gaze went to the stockings.

'Just a little experiment,' explained McLean.

'You mean — bloodhounds?'

'Yes.'

'Can't we come? Can't we be of any use?'

'I'm afraid not.'

He moved towards the door, which Prout opened for him. John caught him by the arm.

'This suspense is terrible,' he said. 'God knows we've been through enough. But father went — so suddenly. This is different — even more horrible. Inspector, do you think that she — that something may — '

'Because we are using bloodhounds it doesn't follow that we think that any harm has come to her,' he said. 'It's just a quick way of tracing her movements.'

John looked far from satisfied as he nodded his head, and went back into the house. A few minutes later the two cars went off, and men and hounds were transported as far as the bridge where McLean had found the footprints. Here Mallory took out his bloodhounds and introduced the stockings to them

'You take Sally,' he said to McLean. 'The pair of them will probably be too much for me. I'll keep Susan. She's a little better than Sally. The conditions are excellent.'

On the farther side of the bridge the two bloodhounds took up the scent at once. McLean felt the leash go taut, and off went Sally, with her nose on the ground, with Susan but a few paces ahead. Twice the scent grew weak, but Mallory got Susan back to it again, and Sally picked it up a moment later.

'Must be nice to have a nose like that,' commented Brook.

'A little inconvenient at times,' replied McLean. 'This hound is about ten-horse power.'

'In a very short time they were at the bridge by the water tower. Over went the hounds at great speed. On the farther side they turned abruptly left, and went across open country in the direction of the wooded islet. Another dyke was encountered, and the hounds went along this at right-angles to their former line of motion. Then there came another bridge, and over this went the party — Brook and Ball getting more and more excited. Ball had already taken a gloomy view of the situation, and was noticeably interested in the deep dyke.

'It's the obvious solution,' he said to Brook.

'Oh, I wouldn't say that,' replied Brook. 'I don't think McLean takes that view.'

'What about Bosanquet and Penny? They both went, didn't they?'

'But this is different,' argued Brook, without knowing exactly why it was different.

The bloodhounds had now left the side of the dyke, and were making across uneven country at a slower speed.

'Scent's weak,' explained Mallory as he watched the animals. 'Some of this may have been under water last night.'

A little later this opinion was borne out by encountering an area still partially flooded. Here the hounds stopped, went off at tangents and then came back again. It was soon evident that the scent was momentarily completely lost.

'It's this damned water,' grumbled Mallory. 'She must have gone through it. Perhaps couldn't find a way round. I'm going across to see what we can pick up the other side. You'd better stay here until I signal to you. Lucky I remembered to wear gum-boots.'

They stood and watched him proceed with Susan — splashing up water as he went. On and on he went, and still there was water underfoot. Finally he seemed to emerge on dry land, for at once he allowed the hound to use her nose, but to no effect. Place after place was tried, and always with the same result.

'Nothing here!' he yelled back. 'I'm going right. Meet you up there.'

He pointed out the direction, and McLean went along the fringe of the flooded area, on a line which promised to bring him to Mallory in due course. But it was a very long time before the junction took place, and during all that time neither of the hounds had recaptured the scent.

'Disappointing,' said Mallory. 'Once I thought Susan had found the scent again, but it wasn't so.'

'Presuming she walked through shallow water, would that effect the scent when she left the water again?'

'I think it would. I propose we go back on this side of the flood and try to continue our former line at some distance apart. There's a chance we may yet pick up the scent.'

This procedure was adopted. The hounds moved round in circles, and made strange noises, but Mallory shook his head, knowing that nothing was being achieved. But they went on for a further half mile, and then came up against another dyke, across which there was no bridge in sight.

'Well, that's that!' grumbled Mallory.

The hounds, having lost the scent for so long, were now showing very little interest, and Mallory reluctantly admitted that the chance of success now was very doubtful. A council of war was held, and it was finally decided that Mallory and Ball should take the hounds back, and that McLean and Brook should continue on foot.

'At least something has been gained,' said McLean. 'There was no doubt about the scent as far as the flood, and that is a mile farther than we got before. Thanks very much.'

'See you later,' called the Superintendent as he took over Sally from McLean.

'Unless we go next,' replied McLean. 'It seems to be a habit in these parts.'

'One o'clock,' said Brook as he looked at his watch.

'You mean lunch-time,' replied McLean. 'Well, take your choice of restaurants.'

He waved a hand at the wide open country, and commenced to walk towards the wooded area, which seemed very little closer than when they had been a mile back.

'There's one amazing thing about all this,' said Brook. 'If Mrs. Bosanquet got as far as the flood-water it must have been dark, as she couldn't have left home much before nine o'clock, and perhaps even later.'

McLean nodded in silence.

'I suppose you had thought of that?'

'Naturally.'

'Of course you would,' muttered Brook. 'Well, anyway, it must have been a pretty urgent sort of call to bring a woman out here after dark, mustn't it?'

'You've answered your own question.'

'So Mrs. Bosanquet isn't quite as simple as she liked us to believe?'

'It depends upon what you mean by 'simple.' '

'Well, we know the man in this case couldn't be Grant, who is in love with her, could it?'

'No. I can't see how it could be.'

'Then we're dealing with a shadow whom we've never seen, and know nothing about.'

'That may be so. I don't know. On two previous occasions we have run into side issues having no relation at all to the Bosanquet crime. It would be very annoying if that happened again.'

'I'll bet my lunch it doesn't.'

'That appears to be a safe bet,' replied McLean, leaving Brook to interpret it as best he might.

22

McLean and Brook returned to Castle House late in the afternoon, having covered a great deal of country without any success. Footsore, weary and hungry, Brook was not in his sweetest mood. The members of the family were anxious to know what had happened, and McLean had to admit that he had nothing new to tell them. Grant, who was with the boys, looked as troubled as they did. He demanded to know what steps McLean now proposed to take, but McLean was not in the habit of divulging his plans. While they were talking Brook managed to get a word with Prout.

'Save my life and bring us some tea,' he whispered. 'I'm as empty as a drum.'

'In the study?'

'Yes. Better come and ask us first. The Inspector can't have the heart to decline.'

'I get you,' replied Prout. 'Weren't the bloodhounds any use?'

'No. They lost the scent at some water.'

'It's all very tragic,' said Prout. 'Her going away — without a word. Well, let's hope it's just loss of memory, or something like that.'

Brook passed into the study, where McLean was now alone, and using the telephone. He got through to Scotland Yard and gave instructions for a police message to be sent out over the wireless, describing Mrs. Bosanquet and the clothing she was believed to be wearing, adding, 'This woman may be suffering from loss of memory.'

'You don't believe that?' said Brook.

'Loss of memory? No.'

There was a knock on the door, and Prout came in.

'Excuse me, gentlemen,' he said. 'I was wondering whether you would care for any light refreshment. There were a lot of sandwiches left over from tea. The young gentlemen have lost their appetites.'

McLean glanced at Brook, who gave him an appealing look.

'Thanks, Prout,' he said. 'That was thoughtful of you.'

Prout vanished and Brook looked very relieved.

'Must have sensed my aching void,' he said.

'Yes — your aching void can become vocal at times. Well, on this occasion you were justified.'

Prout was back very quickly with a large tea-tray, on which was a pot of tea and two cups, also a very fine assortment of egg and ham sandwiches, not to mention cakes and sundries. He wore a neat white linen coat, which had obviously just come back from the laundry, for it was nicely creased and spotless. As he laid out the various things McLean's attention seemed to be unduly centred on him, and when at last he left McLean was gazing abstractedly into space.

'Ah!' sighed Brook. 'Just what the doctor ordered. You don't take sugar, do you?'

McLean shook his head slowly. It was quite clear to Brook that he had scarcely heard what was said.

'Looks good to me,' said Brook, letting his eye range over the plates of sandwiches.

'It doesn't look quite so bad to me — now,' replied McLean as he took the cup of tea from Brook.

'The food?'

'No — the case.'

'I thought that Mrs. Bosanquet's disappearance had put the lid on it.'

'What does 'putting the lid' on things signify?'

'Mucking it up.'

'Thanks for enlightenment. As a matter of fact, it's quite possible that the case is a trifle 'unmucked.' At the moment I'm not making any bets, because our first duty is obviously to find Mrs. Bosanquet.'

From that moment McLean's interest seemed to increase. His eyes grew brighter and his voice crisper. He got the paper patterns which had been made of the footprints, and then roamed round the house. After a long absence he came back to the study with a pair of old shoes in his hands.

'I found them in the bottom of the dustbin,' he said.

'Do they help?'

'I think so. Here's the left one. Just take a look at the sole near the place where the big toe comes.'

Brook did so and saw a mark like a 'V' in the worn leather. McLean then gave him the larger paper pattern, and Brook placed it against the sole of the shoe, and noted the mark which had been drawn on it.

'The unknown man!' he ejaculated.

'A little less unknown since he must be in this house.'

'Don't you know whose shoe it is?'

'Not yet. Ring that bell for the butler.'

Mr. Prout came in response to the summons, and McLean asked him to send in John and Jasper. They entered together a few minutes later. John was comparatively calm, but Jasper looked scared, as he always did when he knew he was going to be questioned.

'Has either of you seen these shoes before?' asked McLean.

'They're John's,' said Jasper immediately.

'That's right,' agreed John. 'But I haven't worn them for months.'

'Where were they kept?'

'I believe they were thrown into the lumber-room, with a lot of other junk. I remember wearing them during the Easter vacation, but they were so worn out I didn't take them back to Oxford with me. I seem to remember seeing them in the lumber-room when I came down in June.'

'And you swear you haven't worn them since?'

'I do.'

'That's true,' said Jasper. 'I remember mother saying he mustn't wear them any more.'

'All right. That's all I wanted to know,' replied McLean.

Brook closed the door after them, and came back to McLean in a state of perplexity.

'I'm all out of my depth,' he said. 'If the two boys are telling the truth, who else is there in this house who might have worn those shoes, and then put them into the dustbin?'

'Why not Mr. Prout?'

'Prout? But for what reason?'

'Can't you think of a reason?'

'Dashed if I can — except to prevent her signing that transfer. We know that he took the telephone message from Pole, and he may have realised what would happen to-day unless — But that doesn't make sense.'

'It certainly would be a bold act on the part of a lady's butler to prevent her forcibly from carrying out her own desire. All the same, I'm quite certain that he put this pair of shoes into the dustbin — after he wore them.'

'Are you going to put that question to him?'

'No — because I'm quite certain he would lie. But I have compared the shoes with a pair of his own. He could have worn them without any discomfort.'

'But we know that Mrs. Bosanquet received a telephone message, and that she acted on instructions. Would she have taken instructions from Prout?'

'She might if she believed Prout was in some kind of trouble.'

'But it was late in the evening, and the rendezvous was obviously out in the marshes. It sounds crazy.'

'It certainly does, but I am not advertising the exact state of affairs to Mr. Prout — yet. Mrs. Bosanquet has to be found, and there will be a lot she will have to explain.'

Before he left the house for the night McLean telephoned to his two other personal helpers, and gave them fresh instructions.

The following morning McLean found that the whole press was giving the case front-page notice. As he had turned away all newspaper reporters, it was clear they were getting information from, or through, Ball. Mrs. Bosanquet's portrait now appeared with the letterpress and heavy headlines. One newspaper showed Bosanquet, Penny and Mrs. Bosanquet across all columns, with the caption 'WHO NEXT?' McLean flung the newspapers aside, with an expression of contempt.

'No one's feelings seem to matter with these people,' he said. 'Get me on to London.'

He spoke to a high official at Scotland Yard for some minutes, during which it was made clear to Brook that no response had come from the wireless broadcast. Then he telephoned the two detectives who had carried out his instructions, and had nothing to report.

'No movement at the house during the night,' he said. 'Well, we must resume the search this morning. I'll get some additional help from Ball, and we'll comb every inch of the marshes.'

'Ponds and ditches?' asked Brook.

'Yes. But I can't think it has come to that. Nothing points that way.'

'Shall I telephone Ball?'

McLean looked at his watch and shook his head.

'Better give him another half-hour. He doesn't believe in early rising. We'll have breakfast first.'

Brook was always agreeable to such a means of filling in time, but they had scarcely started the meal when McLean saw a car draw up outside the dining-room of the hotel.

'I was wrong,' he said. 'It's the Superintendent himself.'

Ball entered the dining-room a few moments later and gave McLean a good morning. He came across to the table.

'Smells good,' he said. 'I had to miss mine. I've got some important news — if it can be relied upon.'

'About what?'

'Mrs. Bosanquet.'

McLean laid down his knife and fork.

'What is it?' he asked.

'A man named Swaith made a statement this morning. He's an old drunk, and heaven knows if we can depend on him. He's still half sozzled, although I've dosed him with strong coffee. I've got him in the back of the car.

Better come out and see him.'

McLean and Brook followed the Superintendent to the big saloon car. The rear part was occupied by a wild-eyed looking fellow, whose clothing was filthy and who exuded a most unpleasant odour. McLean lowered the window before he got inside the car.

'Swaith — tell the Inspector what you told me,' said Ball.

Swaith drew the back of his hand across his mouth.

'It's the truth,' he mumbled. 'You don't believe me, but it's the bloomin' truth.'

'Come,' said McLean. 'Tell me what happened.'

'Well — night before last I was walking across the marsh from Penny Lane to Fenforth, where I live. Saves me a matter of three miles if I go that way. It was late, because I had been held up by the thunderstorm. I was crossing the bridge at Badger's Dyke when I suddenly saw a light moving on my left. It was like a will-o-the-wisp, but when it came a bit nearer I saw something else. It was a man carrying a bundle in his arms — a big bundle. Then the light went out, and I couldn't see a thing. But I heard a sound as if he was coming at me in the darkness. I was scared, so I ran as hard as I could. That's true. I tell you it's true. Maybe

I had had a few drinks, but I saw what I saw.'

'Why didn't you go straight to the police?' asked McLean.

'I had some more drinks when I got home — to steady my nerves, and yesterday I wasn't feeling well and couldn't leave my cottage. It was all like a dream, but last night I was listening to my wireless and heard the police message. It was the late news, and it repeated the message. I couldn't walk all the way to the police station that time o' night, so I waited until early this morning.'

'Were you close enough to see what the man was like?' asked McLean.

'No. The light he had was very small, and it didn't show much. But I know he was carrying something heavy — the way he was bent over.'

'Could you take us to the place where you saw this?'

'Why, yes — course I could.'

'All right. We'll go now.'

McLean went into the hotel and got a hat and the road map. Ball joined him before he returned to the car.

'Sounds promising, doesn't it?' he asked.

'I think so. Do you know the places he mentioned?'

'I know Fenforth. It's just a collection of scattered shacks. But I don't know Penny

Lane. That must be merely a local name. He's lived in the neighbourhood all his life, and probably got the name from his father. I don't think it's in general use now.'

Soon the whole party was in the car, Brook regretting his unfinished breakfast. The Superintendent took the wheel, and Swaith directed him. The car turned left at the Battle road, and then went past the spot where McLean had recently found the footprints. It turned right a mile farther on, and then negotiated some very rough lanes, until finally it reached a spot beyond which there was no possible car track.

'Must stop here,' said Swaith. 'This is Penny Lane.'

'That's news to me,' retorted Ball. 'Well, let's get out.'

Before doing so, McLean scrutinised the map and got his bearings. Then the whole party left the car and set off across the trackless marsh.

23

Swaith led the way unfalteringly. He mumbled that he had been across the marshes by that route a thousand times, and had himself made possible passages across the dykes at shallow points to save time. They negotiated several of these, in addition to the orthodox bridges. Finally they came to a concrete bridge of wide dimensions and here Swaith stopped.

'This be Badger's Bridge,' he said. 'It was here where I saw the light — and the man I told you about. That's where he was — just about abreast of that hole.'

He pointed to a deep hollow in the ground, now half-full of water. McLean had his map folded to suit their present position, and he realised that the site was not a great distance from the waterlogged ground which had baffled the bloodhounds.

'Let's go across,' he said to the Superintendent. 'It links up nicely with our previous search.'

They crossed to the spot indicated by Swaith, and McLean spent some time wandering about the spot. The water-filled hollow was investigated, but yielded nothing. Nowhere was there a single footprint, for the nature of the ground was such as to rule out this possibility. Except in one direction it was open country, where nothing but a corpse could be hidden. The exception was to the north, where the flatness was broken by a considerable hill and woods.

'What lies over there?' asked McLean of Swaith.

'Linfield.'

'What is it — a farm?'

'No, a big house. Gentleman who lives there has got a title. Sir Robert somebody or other.'

'I propose we work in that direction,' said McLean.

'There's an easier way to the house,' said Swaith. 'If you drive the car back along the road we came by, and then turn left, there's a road which leads to the house.'

But McLean preferred to go over the marsh, since that appeared to be the way the man had gone. Provided that Swaith had told the truth, there was yet a possibility of finding footprints.

'Brook and I will work from here,' he said to Ball. 'It might save time if you drove the car to the road which Swaith has mentioned. We'll find our way there.'

'Yes, I'll do that,' agreed Ball, who had no great love for walking.

So McLean and Brook made towards the hill. Fortunately they did not encounter any opposition, and were soon close to the wire fence which surrounded the estate on that side. The house was yet hidden from view by quite thick conifers and other quick-growing trees, all of which appeared to be about forty years old.

'Shall we go over?' asked Brook.

'Yes. If we're caught we shall have to explain matters.'

They climbed over the wire fence and walked slowly up the steeply rising slope. Soon they came to a cutting in the timber, which gave them a view of the house. It was of red brick, rambling and ostentatious in design.

'Sort of thing they did fifty years ago,' said McLean. 'The place looks derelict.'

A little farther on they caught sight of the Superintendent, who was obviously looking for them. He waved a hand and hurried towards them.

'You're quick,' he said. 'I left Swaith in the car. Said he was tired. The house is empty, and there's a sale board at the entrance to it, near the lodge. I knocked at the lodge door, but there's no one there. Hopeless sort of place. They won't sell it in twenty years. Found anything?'

'Nothing at all.'

'Blooming mausoleum. Gardens all over-grown, too. I suppose we'd better break in?'

McLean stopped and picked up a broken stick. It was about half an inch thick, and had quite evidently been trodden on recently.

'Might be a tramp,' he said. 'And it might not.'

They went on slowly towards the house, the ugliness of which was even more pronounced as they drew closer to it. The trees thinned away on the right, and McLean saw something grey amid them.

'A building,' he said.

'Yes. I saw it as I came to meet you. It's only one of those old Martello towers. There are a few odd ones scattered about — off the main line of coastal defence. I suppose there were reasons for doing that. It looks as if the land was bought as a building site half a century ago, and the old tower came into the lot.'

'We'll look at it first,' said McLean.

They changed their direction, and fifty yards farther on McLean found yet another thick twig broken.

'Someone came this way,' he said.

A little later they were free of the trees, and

under the stout walls of the tower. It was exactly like the dozens of others he had seen nearer the sea, with a wooden staircase leading up to a door about five feet from the ground, but owing to its having been in private land for so long it was in better state of preservation. McLean walked up the wooden staircase, and fund himself before a heavy door which bore a padlock.

'No entry,' he said.

Brook suddenly ran round the side of the squat tower and picked up something. He shouted to McLean, and McLean came down the steps. Brook handed him the object which he had found in the long grass. It was a woman's hat — very small and of brown felt. McLean went round to the spot where Brook had found the hat. Above it, in the tower, was a very small barred window. He shouted, but saw nothing on the other side of the bars.

'We'll have to break that padlock,' he said. 'Better go to the car and bring some tools.'

Brook went off at almost a run, and McLean wandered in the vicinity of the tower.

'Looks bad to me,' said Ball. 'Just the sort of place to hide a corpse. As things are, no one would come here in a month of Sundays.'

But McLean found good reason to hope that yet another murder was not to be added to the score. With miles and miles of deep dykes in the neighbourhood it was incredible that a murderer should take all this trouble. In addition, there was every indication that the hat had been thrown through the bars of the window to attract attention.

'We'll soon know,' he said.

Brook executed his errand speedily, and returned with two very large screwdrivers. He was able to get the larger of them through the ring of the staple and, by heavy leverage, the staple was slowly forced free. Brook stood aside for McLean to enter the tower.

The door was pushed open, and a wide chamber came to view, dimly lighted by a small window similar to that which McLean had seen at a higher level. On the right was a stone staircase leading to an upper chamber, and McLean, after a brief look round, mounted the stairs. At the top was another door, but this was not locked. On pushing it open, McLean saw the figure of a woman lying under the window on an old rug. She was hatless and dishevelled, and her face was pallid and drawn. Beside her was a large bottle — now empty.

'Mrs. Bosanquet!' exclaimed Ball, who had now entered the chamber. 'Is she all right?'

McLean leaned over the recumbent woman and shook her by the arm. The eyes opened suddenly and blinked a number of times. Then she gave a little cry, and sat up.

'The — Inspector!' she gasped hoarsely.

'Very glad to see you, Mrs. Bosanquet,' said McLean. 'Are you all right?'

'I'm not hurt in any way, but I've been here for two awful nights, without food. The place is full of rats. I haven't been able to sleep at nights, and I feel terribly sick.'

'Won't you tell me what happened?' asked McLean.

'Not now — please. I want to be back home. Please take me home at once.'

She was evidently very distressed, and McLean was quite willing to postpone his questions until she was in more comfortable circumstances. He gave her a hand and she rose to her feet. Close contact with her revealed an undeniable fact. McLean detected the faint odour of chloroform.

'So you were drugged,' he said.

She made no reply to this, and McLean held his tongue. The party passed through the grounds and were soon in the Superintendent's car. A quarter of an hour later they were at Castle House, having dropped Mr. Swaith at a convenient place and presented him with a nice gift of money, which he highly appreciated.

Prout opened the door to them, and seemed overwhelmed to see Dorinda.

'Oh, madam,' he said. 'This is wonderful.'

John and Jasper came racing from other parts of the house. They left no doubt about the sincerity of their welcome. Jasper even had tears in his eyes as he fumbled his stepmother's hands.

'I'm all right,' she said heavily. 'Just tired. I want to rest for a while.'

When they had taken her away Ball went with McLean and Brook into the study.

'She's mighty secretive,' he said. 'What does it all mean? Why didn't she say something at once? Wouldn't any normal woman who had been treated as she has?'

'The circumstances aren't normal,' replied McLean. 'I must give her a chance to rest and tidy herself. After that I think we shall get somewhere.'

'I'm not so sure,' muttered Ball. 'In this case we never seem to get anywhere but deeper in the mire. Well, I'll look back this evening to see how things are going.'

When Ball had left McLean looked at his watch, and then referred to a railway time-table.

'I'm going to London,' he said. 'But I'll be back here during the evening. Stay on here until I return, and keep everyone here.'

'Suppose Grant calls?'

'That won't matter. I've no objection to Grant seeing Mrs. Bosanquet now. You'd better run me to the station.'

24

On his return from the railway station Brook saw Grant's car outside the house, and when he passed through the hall he heard Grant talking to the two boys in the lounge.

'It's all very mysterious,' John was saying. 'She won't say a word yet. Just wants to rest.'

'She looks ghastly,' put in Jasper.

There was then a dead silence, probably due to the fact that Brook had been seen passing the half-open door. Later Brook saw the trio along the terrace having drinks, and he was successful in catching Prout's eye, with the result that Prout brought a bottle of beer into the study.

'Thanks!' said Brook. 'It's warming up again.'

'It is, indeed,' agreed Prout solemnly. 'It was clever of you to find Mrs. Bosanquet.'

'Not bad work,' replied Brook, with a quick glance at Prout.

'The bloodhounds, I suppose?'

'Oh, no — just experience.'

'But what happened? Did Mrs. Bosanquet get lost?'

'We don't know yet,' replied Brook

tactfully. 'McLean realised that her first need was rest.'

'Undoubtedly. I've never seen her looking so distraught. It must have been a terrible experience.'

His tone was so sincere — so marked with sympathy, that Brook began to wonder if McLean wasn't completely wrong in his deductions. When lunch-time came and Brook wasn't invited to take a meal, he telephoned Detective Stevens and was thus enabled to have lunch at the hotel while Stevens kept an eye on the house.

The afternoon passed uneventfully. Grant and the two boys went bathing and were back to tea. Brook had cause to believe that they had all seen Dorinda, but it was not his duty to prevent this, and so he killed time as best he could. It was late in the evening when a telephone message came from McLean. He said he couldn't possibly get down that night, and that the questioning of Dorinda must wait until the following day. He emphasised that neither Prout nor Dorinda must leave the house, and suggested that Stevens and his colleague should keep a watch on the place during the night.

Half an hour later the Superintendent called, and was disappointed to hear the change of plan. He had obviously been looking forward to an interesting meeting.

'What's the Inspector doing in London all this time?' he asked rather sharply. 'Surely the immediate thing is to have Mrs. Bosanquet's account of what really happened.'

'Evidently there are other things equally important,' snapped back Brook.

'Well, it's his case, but I think he's taking a risk.'

'Of what?'

'Giving her time to make up some fancy story. I've got the feeling she's up to her ears in this business.'

'Probably she is.'

'Then why give her all this rope? If there's an unknown man in the business he'll have plenty of time to get out of our reach, and cover up his tracks.'

'You don't know McLean,' retorted Brook. 'He doesn't let people get away so easily. If something is detaining him it must be important.'

'Connected with this case?'

'I presume so.'

'Well, he's very uncommunicative,' muttered Ball.'

Brook shrugged his shoulders, having nothing to say in response. The Superintendent took his departure, and at nine o'clock Brook signed off for the night, having agreed that Stevens should take over at this hour.

The following morning it was reported that nothing had happened during the night, and when Brook arrived at the house he saw Mrs. Bosanquet downstairs. She still looked pallid and distressed.

'I hope you're feeling better, Mrs. Bosanquet,' said Brook.

'Yes — thank you. Isn't Inspector McLean here?'

'No. But I am expecting him this morning.'

It was actually one o'clock when McLean arrived by taxi. In the interim Ball had telephoned three times. This fact was communicated to McLean.

'Eager for results,' he said. 'Well, we may be able to show him some. Give him a ring and tell him I propose to question Mrs. Bosanquet in half an hour.'

He placed a large square parcel on the table while Brook used the telephone.

'He says he'll be here within half an hour,' said Brook.

'Good! You'd better take the car to the hotel and get a quick lunch. I had something on the train. With any luck we'll finish this case to-day.'

Brook had his lunch and arrived back at the house simultaneously with the Superintendent.

'Sorry about last night, Ball,' said McLean. 'But it simply couldn't be managed. Mr. Grant has paid his daily visit, and the whole family is finishing lunch. I've asked her to come here as soon as possible.'

'But was the delay wise?'

'More than wise, I assure you. Brook, get a couple more chairs from the lounge. We may need them. Oh, one very interesting fact. I had a telephone message from Mr. Pole. He was delighted to hear that Mrs. Bosanquet was safe, and he informed me that she was ready to sign the transfer — with a slight modification.'

'What is it?'

'She wishes to retain for her personal use the sum of five thousand pounds. The balance of the residue of the estate she is still insistent upon transferring to her two stepsons.'

'Hm!' grunted Ball. 'I don't follow it.'

'Probably you will — soon.'

Brook came back with two extra chairs, and McLean disposed of them. A little later there came a knock on the door, and Mrs. Bosanquet entered.

'I hope I haven't hurried you unduly,' said McLean.

'Oh, no, we had lunch a little earlier than usual.'

'Please sit down.'

Dorinda occupied the chair which Brook pushed a little closer to the table. Brook then sat down himself and opened his shorthand book. McLean remained standing, gazing down at some notes which he had made.

'Now, Mrs. Bosanquet,' he said. 'It is most vital that we know exactly what happened on the evening when you disappeared. I must remind you that it may have a very close bearing on this case — in which a double murder is involved.'

'Oh, no,' she said. 'It has no connection at all.'

'I think you are mistaken, but please tell me exactly what happened after Mr. Prout went out.'

She seemed very nervous under the concentration of three pairs of eyes, and for a few moments she hesitated. Then at last she found her voice.

'Mr. Grant left at about a quarter to nine,' she said. 'Prout showed him out, and a few minutes later he came into the lounge and asked me if he might take a walk. I was quite agreeable, and he left me. I spent some time doing a crossword puzzle, and then the telephone bell rang. I went to the instrument and recognised Prout's voice. He told me he was in great trouble, and begged me to come to his assistance at once. I asked him what

352

was the matter, and he said he dared not mention it on the telephone. He gave me some instructions where I might see him, and rang off suddenly. It was getting towards sunset, and I was in a dilemma, for both the boys had gone to the cinema, and I don't drive the car. But finally I decided to follow his instructions, and I walked along the road to Battle, and found a turning which he had mentioned. Finally I saw him, and I asked him what it was all about.'

She hesitated for a few moments, to look at her auditors as if to discover the depth of their interest. Then she resumed in a very quiet voice.

'He said he had my interest at heart, that he knew I was on the point of signing away a large sum of money. He begged me not to do this.'

'Were you standing still all this time?' asked McLean.

'No. We were walking beside a dyke, and it was fast getting dark. I told him it was unforgivable, his interfering in my private affairs — that I resented it, and the way he had brought me from home.'

'What then?'

'He grew very excited. He told me he wouldn't let me do it — that later I would bitterly regret it. By this time I was very angry, and I stopped and told him I would hear no more, and that I was going home. It was then he behaved like a madman. He seized my arms, and said I must give him my word of honour that I wouldn't sign the transfer, otherwise he would take steps to prevent it. I slapped his face, and then he produced a handkerchief from his pocket and covered my nose and mouth with it. I remembered nothing more until I regained my senses and found myself in the Martello Tower, with a bottle of water beside me. I felt so sick I could scarcely move, but later I managed to get to the door, and tried to open it. When night came the place was alive with rats. I climbed up the stone steps to the upper room. It was there I hit upon the idea of throwing something outside in the hope of attracting attention. I chose my hat.'

McLean was silent for a few moments.

'Have you seen Prout in the meantime?' he asked.

'Yes. I told him he would have to go.'

'How did he take that?'

'I — I think he expected it.'

'Aren't you going to prosecute him?'

'No. I believe his intentions were good, and he has been a very good servant.'

'When is he leaving?'

'At once. I think he is packing now.'

McLean who had been pacing to and fro suddenly stopped and stared hard at Dorinda.

'Do you really expect me to believe that you went out late in the evening to meet your own butler in a very desolate part of the marsh?' he asked.

'I know it sounds incredibly foolish, but I really believed he was in great trouble.'

'Didn't it occur to you that he couldn't have got very far in the short time at his disposal?'

'Yes, it did. I thought he must have taken some conveyance.'

'Did you ask him where he was telephoning from?'

'No. It never occurred to me. He gave me very clear instructions.'

'I'm afraid the story won't do, Mrs. Bosanquet,' said McLean.

'Do you take me for — a liar?' she retorted.

'I won't go as far as that. I should say that in order to meet a difficult situation you have gone in for some attractive embroidery. I know you received a telephone message, and that you acted in response to it, but your reason for doing so was other than you have offered.'

'He said he was in great trouble,' she insisted.

'Had you any idea at all of the sort of trouble he might be in?'

'He didn't tell me.'

'But had you any idea of your own?'

'How could I have?'

'That isn't answering my question. But it doesn't matter. We will get to it by another means. What was your maiden name?'

'Gale.'

'Am I right in saying you were one of two children, the other being a boy five years older than yourself?'

'Yes.'

'Was his name Arthur?'

'Yes.'

'Until the death of your widowed mother you lived at Godalming, did you not?'

'Yes.'

'Your brother went to a school there, I believe?'

'Yes.'

McLean dived into a portfolio and produced a photograph of a group of boys round about sixteen years of age. Dorinda watched him, with growing alarm. McLean handed her the photograph.

'Is not your brother in that group?' he asked.

'Y-yes,' she stammered.

'You recognise him quite easily?'

'Yes.'

'The second from the end of the first row?'

'Yes,' she almost moaned.

McLean took the photograph from her and handed it to the Superintendent whose neck had been stretched out like that of an ostrich. Ball's eyelids went up until there was danger of his losing his eyes.

'Prout!' he exclaimed.

'Thank you, Superintendent,' said McLean. 'I'm glad to have a further opinion. Oh, look out — !'

Dorinda had given a curious little sigh, and her head was sagging sideways. Brook sprang to her and supported her with one arm while he patted her hands.

'I'll get a glass of water,' said Ball.

'Thank you,' whispered Dorinda.

The water was brought, and Mrs. Bosanquet drank some of it. McLean waited a few moments.

'I hope you're better?' he asked.

'Yes — better now.'

'Do you now admit that your butler is actually your own brother?' asked McLean.

'Yes. I kept that from you, but my story was true. I felt justified in covering up that fact. It can make no difference.'

'On the contrary, it may make a tremendous amount of difference. How did this

357

strange state of affairs come about?'

'My brother was in difficulties. Up to about two years ago I hadn't heard from him for many years. Then I received a letter from him, telling me he was out of work and penniless. I met him in London and was shocked at his condition. He looked as if he were starving, and ill. He didn't even know that his mother was dead, and had been trying to find her. I gave him what money I could spare and advised him to look for a job.'

'What was his occupation?'

'He had done almost everything. He started as an engineer — '

'After he was expelled from school,' put in McLean.

'Yes. That's true,' she admitted. 'But he hadn't done anything really bad. He was always very impulsive.'

'So impulsive that he stole a car from the engineering works at which he was employed and was sacked.'

'I didn't know that,' she said, expressing surprise. 'But all that happened long ago. He went abroad and I never saw him again until I met him in London. He told me he had been employed in a factory in France, and had served as a steward on a liner. It was the latter fact which gave him an idea later. Our old butler was taken ill and had to give up work. I happened to mention this to my brother when I saw him again, and he suggested that he should take the post. At first it seemed quite impracticable, but he begged me to give him this chance, and was quite sure of his ability to discharge his duties. Finally I gave way, and he came into the house, without my husband suspecting that he was the brother whom I had mentioned, and whom he had refused to help.'

'But hadn't Mr. Grant met him?'

'No. When I first met Grant, my brother was already abroad.'

Brook could tell from McLean's expression that he had doubts about the absolute truth of Dorinda's ready explanation. Somewhere he detected an inconsistency. McLean's next remark seemed to indicate where it lay.

'You have already stated that you were unhappy with your husband. That fact must have been clear to your brother.'

'Yes.'

'When you knew that your husband had received certain anonymous letters, didn't it occur to you that your brother who knew all the circumstances of your married life might have written those letters?'

'Yes — but he denied it.'

'And when you knew that the draft of the new will was missing, didn't you suspect that he might be responsible for that?'

'I didn't know what to think. At that time I was too overwhelmed to think of anything but the dreadful murder which had taken place here.'

'And when you knew that the original will held good and that you were legally entitled to inherit a large sum of money, did you decline to accept it because you were hurt by your husband's intentions to disinherit you, or was there any other reason?'

'What other reason could there be?'

'You might refuse to benefit largely if you believed your brother was involved in the death — '

'No,' she interrupted angrily. 'I never dreamed of it. It was quite impossible. I was with him when the shot was fired. There were, too, other witnesses. You know that.'

'Then this covering up of your butler's real identity was not concerned in any way with the murder of your husband?'

'Of course not.'

'Then why did you not admit the deception when you knew that a murder had been committed? The man who was killed was your own husband. Was that a time to conceal anything from those who were at pains to get justice done?'

This rebuke seemed to hurt her. Her hands closed and unclosed, and her lips trembled.

'I wanted to tell the truth,' she said. 'But my brother was against it. He told me that he was wanted in France, and that if I gave away his identity there might be trouble. Since there was no question of his being involved in the murder there was no real need to embarrass him.'

'So he told you that much!'

'How much longer is this to go on?' she asked. 'In a way I'm ashamed of what I've done, but he's my brother. While he has been here he's been an excellent servant. I'm sure he has done his best to live down the past. The other night he behaved badly, but that was in my interest. Now you know everything. I've been the one to suffer, and you can't expect me to prosecute my own brother for an act which he believed was in my interest.'

'And now you have discharged him?'

'Yes. I can't live here any longer. I want to get away from it all.'

'But on what terms?'

'Terms! I don't understand.'

'Isn't it a fact that you are still prepared to sign the transfer with a certain modification?'

'Yes, but it was John who suggested it.'

'So your stepsons know the position?'

'I felt I had to tell them.'

'They know that Prout is your own brother?'

'They know everything. We had a meeting this morning. Thank God the boys understand. It was John who suggested that I should at least make provisions for my brother. Jasper agreed, and so I telephoned to Mr. Pole accordingly.'

'You are making your brother a present of five thousand pounds?'

'Yes. It is sufficient to start him in a small way of business.'

'Was there no one here who knew the truth about Prout — I mean your brother?'

'No one.'

'Was there any means by which Penny might have got to know?'

'I can't think of any. Why do you ask me that?' she asked sharply.

'Because it might provide a motive for the murder of Penny. You hadn't forgotten Penny, had you?'

Her eyes filled with tears at this remark, and McLean regretted he had put it so brutally. Not yet was it absolutely clear that there had been no collusion between her and the murderer, but every moment he was being won over to belief in her innocence.

'Do you think I can ever forget a single thing that has happened here recently?' she asked. 'Do you imagine that I don't know that there are people who will never believe in my complete innocence? And with that goes my brother's — so far as these crimes are concerned.'

'You are only entitled to speak for yourself,' said McLean. 'There is much in your brother's life of which I believe, and hope, you are ignorant. You may see in his kidnapping of you merely an impulsive act to prevent you doing something which you might later regret, but wouldn't it be greatly to his advantage to have a sister in possession of a big fortune?'

Dorinda rose from her chair, her beautiful face tense with extreme indignation.

'I'm sure you have no right to say such things without a shred of proof,' she cried. 'Please let me go. There's nothing more you can usefully ask me.'

'There is,' replied McLean grimly. Then in a softer voice, 'Mrs. Bosanquet, I only want to prepare you for a big blow to your faith. Please sit down.'

She obeyed as if her own volition had now completely gone. McLean thrust his hand into a suitcase and produced a white linen coat.

'Do you recognise this article?' he asked.

'It — it looks like my brother's working coat. He was asking me if I knew where it had gone.'

'I took it. If you will examine the right sleeve you will see a mend in white cotton. Just there.'

Dorinda didn't even trouble to look.

'I remember it,' she said. 'In fact, I did the mending.'

'When?'

'About a month ago.'

'Did he tell you how he came to damage the coat?'

'Yes — he said he had caught his sleeve on a nail.'

'But the damage couldn't have had that appearance.'

'That is what he said.'

'It wasn't true. If you will look at the sleeve you will see that the mending material has been pulled out. It leaves a small round hole. The microscope shows that the damage was due to a burn.'

Dorinda wrinkled her brows, expressing what appeared to be genuine bewilderment. The Superintendent's bewilderment was no less complete. He couldn't see the relevance of many of McLean's questions — especially those which referred to the white jacket. But

Brook now recalled the occasion when McLean had become interested in the garment, and his immediate reaction on the side of hope.

'Why should he lie about the cause of the damage?' asked Dorinda.

'I shall deal with that later,' replied McLean. 'I have but one more question to ask you. Please give me a direct answer, no matter how much it may shock you. Did you know that your brother killed a man in France?'

At this the Superintendent sat bolt upright, with his eyes fixed on McLean's serious face. Brook broke the point of the pencil he was using, and Dorinda gripped the two arms of the chair in which she was sitting — speechless in her incredulity.

'No,' she cried finally. 'It isn't true. It can't be true.'

'I'm sorry to have to disillusion you about your brother,' said McLean. 'But that is better than that you should suddenly discover — '

Again she lost control of herself, and Brook rose and poured out a glass of water. But this time she was in a dead faint, and the water had no immediate effect.

'Better take her into the lounge,' said McLean. 'Then I'll see Mr. Prout.'

25

In the lounge John and Jasper and Grant were waiting the outcome of the questioning of Dorinda. John saw nothing in the matter of the abduction which affected the police since Dorinda had not the slightest intention of taking any action.

'What's it got to do with the police?' he asked. 'This is a purely domestic crisis. I don't blame Dorinda for wanting to help Prout — can't help calling him that. He's been the best servant we ever had, and he had the guts to do something about Dorinda's inheritance. It didn't succeed, but he did try.'

'He certainly did,' agreed Grant. 'And didn't stop even at chloroform.'

'Yes, that was a bit thick,' said Jasper. 'But Dorinda forgave him, and I like her even better for that.'

'Why are they keeping her such a long time?' complained John. 'Damned inconsiderate I call it. Can't they see she's not well?'

Grant looked worried, as he lighted a cigarette very slowly.

'McLean sees some connection,' he said.

'Connection with what?'

'He won't accept the recent affair as something quite dissociated from the two crimes. This house is being watched day and night.'

'What!' cried Jasper.

'It's true. I can't pretend I can read what's in McLean's mind, but I'm certain that his long absence meant something. I've been gleaning all the information I can get about him. He has the most wonderful record — never lets go of a case. It's curious that he permits us all to foregather, if he believes that the murderer is in, or closely associated with, this house.'

'But that's not possible,' said John.

'Not from our point of view, but the police have the power to get information denied to lesser mortals.'

'I say,' said Jasper. 'Isn't it queer about Prout's white jacket.'

'What's this about Prout's jacket?' asked Grant.

'It's missing — you know, the one he wears in the mornings. Of course he's got two of them, but the one he has been using this week suddenly vanished. He was making an awful row about it. Do you think the police are dumb enough to think that Prout had something to do with the murder?'

'How could he? They know perfectly well

that he and Dorinda and the Chatleighs were all together when — '

He stopped and gasped as the door was pushed open and Brook entered, carrying Dorinda in his arms with the utmost ease. Grant and John leapt up from their chairs.

'It's all right,' said Brook. 'Must have been the heat.'

'Heat!' snarled John. 'You're worrying her to death. Oh, be careful!'

Brook laid Dorinda on the couch close to the window, and pulled back the long curtains to their fullest extent. Grant began to chafe her hands gently.

'She's coming to,' said Brook, as Dorinda's eyelids fluttered. 'Now I want Mr. Prout — I mean Mr. Gale.'

Grant looked up at Brook, and the two boys also concentrated their gaze on Brook.

'So you know that?' said Grant.

'Yes — and more,' replied Brook. 'It looks as if we shan't have to haunt this house much longer.'

Dorinda had opened her eyes, and was evidently trying to grasp what Brook was saying. Grant turned to her with a smile.

'Better now?' he asked.

'Yes, Bob. It was silly of me. Oh!' She seemed suddenly to remember something. 'I must go back. The inspector said something.

It wasn't true. It couldn't be true. Mr. Brook!'

Brook stopped on the threshold of the door.

'I'm sorry, Mrs. Bosanquet,' he said. 'I have my instructions. If the Inspector needs you again he will let you know.'

Dorinda jumped up as the door closed, and pushed back her dishevelled hair.

'I can't stand this,' she said. 'I should be near him. There's some mistake — some awful blunder — '

The door opened softly and into the room came the late 'butler.' He looked strange out of his drab uniform. He now wore a neat lounge suit, and a soft silk shirt. His whole posture was different. The placid, almost obsequious butler had disappeared, and a new man had taken his place.

'Arthur,' gasped Dorinda. 'Brook is looking for you. You are wanted in the study.'

'I thought I might be,' he replied. 'But what has been happening to you?'

'They've been putting her on the rack,' said Grant.

Dorinda shook her head.

'No. They were kind enough. Arthur — there's something I must ask you. Have you been honest with me? Is there anything you haven't told me?'

He smiled and patted her arm.

'Don't worry. Everything is all right. Stay here and rest, and I'll be back in a few minutes.'

'No. I'm coming with you.'

'So am I,' said Grant. 'This is a private house, not a police station.'

'That's right,' agreed John. 'Come on, Jasper.'

Brook came down the stairs to see all of them outside the study door.

'Hey!' he called, hurrying towards them. 'You can't go in there. Only Mr. Gale.'

But the door was already open, and McLean was staring at the intruders.

'I told them not to come,' said Brook, bringing up the rearguard. 'Now, Mrs. Bosanquet — '

'Wait!' interrupted McLean. 'I have no personal objection to their being present. But I doubt whether it is a wise course on their part.'

The intruders glanced from one to another, but none of them made any attempt to move.

'Very well,' said McLean. 'Mrs. Bosanquet, I think you had better sit where you did before. Mr. Gale, please take the chair at that end.'

There was dead silence for a few moments while McLean went through some papers.

Then he took up a sheaf of them, and directed his gaze on Gale.

'Will you admit that you are Arthur Gale, brother of Mrs. Bosanquet?' he asked.

'Yes,' replied Gale in a curious toneless voice.

McLean handed the three anonymous letters to Gale.

'Did you write those letters?' he asked.

'Yes,' replied Gale, and caused Dorinda to utter a little cry.

'What was your object in writing them?'

Gale looked at his sister for a moment, and then thrust his head forward.

'I thought it might bring some scrap of human affection into his heart,' he said. 'Bosanquet was the meanest man alive. He treated my sister — and his two sons — abominably. His thoughts were as mean as his actions, and yet he loved to regard himself as a very righteous person. I disguised my handwriting and used some odd sheets of notepaper which I found in the house. My sister never knew. I didn't want her to know.'

'Did those letters have any effect?'

'No. He grew even more impossible.'

'Did you then decide to take some stronger action?'

'No.'

McLean took back the letters, and then

produced a document from the sheaf which he held.

'Did you live and work for several years in France?' he asked.

'Yes.'

'And did you adopt the name of Henri Calmet, and pass yourself off as a Fleming?'

'I did.'

'Do you admit being charged at Clermont Ferrand with the murder of a man named Calloud?'

'Yes.'

A heart-rending little cry came from Dorinda. Gale's mouth twitched as he gave her a glance.

'Was the sentence of death later commuted to a life sentence on Devil's Island?'

Gale's eyes flashed hatefully.

'Yes. But I didn't want it. Death would have been better. You must let me say a few words. Calloud was a monster — everyone knew it. He lived by exploiting women of the poorer classes. He lived in opulence on their immoral earnings. I shot him dead, and was glad to do it — am still glad.'

There was something quite impressive in the way he flung back his head and glared challengingly at his auditors. The Superintendent, who was enjoying himself immensely, looked as if he was on the verge of clapping his hands. Dorinda was weeping softly.

'Mrs. Bosanquet, if you would prefer to leave — ' said McLean.

She shook her head and McLean went on.

'After spending three years on Devil's Island you made a very clever escape. You finally managed to land in England, and you looked up your sister. Did you tell her that you were an escaped convict?'

'No. I gave her to understand that I had been in trouble in France, but she believed it was some trivial matter. I needed a hide-out, because I knew that every police force in the world would be furnished with full details. In this house I considered myself safe, and, believe it or not, I've been very happy here, apart from witnessing my sister's unhappiness. I tried to give good service.'

'That's true,' interrupted John.

Brook waved a finger at him, and Ball turned to frown. Dorinda was still sobbing, and trying to smother her sounds.

'Now, Mr. Gale, I propose to deal with matters directly relevant to the murder of Mr. Bosanquet, and the later murder of the chauffeur.'

'What have they to do with me?' asked Gale quietly.

'Yes — what?' demanded John.

'I must ask you not to make interjections,' said McLean.

'Out you go, young man, if you do it again,' threatened the Superintendent.

'Do you deny that you had any hand in the shooting of Mr. Bosanquet?' asked McLean.

'You know I didn't,' replied Gale.

'On the contrary, I know you did,' retorted McLean, and caused the rapt audience to draw their breaths. 'This jacket, I believe, belongs to you?'

Gale gazed at the white jacket and nodded his head.

'Will you tell me how you managed to burn a hole in it, and why you lied to your sister afterwards?'

'How did I lie?'

'That hole was never made by a jag on a nail. It was the result of a burn. How did you manage to burn it in that particular place?'

'I forget. I don't know what it all means.'

McLean opened a drawer and produced the book with the burn on the paper jacket.

'When I questioned you about this book on a former occasion you were quite unable to account for the burn on the edge of the wrapper.'

'That's true.'

'Would you care to be enlightened?'

'No. I'm not interested.'

Ball screwed up his face as he stared at McLean. What on earth had all this to do with the two murders? From the floor McLean lifted the square package which he had brought with him in the car. He undid the string, and then opened out some paper, and exposed a large square cardboard box. From this he took, with great care, the fish-bowl which had been shot to pieces. It was now very cleverly mended, and was quite complete, with the exception of two small gaps at the top of it.

'On the occasion when the shot was fired through the window,' said McLean, 'this was the target — not me. It happened after I had raised questions about the burn on the book wrapper. Some person didn't wish the fish-bowl to stand there suggesting ideas to an investigator. There was no possibility of disposing of it except by the means adopted, because when we weren't here the room was locked up. Had the bowl been broken in our absence that would have looked a little significant, but by shooting it to pieces while we were here the murderer believed we should interpret his act as an attempt on my life. The same weapon was used as that which killed Bosanquet, and the culprit was really brilliant when he chose a heavy thunderstorm to smother the sound of the shot, and thus permit himself time to get away. That man was you, Gale.'

Dorinda seemed too horrified to utter a sound now. Her tears had ceased to flow and she was staring at her brother, who, to everyone's amazement, was perfectly calm — even to the extent of disinterestedness.

'I should like to know how you arrive at that astonishing conclusion, Inspector,' said Gale.

'You shall,' replied McLean.

He lifted the reconstructed fish-bowl on to the end of the table where it had hitherto stood. Then he produced a can of water from under the kneehole table and emptied it into the fish-bowl until it was within a few inches of the top of the bowl. The curtain at the window was partly drawn, and the bowl was now in the shade. McLean drew back the curtain, and immediately the bowl became strongly illuminated.

'This is what happened some months ago,' he said. 'Gale suddenly discovered something interesting about the fish-bowl. He must have been standing by the table — his right elbow resting on it. Perhaps he was sitting, as that would be the more natural attitude to bring his elbow to the required position — like this.'

He took the white jacket, laid the right

sleeve of it against his own, and then moved it fairly close to the bowl. In a few moments he found the position he wanted, and a few moments later smoke arose from the jacket.

'Good God!' ejaculated Ball. 'A burning glass!'

McLean nodded and turned to Gale.

'Look at the new hole — exactly like the one you made, and lied about. Even at that time you must have realised how you could kill Bosanquet and not be suspected.'

'I don't see how,' replied Gale, still apparently unmoved.

'You shall see how. Bosanquet was shot with a thirty-two Colt automatic. Yesterday I procured such a weapon, and a gunsmith swiftly made certain alterations which would permit a concentrated heat-ray to play on the back of the cartridge. Here is the actual weapon.'

He produced the rather big pistol and showed where the metal at the rear end of the barrel had been cut away. A blank cartridge was in the chamber, and the back of it could be clearly seen.

'This, I believe, is an almost exact replica of the weapon used. But for the weapon to be operative in the circumstances it had to be so placed that the concentrated rays of the sun struck full on the percussion cap. For that purpose two or more books were used. The bottom one on which the barrel of the pistol rested was this book with the burned wrapper. The murderer should have placed the weapon so that the end of the barrel came over the wrapper. As it was, it came about an inch short, and when the shot was fired the flame from the muzzle scorched the wrapper. The pistol fell to the ground on recoil. I was puzzled by the fact that there was no ejected cartridge-case left behind, because it seemed incredible that after firing the shot the murderer should have waited to find that empty case. It had to be found, because if it came into the hands of the police they would see at once by the absence of any striker mark on the percussion cap that it had never been fired in the normal way. Who was it who first came into this room after the shot was fired? You — Gale. You had time to pick up the pistol and the cartridge-case and to replace the books in the book-case before you called the family. That is the reason why Penny failed to see any escaping man. You knew Bosanquet's habits. You knew he would fall asleep soon after he came into this room. You had the opportunity to steal in and arrange the matter. The plot worked. It worked this morning in London, when it was tried out. I am going — '

Gale stopped him by waving his hand. His eyes were half closed and his whole demeanour was changing.

'Let me say something before you caution me,' he said. 'Your helpers aren't very expert, Inspector.'

'What do you mean?'

'I saw them from the window upstairs, waiting for me in case I tried to do something silly. And there was a familiar gentleman in the car which you kept waiting. I recall him quite well. I could see his features quite clearly through a pair of field-glasses which I had in the bedroom. He is thought a lot of at the Sûreté in Paris. It was he who arrested me for giving Calloud what he deserved, and I presume he flew across from Paris with the idea of shoving me back on Devil's Island, in the event of your being unable to get me for the Bosanquet murder — perhaps to identify me if I denied I was the man in question. I killed Bosanquet because he was planning to disinherit my sister. It was I who intercepted that draft will and destroyed it. It was I who killed Penny. I had to, because on that evening he overheard a conversation between me and Dorinda. I saw him stealing away after eavesdropping. He must have known I was Dorinda's brother. I couldn't afford to risk that knowledge being spread about. I'm not afraid of dying, but I *am* afraid of Devil's Island, and so, McLean, I'm sorry I can't give you all the pleasure of presenting me at court — good joke that, for a man in my position. And I would have spared Dorinda — the knowledge — that I provided the key — the key — '

He stopped, and there was a sudden collapse of his curious rigidity. Brook looked sharply at McLean, and the Superintendent became alive to the situation.

'He's taken something,' he said excitedly. 'We ought never to have given him that opportunity. Hadn't you better do something about it?'

McLean picked up the telephone receiver as Dorinda, with a wild cry, rushed to the side of her brother.

'Dr. Galbraith's number?' he asked John.

John gave him the number in a whisper.

* * *

It was all over. The doctor had come and gone and the corpse of Arthur Gale now lay in an upstairs bedroom. McLean had cleared up his papers and was walking round the garden in the warm afternoon sunshine. Brook came to him from the car.

'Everything's inside,' he said. 'Has the

Superintendent gone?'

'Yes. I think he has a friend on the press who relies on him for an occasional good story.'

'Well, he's got one this time,' said Brook. 'I'm sorry for Mrs. Bosanquet, though. She believed in him so deeply — I mean her brother.'

'She's been through hell, but I think it will all turn out right for her.'

'You mean — Grant?'

'Yes. He won't let her go far.'

'Not if he has any sense. I wonder what Gale did with the pistol and the empty cartridge-case?'

McLean gazed out towards the marshes.

'There are miles and miles of dykes out there, and a pistol is a small thing. It can stay where it is so far as I'm concerned.'

'Could the pistol have been used in normal fashion after it had been altered?'

'Yes. I satisfied myself on that point.'

'Well, he had brains.'

'And courage.'

'Plus more than a little personal charm,' said Brook. 'What was it he took?'

'We don't know yet.'

'The Superintendent thought you were a little careless in giving him an opportunity to see the French detective waiting in the car.'

381

'It did seem a little remiss on my part, but then perhaps Superintendent Ball has never seen Devil's Island and its inhabitants. I did — once.'

Brook shot him a glance, but McLean was staring down at the colourful fishes in one of the pools.

'I'll fill up the radiator and then we're ready,' said Brook.

'Do. I'll join you in a minute or two.'

He walked through the deserted garden back to the terrace. A breeze had got up and was rustling the leaves of the trees. It was cool and pleasant after the fierce heat of the past weeks. Away to sea there were white crests on the waves, and out on the horizon a great liner made her way down channel. On turning the corner of the house he came upon the three men, sitting together on a bench.

'I'm leaving now,' he said. 'You must all hate the sight of me.'

John shook his head and held out his hand.

'You've brought us what we all craved,' he said. 'Peace at last. In a short time we shall all be on a ship like that.' He pointed to the great liner. 'All we need now is time to forget — time to start all over again, and there's not going to be any harking back. All through you've been marvellous. Dorinda wanted me to tell you that.'

'That was kind of her. How is she?'

'She's all right,' said Grant. 'If Prout — I mean Gale — had been arrested and she had had to undergo the horrible strain of his trial I believe she wouldn't have survived it. Did you know that? Did you anticipate — '

'Mr. Grant, my duty is to bring criminals to trial,' interrupted McLean. 'But if Mrs. Bosanquet has benefited by a careless slip on my part, it is some consolation to me. I wish you all the best of luck, and please tell Mrs. Bosanquet that she's needed in the garden. It's a little dull without her. Perhaps one day she'll come back to it and make it live again. I hope she will.'

Five minutes later the car went down the drive, and from the terrace there came a waving of hands. McLean sighed as they turned into the main street, but Brook's attention was taken up in avoiding holiday-makers in the weirdest garments. Then the old castle, and later the winding road through the open country.

We do hope that you have enjoyed reading this large print book.

Did you know that all of our titles are available for purchase?

We publish a wide range of high quality large print books including:
Romances, Mysteries, Classics
General Fiction
Non Fiction and Westerns

Special interest titles available in large print are:
The Little Oxford Dictionary
Music Book
Song Book
Hymn Book
Service Book

Also available from us courtesy of Oxford University Press:
Young Readers' Dictionary
(large print edition)
Young Readers' Thesaurus
(large print edition)

For further information or a free brochure, please contact us at:
Ulverscroft Large Print Books Ltd.,
The Green, Bradgate Road, Anstey,
Leicester, LE7 7FU, England.
Tel: (00 44) 0116 236 4325
Fax: (00 44) 0116 234 0205

Other titles in the
Ulverscroft Large Print Series:

DEAD FISH

Ruth Carrington

Dr Geoffrey Quinn arrives home to find his children missing, the charred remains of his wife's body in the boiler and Chief Superintendent Manning waiting to arrest him for her murder. Alison Hope, attractive and determined, is briefed to defend him. Quinn claims he is innocent, but Alison is not so sure. The background becomes increasingly murky as she penetrates a wealthy and ruthless circle who cannot risk their secrets — sexual perversion, drugs, blackmail, illegal arms dealing and major fraud — coming to light. Can Alison unravel the mystery in time to save Quinn?

MY FATHER'S HOUSE

Kathleen Conlon

'Your father has another woman'. Nine-year-old Anna Blake is only mildly surprised when a schoolfriend lets drop this piece of information. And when her father finally leaves home to live with Olivia in Hampstead, that place becomes, for Anna, the epitome of sinful glamour. But Hampstead, though welcoming, is not home. So Anna, now in her teens, sets out to find a place where she can really belong. At first she thinks love may be the answer, and certainly Jonathon — and Raymond — and Jake, have a devastating effect on her life. But can anyone really supply what she needs?